THE WINTER BEACH

THE WINTER BEACH

(THE ROSE SISTERS, #3)

SIENNA CARR

CHAPTER 1

GINNY

"I will always be there for you, little one." Ginny cradled her baby bump, her hands gently caressing her swollen belly.

She sniffled, fighting to hold back the sob that threatened to break forth from her throat. "You will never, ever be alone." But those whispered words shattered the fortress of the walls she'd put up around her, and her emotions broke.

Ben had cheated on her. A second time.

Her friend, Talia, had confirmed it. Ginny already had her suspicions, but when Talia told her that Ben hadn't been in the car alone, that he'd been driving late at night when he'd had that fatal car crash, and this woman had been the other passenger, it was another crack in her already fractured heart. Other friends told her how they'd seen Ben and Rhonda together a few weeks before. It had been round about the time she'd noticed Ben being aloof and distant with her.

1

A solitary tear trickled down her cheek, and she fought to hold back her cries. Most days she sobbed into the early hours of the morning, unable to sleep until dawn broke and the birds started to chirp outside. She'd wake up late, around noon, tired and groggy. Those first few seconds of opening her eyes, she would forget the horror of what had happened. She'd be content, as if life were normal, and then in the blink of an eye, it would all come rushing forth.

Ben's death.

His cheating.

And now she was left to bring up a new baby by herself.

She'd been so ill after the funeral, and had lost the will to live as the reality of her new existence sank in. She grappled to come to terms with the shocking news not only of her ex-fiancé's death, but the idea that he had been with another woman.

The other woman had been fine. She'd walked away and continued with her life while Ginny's life fell apart. Now she was left feeling sad, angry and humiliated. So broken that she would never be able to put herself together again.

So many emotions meshed and mingled inside her. It was hard enough dealing with her pregnancy problems; recently her thirty-two-week scan had shown that her placenta was still lying low. It was more bad news she didn't need, and it wasn't fair.

Life wasn't fair.

She'd been doing what the doctor had advised. She'd had lots of bed rest, had taken things easy, had stopped working at the bridal shop. But this late in her pregnancy her condition hadn't improved.

She would need to have another check up in a few weeks' time and it was highly likely that she'd need a C-section. She was a failure. She couldn't even carry a baby to term and give birth naturally.

Her sisters, Ashleigh and Eloise, constantly worried about her. Ginny could see it in the way they stared at her, their eyes gaunt, their faces pale. She could see it in the way they fussed over her; telling her she couldn't go to work for the foreseeable future, that she needed to think about herself and the baby she carried.

They constantly preached to her that she couldn't change what had happened, and she had to move for the sake of her baby.

Her sisters had never been fond of Ben. They'd tried to hide it, but with the revelations of a possible other woman, she couldn't defend him. She would never know, because he wasn't here to tell her the truth, what had happened; why he'd been with someone else. Why he'd turned distant towards her.

She'd made a mistake in getting back with him. A fresh start, she'd told herself. A baby needed a father, and she could overlook his previous infidelity, for this new life.

But Eloise had been right. People never change who they really are.

And now, Ben was gone. His parents wanted to be part of her life, part of their grandchild's life, which put Ginny in a difficult position. She felt for the grieving broken people who had lost their only child, but she didn't want to be constantly reminded of Ben and the past.

The nights were the hardest; she tossed and turned in bed, grasping at slivers of sleep. Bitterness and regret mixed with humiliation and hatred. Unable to sleep during the night, and then unable to get up in the morning, unable to work, or cook, or clean, or participate in anything, she was good for nothing. She tried to move on, but she was in such a bad place, couldn't summon the energy to pretend.

In quiet moments, alone with her thoughts, she would place a hand on her baby bump and close her eyes, trying to imagine the life inside her. She would try to conjure up a future where everything would be okay, when her days would be filled with lightness and laughter. But it was hard, almost on the verge of impossible, for she couldn't see or imagine such a time. Her life had been in freefall for a while now.

Focus on your baby.

That's what she tried to tell herself when she fell down the dark abyss. Her thoughts encircling around her like poison arrows.

Focus on your baby.

She couldn't feel sorry for herself. She had to be strong. She was going to be a mother, responsible for a new life, for a girl, she hoped, and she would be busy with the new baby. It was something to look forward to. Something that would distract her from the harsh reality of her messy life.

Wiping her cheek, she slowly waddled over to the closet. A new life, a small human being would soon rely on her for everything. Her little girl would dictate all her thoughts and actions. Luckily, Ash and Eloise, with Ford and Liam, had helped with the nursery. Painted a pearly white color with hints of yellow and orange, it was a warm and wonderful room.

It held a promise.

Of good things.

Of happier days.

And these were the things she tried to focus on.

She opened one of the drawers of the wooden dresser, her breath catching in her throat at the neatly folded piles of baby clothes. Her sisters had been so generous and had bought so many things.

Ginny reached out and grasped a soft white bodysuit. It was so tiny. She couldn't believe her baby would be wearing this.

Setting it down, she reached for the soft, fleecy blanket next to it. It was white with baby toys in pastel colors printed on it. Unfolding it, she held it to her face, closing her eyes and luxuriating in its softness. "We're going to be fine, little one," she whispered.

A sharp pain—like a screwdriver plunged into her belly—shot through her. She doubled over in pain, holding her stomach, and when blood pooled on the wooden floor, she let out a blood-curdling scream.

"My baby! My baby!"

CHAPTER 2

ELOISE

"*I*t's going to be okay, Elle. Ginny's going to be fine." Liam's arms encircled her waist and he hugged her closer; the solid wall of his body filling her with strength.

Opposite them, in the small private waiting room at the hospital, sat Ashleigh and Ford, each on one end of the sofa, with a gaping wide chasm between them.

Ford nodded. "She's going to be fine. Ginny's a fighter. We all know that, right?" He attempted a laugh, but he didn't hide it well, the tightness around his eyes was new. Eloise hated that Ford and Ashleigh were no longer together. Her older sister was miserable, and Ford looked like a changed man. Gone was the jovial big guy she'd come to know again. These days he was introverted, serious and somber. But it didn't stop him from coming over to check in on Ginny every now and then.

He still cared about them all. He'd been shocked about

Ben's untimely passing, and was as worried as they were about Ginny. While the atmosphere around him and Ashleigh was still prickly, Ford didn't let that get in the way of his concern and self-appointed sense of responsibility for the Rose sisters. He'd usually come over a few times a week to check in on them all.

Earlier today they'd been talking about their plans for the New Year now that Christmas was over. That's when they heard Ginny's scream, and they rushed upstairs.

Eloise recoiled at the memory of seeing the floor drenched in blood. Of the fleecy white blanket that had turned maroon. She'd never been so scared.

Everything happened quickly. Ford called 911 who'd come almost instantly. It felt surreal, like a deja vu of when this had happened before around the time they'd heard the news about Ben. Poor Ginny. She just couldn't catch a break. She'd suffered so much and it seemed as if there was no let up.

Ashleigh wiped her hands over her face, her face pale, her eyes haunted by worry. They were already struggling to take care of Ginny while also running the family business. They'd come to rely on their assistants, Rachel and May, more and more. But now that this had happened another dark cloud loomed over them.

They were already at the end of their tether. How would they cope now, with a newborn, as well as Ginny?

"Hey." Liam dropped a kiss on her head. "She's in good hands here, and she'll get the best medical care."

The door opened and they all rushed to stand. In that first split second, Eloise felt the blood pounding through her ears. Her eyes scanned the doctor's face, and she braced herself for the news.

"Your sister has given birth to a baby boy."

"A boy?" Ashleigh cried.

"A baby boy?" Eloise turned to her sister and they hugged one another tightly before bursting into tears.

"You're aunts! Congratulations." Ford's hand landed on their shoulders from behind.

"Congrats! Told you she'd be fine." Liam whispered, as his lips brushed her earlobe.

"Can we see them?" Ashleigh asked.

"Soon. The baby is six weeks premature and he's small. He weighs five pounds three ounces. He can't breathe by himself yet, so he's in the neonatal ICU."

They let out a collective gasp "What?" Eloise remembered the blood on the nursery floor, and on the blanket, and running down Ginny's legs. She couldn't get the sound of her sister's sobs out of her head. She trembled, fearing the worst.

Ashleigh sat down, her hand clutching her chest. "He's going to live, isn't he?"

"He's going to be fine," the doctor assured them, "but he can't go home. Not for a few weeks. You should also know that your sister has lost a lot of blood and she'll need several blood transfusions."

Ashleigh let out a cry and Ford placed his hand on her shoulder. The doctor cleared her throat. "She's weak and she needs lots of rest and recovery, but in time she'll be fine. We were lucky she got to the hospital so quickly."

The tone of her voice sent a shiver down Eloise's spine. "And if we hadn't?"

The doctor looked her directly in the eyes. "But you did. Mother and son are fine. I'll send one of the nurses in when your sister is able to see you. Genevieve had an emergency C-section, so it's going to take time for her to heal. Please don't look so worried. She will recover but it will take a while."

The sob she'd been trying to hold back burst and tears

rolled down Eloise's cheeks when the doctor left. "It's not looking good, Ash."

"Stop." Liam put his arm around her and hugged her closer. Ashleigh started to cry. Ford shook his head. "Don't, Ashleigh. Don't lose faith. You heard what the doctor said. Ginny's going to be fine."

Eloise watched and waited, but Ford didn't pull her to standing, or hug her. He just placed another hand on her shoulder. Like a friend would. Eloise felt sorry for her sister. At a time like this, Ashleigh didn't need him to be just a friend.

~

ASHLEIGH

Her baby sister was a mother.

A mother.

Ashleigh repeated the words over and over again, like a mantra, holding Ginny's face in her thoughts. Praying, hoping, willing her sister to get well and fully recover.

Ginny is a mom and she's going to be okay.

But, as much as she tried to convince herself of this, she couldn't erase the image of blood all over the nursery floor.

Up until that moment they'd all be sitting around the kitchen table, talking about how they'd spent Christmas Day. Liam and Eloise were annoyingly lovey-dovey, hugging and laughing, and kissing, all of which made Ashleigh's stomach turn.

Liam was here most days for dinner, and he and Eloise were inseparable. Ashleigh breathed easier when they disappeared to Eloise's house, just a short walk away. Eloise had moved out, but not completely. She still stayed here, at the main house, for most nights and they often ate together.

Ginny worried them. She'd fallen apart after Ben's death, and the rumors of infidelity didn't help. Added to this, she was having a hard time during her pregnancy and most days she was grieving, and angry, and sad.

They'd forbidden Ginny from working at the shop, which meant that Ashleigh and Eloise now had to do everything. She didn't want to think about what would happen now that there was a little baby to take care of as well.

A nurse walked into the room and announced that they could see Ginny, but only two people at a time and only immediate family for now. She and Eloise rushed towards the door and followed the nurse into the room where Ginny was.

Ginny looked like a ghost. Like a spent, listless ghoul, deathly white and with her eyes closed.

Eloise uttered a shocked cry, but Ashleigh managed to keep it in, her hand on her mouth blocking the sound of her reaction. "Is she … is she going to be okay?" she asked, afraid to hear the answer.

"She's going to need a lot of rest. She's very weak, and it will take time. She won't be able to feed the baby, or hold him much at the start, but if she gets lots of rest, there's no reason why she won't go on and be completely recovered."

"She looks so pale." Eloise took Ginny's hand and peered down at their sleeping sister. Ashleigh moved to the other side of the bed and caressed Ginny's cheek. Ginny stirred, slowly opening her eyes.

"Hey, Gin." Eloise's voice was a whisper. Ashleigh faked a smile, even though she was sick with worry. Ginny looked so unwell. She didn't seem to have the energy to keep her eyes fully open. When her eyelids fluttered closed again, she and Eloise exchanged worried looks.

"The doctor said she needs lots of rest," Eloise reminded her.

"She will have all the rest she needs," agreed Ashleigh. They'd find a way to take care of everything. The business, the baby, and Ginny. They'd find a way to put back her broken heart. Hope blossomed inside her. Ginny had a purpose now. She had a little boy. A beautiful gorgeous little boy. Things would be easier now that Ginny had a future to look forward to.

They sat by Ginny's bedside for what seemed like hours, but was a relatively short time when Ashleigh looked at her watch. A nurse came over, and told Ginny that she could see her baby now. Ginny didn't look as if she wanted to move, let alone get out of bed. She looked so fragile, but with their help and the nurse's they were able to get her into a wheelchair and wheel her to the ICU.

The nurse took her right up close to the big, glass incubator. Ashleigh's heart somersaulted inside her ribcage at the sight of the tiny baby. He looked like a doll. So thin, so weak, so scrawny. He was connected to wires and tubes. It looked so painful. She shrank away in fear.

"You have a beautiful, little boy, Genevieve," the nurse said. Eloise's face was lit up with love. "Awww. He is *so* adorable."

"He is, but he's *soooo* tiny! We'll help him get bigger and get well and get out of here." Ashleigh's voice wavered, even though she'd tried to be brave. Consumed by worry, she prayed that this little boy would be okay. This family could not go through another tragedy.

"We can't take him out yet, and unfortunately you can't hold him or get any skin-to-skin contact, but you can gently touch him if you slip your finger through this little section here." The nurse demonstrated to Ginny, but she turned her head, refusing to look at her son.

"Look at him, Ginny," Ashleigh pleaded. "You have a beautiful little baby."

"He's so cute, Gin!" Eloise squealed, her voice wobbling. "He's your son, and he's so beautiful."

A heavy feeling settled in Ashleigh's stomach. This wasn't how it was supposed to be. They'd all pinned their hopes on the baby giving Ginny a reason to embrace life again. "Ginny, open your eyes, look at him. He's so—"

Ginny's face twisted into an ugly scowl. "I don't want to. I don't want to be here. Take me back to my room."

Ashleigh's insides flinched and she locked eyes with Eloise.

"I don't want him!" Ginny screamed, the anger in her voice making them jump. The nurse started to wheel Ginny away.

Ashleigh's jaw dropped. Of all the reactions she'd expected from Ginny, this hadn't been one of them.

"She's tired," said Eloise, clearly shaken. Ashleigh nodded. They couldn't talk about Ginny in front of her. They followed the nurse who wheeled Ginny back to her room.

"You don't have to stay here," Ginny said, when the nurse left them alone.

Eloise stood up and took Ginny's hand, but her sister moved hers away.

"We want to be with you," Eloise told her.

"I want to be alone." Ginny stared out of the window.

Maybe they needed to let her get some rest. Ashleigh nodded towards the door, indicating to Eloise that they needed to leave. She patted Ginny's arm. "We'll let you get some sleep."

No sooner were they out of the room, than she and Eloise faced one another. Worry lines filled Eloise's brow. "She doesn't want him."

Ashleigh didn't want to believe it. This was a reaction

because Ginny was in pain. "She's lost a lot of blood. You heard the doctor."

"After everything she's been through, the birth, the blood transfusions, the doctor saying she's going to need time to recover … how will we cope?" Eloise asked.

Ashleigh didn't have an answer for that. The thought hadn't been far from her mind. She and Eloise had struggled to take care of Ginny after Ben's death. Their youngest sister had sunk into listlessness; not wanting to get out of bed, not wanting to eat, not wanting to do anything. She was silent, almost invisible, most days. Even when they forced her to come downstairs, she would lie on the couch staring at the TV which often wasn't switched on.

Sometimes they had to feed her, just in order to get her to eat. Because of the complications with her pregnancy, they didn't dare leave her at home alone, which meant that only one of them could be at the bridal shop at any given time. Thank goodness for their shop assistants.

Now, with the baby here, it was all going to become so much more difficult. It had been one thing after another ever since Ginny had broken up with Ben and called off the wedding. Ashleigh didn't want to think about it.

"What are we going to do?" Eloise asked, her voice shaky.

"I don't know yet." She would think about it. Sleep on it. Come up with a solution. They'd weathered bad situations before. They would do so again.

They walked back into the small waiting room. Ford and Liam rose from their seats and stared at them expectantly. "And?" They asked in unison.

"It's not good." Ashleigh shook her head, but couldn't bring herself to elaborate. She listened as Eloise explained what had taken place.

Ford paced around the room, his brow furrowing as if this affected him personally.

"She wouldn't even look at the baby," Eloise told them. Ashleigh wiped a hand over her face and listened to the conversation, watching the shock and surprise as Ford and Liam took in this news. A mother rejecting her baby. How worse could things get?

"Can we go and see them?" Ford's voice up close and behind her, gave her palpitations. She could feel the heat of his nearness, and an instant thrum started low in her belly. She'd made the mistake of taking him for granted, and now that he was no longer hers, she craved him even more. Whenever she saw him, she felt even more acutely the void of him no longer being in her life.

She turned around and stared up at him, wanting to fall into his arms, to lean against his chest, to have him hold her and hug her. She didn't need him to tell her that everything would be fine. The Rose sisters lives had been full of ups and downs, mostly downs, but they persevered and had gotten over it. Lately, though, it seemed as if life was getting more difficult.

"Ginny needs to rest, but we can check with the nurse and see if it's okay for you to see the baby."

"Cool." Liam took Eloise's hand and they moved towards the door.

Moments later they had the nurse's permission to visit the little baby. They stared at him in awe, as he lay fast asleep, a delicate little bundle.

Ashleigh's eyes welled with tears. "Oh, baby. You sweet, sweet thing." His eyes were closed and his little cherub lips were sealed together into a peaceful smile. She couldn't stop herself from gushing. "Isn't he beautiful?"

Ford's eyes were shiny. He nodded. "He sure is."

"Awww!" Eloise squealed. "I can't wait to hold him."

"Me, neither." Liam had his arms around her as she rested her back against his chest.

Ashleigh swallowed, a deep sadness washing over her. In happier times, she and Ford would have had their arms around one another. At the very least he'd be holding her hands now and making sure she was okay as another drama engulfed the Rose family.

But this time he kept his distance.

Just like a stranger would.

CHAPTER 3

GINNY

hankfully, Benjy was asleep.

Benjy.

Ashleigh and Eloise had asked her for a name, but she hadn't cared much about it. Didn't want to think about it. Couldn't think about it because everything hurt. Her stitches hurt, her body hurt. Her brain was still in a fog. Her breasts were engorged but she couldn't get the baby to latch on, and that pain was excruciating. When she slept, or tried to sleep, her back hurt.

Each time the baby cried, she wanted to pick him up, but the wound on her lower belly was still painful to touch. It hurt when she sneezed or coughed, or moved, but the nurses had told her she had to move, to reduce the risk of blood clots.

She felt awful. Weak and helpless. Sleepwalking through her days.

She'd wanted a girl, and she'd had a boy, instead. A boy

who looked like Ben. Life had a way of never giving her what she wanted. It wasn't right or fair. She saw it as a punishment to see the face of her cheating ex-fiancé reflected back at her each time she looked at her child.

After spending three weeks in the hospital, when the baby was able to breathe by himself, they were allowed to go back home. She'd been glad of the rest herself, that someone else had been taking care of him, because she felt incapable of doing that herself.

Those first few days after the birth had been so difficult. She'd been in so much pain, and the nurses had told her to walk, to be up and about. They wanted her to be mobile and had encouraged her to spend time with the baby. She'd stroked his skin, but it felt so different; nothing like she imagined it would be.

Were it not for her sisters, she would be totally lost. She'd been home only a few days now and already it was hard having to take care of him. It was so overwhelming and unbearable. The baby cried all the time and she was convinced he hated her. Every time Ash and Eloise tried to hand him to her, he cried as if she were the devil.

Even he could tell she was bad luck.

Even he didn't want to be with her.

She stared out of her bedroom window. The dark, bare and solitary branches of the tree outside reflected her own life.

"Hey Gin." Eloise walked inside, carrying the baby. Ginny's breath hitched. Anxiety clawed at her insides. He was quiet now but in a few seconds he'd be screaming again.

"He's hungry. Do you want to see if he'll feed from you again before he starts screaming?"

The baby made mewling noises, and funny expressions with his mouth. "He's so funny!" Eloise giggled. "Shall I hand him to you?"

Ginny shrank back, a growing sense of restlessness creeping over her. "Can't you feed him? Just give him formula milk again." She'd tried to give him her own milk, but he never seemed to latch on to her breast. All her attempts had ended in nothing, with the baby getting more frustrated and then screaming his lungs out when he didn't get any milk.

It made her feel even more of a failure.

Eloise held the baby out to her. "The nurse said it was important to keep trying otherwise your milk will dry up."

Unease crawled up Ginny's back like a spider. "It's not working, and I don't want to keep trying. I'm so tired. I didn't sleep much again last night."

Eloise sat on the bed slowly, angling the baby towards her. He looked so much like Ben, but at least he had her forehead. She'd been taking photos every day, and when she compared them all she could see how much his face had changed in such a short span of time.

Being back home, in the familiar comfort of her room, with the unfamiliar, almost alien, idea of being a mother and having a baby who needed her, it threw her. Made her feel out of sorts.

"Just try, Gin," Eloise persisted, but Ginny was reluctant to take him. It was easier to observe him when he was asleep. During those peaceful times she would stare at him and marvel at his tiny lips and his little features, feeling nothing but love for this small bundle she had produced. But when he was awake she was scared he would cry. And now Eloise was forcing her to have him again, even though Ginny was certain he'd start bawling any second now, getting frustrated because he could smell the milk but couldn't have any. She'd only feel worse than she already did.

"You're so difficult to deal with sometimes!" Eloise glared at her and hugged the baby to her chest. Then her expression softened. "I'm sorry, Gin. I'm so tired. It's been a long day and I don't know what you want sometimes."

"I want to be happy." She so badly wanted to be happy and to love her child. She wanted to be a mother, to take care of him, to feed him, to cuddle him, to hold him, but she couldn't. She didn't feel like taking him, not when he was crying. Even when he was quiet, he'd often start crying moments after she held him. She didn't want or need another rejection.

"You will be, honey," Eloise told her but her smile didn't quite reach her eyes. "You will be," she said again, as if she were trying to convince herself. "Just try. Don't give up."

Ginny shook her head. She hated it when her sisters were so overbearing. Eloise wouldn't leave until she did, so she had no choice but to take him. She held out her arms like a robot and took him. The baby stirred, his eyes blinking open, and then his lips formed into that familiar little scowl.

Her body stiffened in expectation. It was coming. A few seconds later, the baby started to cry. "Told you he doesn't like me!" Ginny cried, desperate for her sister to take him.

"He's hungry!" Eloise refused to give in. "He can smell your milk, Gin. He knows its feeding time. Try again—"

But the baby's cries turned louder, shriller. "Take him! He doesn't want me."

Eloise's eyes turned glassy. "He needs you, Gin. He's your son. He *needs* you."

"But I don't need him. I don't *want* him. Take him. *Now*."

"You're impossible sometimes," Eloise hissed, storming out of the room with the baby. She slammed the door behind her, leaving Ginny alone in her room.

She didn't deserve to be here, let alone be a mother to a little boy who'd had such a struggle to be born. He'd needed a machine to help him breathe during the first few weeks of his life. She couldn't even carry him to term. Couldn't even have a baby like most women did.

This baby didn't want her, just like his father didn't hadn't wanted her.

~

ASHLEIGH

She had finished updating Darcie on how badly things were going between mother and baby when she heard the baby's cries. Eloise appeared with him in her arms.

"She didn't try?"

"She barely held him." Eloise took the bottle of formula milk that Ashleigh had prepared, just in case. Liam pulled out a chair for Eloise and she sat down to feed the baby.

Ginny had refused to give the baby a feeding. She hadn't bonded at all with him. Had barely held him, or bathed him, or changed his diaper. When he cried in the middle of the night, and every few hours after that, it was Ashleigh or Eloise who got up to tend to the little boy.

Their sister lay in bed, hopeless and useless and not helping herself. One night Ashleigh had been so overcome with tiredness that she'd shouted at Ginny. Told her to pull herself together and do something.

But her sister had looked at her with a blank expression.

Darcie nudged her gently with her elbow. "You have to get help."

"We're doing what we can." Ashleigh watched as Liam looked over at Eloise and the baby, a smile curving up on his lips.

"You're a natural at this, Elle," Liam murmured as she and

Eloise continued to fuss over the baby. Liam had such a tender expression on his face; something that resembled longing. It seemed at odds with a hefty, bearded man like him.

"Don't go giving her any ideas," Ashleigh said, shifting uneasily in her chair. She felt like an outsider at a family event. She was happy for Eloise, but right now, the last thing she needed was for these two to get married and ride off into the sunset.

She didn't want to be left here, having to take responsibility for Ginny and the new baby forever. She would always be here for her sisters, but there was a danger that this could end up being her new life and, having already tasted some freedom, traveling and spending time alone, meeting new people, she yearned for more adventure.

It was hard enough trying to slip back into Whisper Falls after her whirlwind European tour was cut short. She yearned to return to that carefree life again; with no timetable and no cares, no worries, and no stress. She had plans to go back and see the places she'd missed, and maybe this time she would return with Ford. Her heart skipped a beat at the thought. It seemed unlikely now that he'd told her they needed space apart. He felt he'd pressured her into getting back with him again.

She'd hurt him, but she hadn't meant to, yet even though they'd broken off their short-lived second chance romance, he hadn't left her side, not through any of the recent hard times with Ginny. It was as if he were a member of their family. He was there for her, even if they weren't together.

But Liam and Eloise were inseparable.

It was bittersweet watching them sometimes and she couldn't help thinking that if it was hard for her to see these two in love, how much harder was it for Ginny to watch, after everything that had happened?

"Did you hear what I said?" Darcie nudged her again. "You

need help. Someone else to come in and help you with Ginny and the baby until Ginny is well enough to take care of him herself."

"Help? That would be great, but help from where?"

"I know just the person. Leave it to me."

CHAPTER 4

RYAN

"It won't be for long, I promise." Ryan threw a quick glance at his daughter who was sitting on the stairs putting on her shoes.

"Stay as long as you want. For as long as you need. I have this whole house to myself and its gets lonely sometimes and, to be honest, as sad as this situation is for you, I'm glad you and Daisy are here."

Ryan inhaled a sharp breath. His sister Kayla was being generous as always, and he needed her more than ever now that life had thrown him a curveball he hadn't seen coming.

"Does mommy know where we are?" Daisy asked.

A knife twisted in Ryan's gut. "She knows where we are, sweetie."

"Will she come and see us here?"

"I don't see why she couldn't." He smiled at her, not

wanting to lie. This was the best answer he could give. His precious little five-year-old was starting a new school in a new town. His heart broke for her. She would know no one. Friendships would be already set up, and his little girl would be a stranger. He didn't want that for Daisy.

He wished he could make everything better for her. It was bad enough that she'd been uprooted from the only home she'd ever known. Young enough to not understand everything, but old enough to know that something wasn't quite right.

His eyes welled up and he forced himself to be strong. Kayla placed a placating hand on his shoulder. He had to man up. He couldn't break down in front of his daughter, even though this starting over was so painful.

"You being here is timely for me, and it helps. That family needs my help, but I won't get behind the wheel of a car yet. This works perfectly, don't you see? It works for both of us."

Kayla had taken on a new temporary job, 'helping a friend of a friend.' His older sister had been suffering from a nasty inner ear problem which affected her balance and made her dizzy and nauseous. It had taken a while to diagnose but it had severely affected her and she'd taken time off school. During a particularly nasty dizzy spell while driving one day, she'd hit a tree. Thankfully no one was injured. The car was dented, and the tree stood firm but this accident, coupled with the slow recovery from her illness, had battered her confidence. He and Daisy had visited her a few times in the past year to see how she was. Though she was better, she'd taken extra unpaid leave and wasn't scheduled to return to school until some time after Easter. Ryan had offered to sit with her in the car so that she could regain her confidence again when she was ready to get behind the wheel.

"I don't want to be in your way for too long."

"You're not. You're my brother. I hate what you're going

through, but we are family, and I don't want you to rush just because you think you're in my way. You're not, okay? So, take your time in deciding if you like it here. You don't need to rush into anything."

He let out a breath. It was his first day at a new place of work. "Thanks. That means a lot." He needed to get his life back together, and he was sure how things would turn out in this arrangement. He hoped he and Kayla wouldn't fall out. They hadn't lived together since he was a teenager. Six years older than him, she'd left home soon after college, moving around the country in various teaching jobs and finally settling here. While she was a caring older sister, she was also nosy and judgmental.

Kayla lowered her voice. "You have to be strong for Daisy. This needs to be a happy new start for her. Wipe that sad look off your face."

Instantly, on cue, he slowly forced a smile he didn't feel. "It's a first day for all of us. Are you sure you're up to the task?" he asked, worried about Kayla.

"It's a good way for me to get back into working."

"Looking after a new mom and baby? That's hardly the age range of kids you were dealing with before." New babies were demanding. He knew too well how difficult things had been when Vanessa had Daisy. His wife ... his -ex-wife, had been tired and the new baby's feeding demands had been relentless.

"I can look after a baby," Kayla insisted. "They sleep most of the day. I've looked after a class of kindergarten kids, and I'm a childminder for a lot of my friends."

Ryan didn't want to say anything to shatter his sister's confidence. Looking after a class of young kids was so different compared to taking care of a baby all day. He'd overheard his sister on the phone to her friend, and it seemed that the mother had had a difficult birth and was unable to do much at the moment.

Poor woman.

"And I'd like to help. Ginny isn't well."

"Ginny?"

"The mom. The sisters run the bridal shop in town and—"

"I'm ready, Daddy."

Daisy stood up, and he couldn't help but notice her shiny new shoes. "I'm ready, too."

"Honey, you look so smart and pretty." Kayla walked towards her niece with outstretched arms. Daisy rushed into them and gave her aunt a big hug.

"Come on, Dee. Let's go." Ryan winked at her.

Kayla glanced at her watch. "We should leave now. I told Ashleigh I'd be there by eight."

The family Kayla was helping lived near Daisy's new school, and this was a blessing. "Are the family okay with you going to pick Daisy up from school?" He hated inconveniencing his sister, and he didn't want anything to affect her temporary job.

"It's a short distance from the Roses' house and I can easily walk there. I told Ashleigh about you and Daisy—not everything—just that you were living with me for a while, and she assured me it would be fine. They're desperate for my help, and they're perfectly okay for Daisy to stay there for a few hours until you pick us up."

"Good to hear." It was a relief, in a rollercoaster year. "Things seem to be falling in place for us around here," he said, giving a rare smile.

"Whisper Falls is a great place to live. You should consider it."

There was nothing for him in Lansing anymore but coming from a big city to this small town was going to take some adjusting. He lowered his voice. "It's a new start for me and Daisy. It's not going to be easy trying to put a failed marriage behind me."

Kayla gave him a stern school-teacherly look. "Your marriage failed because your wife cheated."

CHAPTER 5

GINNY

"For goodness' sake, Ginny. Kayla's here. You knew she was starting today. Why are you still in bed!" Ashleigh's face twisted in anger.

"Is it safe to leave her today?" Eloise stood behind her, her gaze bouncing from the baby to her.

Ginny opened her mouth to protest, resenting this early morning intrusion. "I'm here. I can hear you." She groaned loudly, not wanting to get out of bed. She wanted to curl up under the duvet and sleep again. She'd been up all night, had heard the birdsong in the morning. The baby had woken up crying a few times and she'd fed him with the formula milk. She was done trying to get him to latch on to her.

"Then get out of bed," Ashleigh ordered. "The doctor says you need to be up and about and active."

Eloise sidled closer. "You liked Kayla, didn't you?"

"Yeah." Ginny had met the woman, the new 'helper' her

sisters had found, last week. She'd found her pleasant enough, if a bit stiff and formal. She'd come over and looked after Benjy for an hour, and the two of them had talked. Ginny was relieved when she left. "But I don't need any help."

"You do need help," Eloise pushed back. "And Kayla's come at such short notice. Ash and I can't keep doing this and you need to pull yourself together. We're exhausted trying to take care of everything, what with the shop as well, and now Benjy. You need to start doing more instead of just moping around in bed all day. She'll be a great help around the house, and Benjy liked her."

Ginny gritted her teeth. *Benjy.* Her sisters had given him that name because they'd gotten sick of waiting for her to name him. At first she hated the reference to Ben, but she was growing to like Benjy.

It was cute, and sweet and fitting.

She would call her son Benjamin Rose.

The doorbell rang and her sisters stared at one another.

"Don't just stand there!" Ashleigh glared at Eloise. "Get the door! She'll think we're so unorganized."

"We *are* so unorganized," Eloise retorted, her hand on the door frame, poised to go. "Get up, Ginny! It will look rude if you don't come down to greet her."

Ashleigh nodded towards the door. "Just get the door, please." Ashleigh's hard stare fell on Ginny once more. "I'm collecting the pills from the pharmacy later. Those should help you."

"I don't want to take pills."

"They'll help, and you can take them now that you've given up on breastfeeding."

"I tried it. I didn't give up easily," Ginny hissed, resenting the implication that she hadn't.

"Taking the pills could help, so you should take them

instead of arguing with me." Her sisters had spoken to the doctor who had come to see Ginny. He'd prescribed a course of anti-depressants. "Get up!" Ashleigh was furious. Ginny let out a sigh. It took such effort to make herself to anything. Even something as simple as lifting her legs onto the floor and standing up. She didn't want to.

Ashleigh looked like she was going to explode. "Kayla is recovering from an illness herself. Don't stress her out. She's here to help you, not do everything while you mope around."

Ginny got out of bed slowly. "She didn't mention anything about an illness to me. And I don't understand how she's fit enough to look after me if she's recovering."

"She had a problem with her balance a few months ago, but she's fine now. She's going back to work at the school in a few months' time."

Ginny slowly climbed into her leggings. "I'll be fine. I don't know why you two are insisting on getting me this help. You just need to get to work, and leave me to it." She wanted peace and quiet, and for her sisters to leave her alone. She would take care of the baby because she'd have to if no one else was around. They weren't giving her a chance and it was always easier for her to let Ash or Eloise take charge. She didn't want people to be in her face and her space, watching and judging her every move and making her feel even more inadequate than she already did.

"I hate it when you're like this," Ashleigh snapped. "Hurry up and put something decent on. We've put up with this behavior for weeks and you need to grow out of it."

Ginny flinched, and threw on a sweatshirt quickly. She'd never heard that much vitriol in her sister's tone. "You don't have to keep having a dig at me."

"I wouldn't if you weren't so lazy—," Ashleigh stopped midsentence.

Lazy. That's what they all thought she was. Bone idle and lazy. But that wasn't true. She wanted to take care of Benjy, but she couldn't. She felt heavy, unable to move, not wanting to do anything. She wasn't being lazy, even though it probably looked like that to her sisters. She was trying but it was difficult to want to do anything when she constantly felt sad and had no energy. She felt tearful and tried hard to hide it from her sisters. They were worried about her and fussed over her and tried to take care of her and the baby. She hated being a burden to them but she couldn't get out of this dark hole.

Ashleigh rushed around the room like a mad woman, making the bed and tidying up while Ginny stood there, watching her and unable to move. She slept so poorly that when sleep did come, very late, it meant she woke up late, often not getting up until noon. There were days when she didn't bother to brush her hair or even get changed because it was too much effort. She didn't like her body; the way it had turned soft and flabby, and she didn't like how she looked and felt.

She didn't like anything.

This was horrible.

It wasn't how she'd imagined motherhood would be. With both her sisters at home taking care of her and the baby, it meant that she was free from taking responsibility herself. They made it easy for her to do nothing, and now they were enabling her even more by hiring help.

"Ginny, for the love of God, *do* something!" The crying started, and Benjy was awake. Ginny picked him up and tried to quieten him. Holding him to her chest, he smelled like freshly laundered cotton. It was a miracle that this little bundle who pooped and drank milk, and burped and sometimes threw some curdled milk out, still smelled so good. In comparison, she smelled like bad cheese.

She paced around the room, trying to hush him and

miraculously, he quietened within seconds. Ashleigh rushed towards the door and held it open. "Pull yourself together, for your sake and the baby's. Now get downstairs and be nice to Kayla."

Ginny reluctantly followed her sister, holding Benjy in her arms.

Maybe this could work. Her sisters would be out of her hair, out of the way, no longer whining and complaining about her. Maybe a little help wasn't such a bad thing, because the way she felt right now, she couldn't do it all alone. She couldn't take care of him and herself.

Any trepidation she felt about being at home left alone with the baby disappeared when she saw Kayla again. Bespectacled. Schoolmarm-ish. Dressed older than her years. Ashleigh had mentioned that she was almost forty. Ever since her sister turned forty she'd had a pre-occupation with people's ages.

"Good morning!" Kayla's voice brimmed with a cheerfulness that Ginny couldn't relate to. She imagined that was how Kayla probably greeted her class every morning.

Benjy had fallen asleep through the chatter, his head resting on her shoulder.

"We're going now," Ashleigh announced. "You're in Kayla's good hands."

Ginny plastered on a smile. "Okay. 'Bye."

"Call if … if there's anything urgent," said Eloise.

"I will." Ginny nodded.

They hurriedly said goodbye and left. In the silence that fell Ginny and Kayla faced one another. Then, for no discernible reason, Benjy started to whimper again. Ginny looked at him, warily afraid of what might follow. It took no more than a few seconds for him to go start screaming from the top of his lungs. That was what she didn't understand. He was so changeable.

One minute he would be content and quiet, and the next he'd turn into a screeching Banshee.

"He must be hungry. Do you want to feed him?" Kayla asked.

Ginny swallowed. No, she did not. The baby made her feel inadequate. She stared at him vacantly as the noise filled the room.

"Here, come and sit down." Kayla stepped into the living room and adjusted the cushions on the couch. "Why don't you sit here and feed him? I'll get some porridge on." Kayla asked, her voice louder so that she could be heard over Benjy's crying. Ginny froze. The baby's screams pierced through her and made her more jittery. She wanted the noise to stop. She wanted the baby to be quiet.

"Ginny?" Kayla asked again, as Benjy let out a piercing shriek. "Why don't you—"

"I can't." Ginny held the little bundle at arms' length. "I c-can't feed him. He doesn't like me."

Kayla didn't take the baby, but looked confused.

"Take him!" Ginny cried. "Please take him." Kayla grabbed the baby, a look of surprised shock in her eyes. She mumbled something about there being formula milk in the kitchen and headed presumably to get it.

Ginny slumped against the wall. Engulfed in a thick fog, a feeling of dread hung heavy over her. She felt anxious about everything; about the baby, about not bonding with him. About feeling a failure.

"There, there." She heard Kayla trying to soothe her son, and she buried her face in her hands. Tears rolled down her cheeks. She was a mess. Broken and falling apart. She would never be a good mother.

The hard thump of the door knocker boomed over the new quietness. Her sisters had forgotten something. Ginny looked towards the kitchen. Kayla obviously had her hands full. Getting up slowly, she opened the door to find a pair of eyes, the color of mocha, staring back at her. His light brown hair, swept back, contrasted well with his dark business suit. He looked slick, and sharp, and like he was out of town.

"My sister forgot her phone." There was a confidence in his voice that made her take note. His eyes narrowed and she could feel the trail of his gaze over her face, assessing, thinking. "Are you ... okay?" he asked, reminding her that she hadn't yet uttered a word.

"No. I'm not okay." The words tumbled out, an automatic response to a question nobody had asked her.

"I'm sorry to hear that. Can I help?" His smile was warm and friendly, and she noted the thin lines fanning out from the corners of his eyes.

She raised her hand to her hair, knowing it was messy, knowing that her face was wet with tears, knowing that she looked haggard after a night of little sleep. She opened her mouth to say something but failed.

"Daddy, I'm going to be late!"

She saw, over his shoulder, a small child. A young girl who looked ready to go to school.

"Ryan, what are you doing here?" Kayla appeared, with the baby on her shoulder.

"You forgot your phone. I'll leave it here." He handed it to her.

"Oh, shoot. I needed that. Thanks."

"Is everything okay?" he asked his sister.

"Daddy!! I don't wanna be late on my first day."

"You should go. You don't want Daisy to be late. Good luck to you, too."

Ginny listened, feeling like a guest, standing on the sidelines in her own home with two strangers, one of whom was taking care of her baby. She felt even more helpless than usual; unable to step up and become the mother she needed to be.

The man gave her a look before he turned. His soft brown eyes were filled with something that looked like concern. That look was more than anything she'd had from Ben. That look was of a man who seemed kind. Who seemed worried. Who looked like he cared.

A beat tripped inside Ginny's heart; and she felt something odd and alien. Clearly the man had a family, and it was wrong for her to feel anything. Tired and overwhelmed, she longed for rest. "I didn't sleep too well last night," she told Kayla. "I need to have a nap."

Kayla nodded. "Benjy's gone back to sleep. I've put him in the crib downstairs. Come and have some breakfast, then take your nap."

CHAPTER 6

RYAN

"Why did you come out of the car, Dee?" Ryan fixed Daisy with a stern stare.

Or at least he tried to. She looked so sweet in her shiny shoes and with her pigtails, smartly dressed for her first day. But something was missing. Her mother.

He tried to keep his daughter busy and fill her days with distractions but there was a void he couldn't fill. He just prayed that she would settle in well at this school and make lots of friends.

"I don't want to be late, Daddy. Everyone is going to stare at me." Daisy's lower lip stuck out in a pout.

"I'm sorry. I'm sorry." He leaned over and kissed the top of his daughter's head. "We're not going to be late."

"What's Aunty Kayla doing there?"

"She's helping someone who's had a baby."

"Why?"

Good question. "Uh … because she just needs help." He struggled with an answer because he was curious about her. That woman had obviously been crying. Her wet face, her soft brown doe-like eyes were ample proof of that. Kayla had said something about the family and how the new mother needed help. He guessed that the woman who'd opened the door was the new mom.

"Why can't she do it?"

"I don't know."

His mind churned over what he'd seen, and it didn't make sense. Maybe she was suffering from post-partum depression. He'd read up all about it before Daisy had been born. He wanted to be prepared, wanted to know all about pregnancy and a newborn and how best to support his then wife. Depression after childbirth was common, but, thankfully, Vanessa hadn't suffered from it.

He drove up to the school and parked up. Maybe this is how it was meant to be. The school wasn't too far from where Kayla was, though his drive to work was another forty minutes yet. He wouldn't have been able to do this alone, and he was grateful for his sister's help.

He turned and stared at his daughter. "Ready?"

Daisy's eyes lowered.

"It's both our first days," he said, his voice turning softer while his heart ached. It was much harder for his little girl. Walking into a class where she would be the outsider. He prayed the children would be nice and make friends with her.

"Are you scared, Daddy?" Daisy stared at him with big, shiny eyes. His heart thumped loudly. "No. What I feel is … excitement." He could see her fear. Could sense her trepidation. So much had changed for her in such a short time. "Do you know how I'm going to deal with my first day at work?" he asked, hoping to give her ideas. "I'm going to think of all the nice friends I'll make, and the new work I'll be doing. It'll be the same for you in your new school, with … with …" He struggled to paint a rosy picture when his mind was filled with nothing but worry. "With new friends to make, and new adventures to have."

"I want Mommy to pick me up or drop me off."

He pressed his lips together and his insides turned hard. Vanessa had turned her back on them. He could understand her doing it to him, falling out of love and falling into it with someone else, but what he would never understand for as long as he lived was how a mother could turn her back on her child, for another man.

In his eyes, that was an unforgivable sin.

He shrugged. He didn't want Daisy to become bitter and twisted, not ever, but it hurt him to know that she still hungered for her mother. He hated his ex-wife with a passion that scared him at times. "She might surprise you, one day."

Daisy's face lit up like a torch. "She will?" He blinked, unable to say anything as his daughter filled with excitement and looked raring to go. He hated giving her false hope and his insides hardened when she threw her arms around him. "I love you, Daddy."

He crouched down, his face was level to hers. "I love you more than you know. I want you to have a great first day, sweetie."

"You too, Daddy. You have a great first day at work as well."

She was wonderful. So young and so lovely, despite what had happened. He wondered what she made of it all, leaving their home, moving, starting over. But Daisy wouldn't see it like that just yet. For her he had to keep up the pretense.

~

His first day at work hadn't been so bad.

Coming from a big city where he'd headed a technical team of over thirty, and now moving to this place seemed like he was going backwards in his career. He'd been unsure about accepting a job as a technical manager for a much smaller team, working at an insurance company, but his day had been good. There was no traffic, a relatively easier commute and a lovely building surrounded by greenery.

It was not an urban concrete jungle, and the people seemed nice and friendly too. An added bonus was that he was back to pick Kayla up by six o'clock. He hoped that Daisy hadn't gotten too bored at the house. He'd have to worry about what he was going to do once Kayla returned to school, and he would need someone to take care of his daughter after school while he was at work. As with most things in his recent life, he didn't have the answer to that.

He stared up at the house, wondering whether to call Kayla to tell her he was outside. He sent her a text, not wanting to call in case he disturbed the baby who might be sleeping.

But when she didn't respond to his texts, he decided to knock on the door. For the longest time no one answered and just as he was about to head back and wait in the car, Daisy opened the door. "Why are you opening the door?" he asked, alarmed.

Daisy looked sideways before whispering, loudly, "She's sad."

He stepped inside, and looked around, unsure of what to do. "Who is?" he asked in a whisper.

"The baby's mom."

"Where's Aunt Kayla?"

"She's changing the baby's diapers upstairs. Come and say 'hi' Daddy."

Before he had a chance to object, Daisy grabbed his hand and led him into another room. He saw the woman from the morning, sitting on the couch, hugging a cushion to her chest. She was watching a sports channel on the TV, which surprised him. When she didn't turn to acknowledge him, he coughed lightly. "You're into sports?" he asked, hoping to break the awkward silence.

The woman turned to him just as Daisy loudly whispered, "Her name's Ginny."

"Sports?" the woman echoed, her face devoid of emotion.

He looked over his shoulder, thought he heard something. "Ryan!" Kayla beckoned him from the shadows. He went back into the hallway and followed her into what looked like the kitchen. "I don't know if I should leave her with the baby. She doesn't seem to be very comfortable with him. Ashleigh said today was the first time they were leaving her alone with him."

"She's not been alone, though, has she? You've been here."

"That's what I mean. I don't know if I should leave before her sisters get back."

"Is she alright?" he asked, even though every fiber in his body told him she wasn't. Kayla let out an exasperated sigh. "I don't think so, given the circumstances."

"What circumstances?" His curiosity piqued.

"Her fiancé died in a car crash and she had a difficult pregnancy and birth. Of course she's not going to be okay."

"That's my Daddy!" Daisy sounded happy. He turned around to find her pointing at him with the woman standing behind her. He sucked in a breath, hoping she hadn't heard.

"You can go home, Kayla. I'll be fine." The new mom, Ginny, had heard. Kayla scrubbed the back of her neck, looking hesitant. "I can stay until your sisters get back."

"There's no need. I can look after him."

"Are you sure?

"I'm sure. And anyway, he's sleeping now."

"I don't know …" Kayla didn't seem too keen to leave.

"I can wait outside for a while," he offered, speaking to Kayla.

"I'll be fine." There was a steeliness in the woman's voice which he couldn't ignore.

"Okay, if you insist," Kayla said, still looking unsure. Ryan could tell that his sister wasn't okay with this.

"Can we go now? I have homework," Daisy announced proudly.

"You've got homework? Already?" Ryan bent down, happy to hear his daughter sound enthusiastic.

"Yeah! I have to read a book."

"A book?"

Daisy nodded, and her pigtails bobbed about. "Will you help me read it?"

"Of course I will."

"I'll see you tomorrow, Ginny," Kayla said as they turned to leave.

"'Bye," Ryan said,

"That's so tragic about her fiancé," Kayla said as soon as they got into the car. "I remember hearing about that crash. It was horrific."

"That is tragic," he said, staring straight ahead.

"She split up with him before, but they got back together again."

"She told you all this today?"

"Darcie told me. She wanted me to know so that I was prepared."

"Prepared for what?" For the first time in a long time he stopped thinking about the mess that was his life. Hearing someone else's problems put things in perspective.

"Prepared for the way she would be. I can see why her

sisters were desperate for someone to help. That girl is suffering from depression."

He looked in the rearview mirror to find Daisy listening intently. This wasn't a conversation to be held in front of little ears. He and Kayla could talk later. "How about you tell us how your first day at school was, sweetie?"

CHAPTER 7

GINNY

Ginny slunk against the door when Kayla left.

The sound of silence was pure bliss. Ginny leaned against the door and closed her eyes, reveling in the silence.

She hadn't had a moment like this for a long time. She hadn't been truly alone for months. But now there was no Ashleigh or Eloise, no Kayla, no Darcie, no Ford or Liam.

She let out a grateful sigh. Sliding to the floor, she bunched up her knees, folded her arms and rested her head on her knees.

Benjy's piercing cries ripped through the air, jolting her. She lifted her head and looked at the stairs. Her heart hammered in her chest and her armpits turned sweaty. The baby's wails grew louder.

"I'm coming …" she whispered, but she didn't move. Her heartrate rocketed, and her hands grew clammier. She wanted to rush to Benjy, but she was scared to pick him up, scared that she couldn't quieten him. Scared that he didn't want her.

Her breath stuck in her lungs making it harder to breathe. It was a familiar feeling. Something she battled with daily; rejection, failure and not being enough.

And then it came, a montage of images and feelings tinged with sadness. Images of Ben and the girl on his bachelor night.

Of the photo she should never have seen.

Of her wedding dress, unworn and hanging on the clothes rail for days.

Of discovering she was pregnant, and trying to hide it.

Of reaching out to Ben again.

Of taking a misguided leap.

Of having the silly idea that he might have changed.

Of having him back in her life only to analyze and second guess his every move and sentence.

Of never fully trusting him, but wanting and needing everything to work out.

She was frozen in place, thinking about the past, with Benjy's screams amplifying tenfold in her head.

Then the key turned in the lock and Ashleigh and Eloise walked in.

She stood up shakily.

"What are you doing just standing there?" Ashleigh hollered, dropping her handbag to the floor. "Can't you hear Benjy crying?"

"Ginny!" Eloise hissed, before running up the stairs.

"Your baby's crying. *Wailing and screaming,* for goodness sake." Ashleigh's voice was hard and cold. Like steel. Eloise's soothing voice floated down the stairs. She had the baby in her arms.

Ginny cowered when her sisters stared at her in disgust. She felt completely useless. "I was about to go to him but ..." The excuse died on her lips. They wouldn't understand.

Not in a million years.

She wanted to go him but, but she couldn't. Her mind knew what needed to be done, but her body didn't obey. Didn't let her do what needed to be done. It couldn't.

"What are you doing, Ginny?" Ashleigh stormed into the kitchen in a huff. Eloise passed by with the baby who was now quiet and gurgling in her arms.

Just over a month old, he was still so tiny and fragile and she was scared she'd hurt him by not holding him properly, or panicking and dropping him. She'd run through so many awful scenarios in her head. She didn't want to hurt him; she loved him, with all her heart but each time she tried to pick him up or touch him, he cried.

She followed her sisters into the kitchen. Ashleigh started getting things out of the fridge and cupboards, in preparation for making dinner. Eloise sat in the chair, making funny faces at the baby who rested in the crook of her arm.

They gave her the cold shoulder for a while. Then, "I got your pills. They're on the table," Ashleigh told her. "So, how was your first day without us?" her sister asked, throwing her a glance over her shoulder. "How did you find Kayla?"

Ginny folded her arms. She hadn't done much. She'd been watching how quickly and easily Benjy had taken to Kayla, a complete stranger, and how she was able to quieten him, and feed him, and put him to sleep, and play with him. The woman wasn't even his mother. "It was okay."

"Just okay? What did *you* do?" Eloise looked up, her fingers lightly stroking Benjy's cheek. He was staring up at her, his lips in a goofy smile.

Ginny's insides crumpled. He never looked at her like that. "I watched TV." Her cheeks heated as she suddenly felt a blush of guilt and embarrassment. From the periphery of her view she could see her sisters exchanging glances.

They thought she was pathetic, but they didn't understand. Grinding down on her teeth, she turned and left.

~

ASHLEIGH

"I'm *exhausted*."

Ashleigh flopped onto the couch like a deflated balloon. Her feet were sore. Her body was bone tired. "We need to do something about Ginny." She pressed her fingers along her eyebrow, trying to soothe out the knot of tension along it.

Eloise yawned. "We did do something. We got her some help."

"She needs more than that. She needs therapy or counseling, or *something*." Ashleigh was at her wits end. It seemed like she and Eloise were always worrying about Ginny. For so long now their sister's life had been a downward spiral of descending into darkness and she and Eloise were at a loss with what to do. They had suggested to Ginny that she get some bereavement counseling to help her come to terms with Ben's death, but Ginny wouldn't hear about it. They'd just about managed to convince her about Kayla.

She hoped that Ginny would take her medication. It would be a start.

Eloise grinned as she texted on her phone, and Ashleigh became even more irritable. "You're not seeing Liam today?" she snapped, wishing she had someone special in her life, someone she could text and talk with and go and see. Someone who would take away the stresses of her daily life. Someone she could escape with and who would get her out of this daily grind.

Eloise giggled at the phone, and didn't answer. She was madly, annoyingly, irritatingly in love. Ashleigh looked away and tried to block out Eloise's girlish giggles.

She missed Ford.

She didn't think so much about her recent trip as she did about Ford and how much she missed him.

Gone were the days when he would text or call and they would talk for hours. These days he barely said much. He spoke more to her sisters than her. She'd learned that his elderly mother had recently fallen and broken her hip, and she knew he was busy taking care of her. If things had been fine between them, she'd have helped him. She had offered to, and had wanted to visit his mother when she'd been in the hospital and later when she'd come back home, but Ford told her his mother didn't want any visitors. Ashleigh wasn't sure if she believed him.

Ginny was their problem, not Ford's. It was good that he came by as much as he did, to check in on Ginny, but lately she'd noticed that he'd been more somber than usual.

"I might as well talk to myself," Ashleigh muttered, when she didn't get a response from her sister?

"What's that?" Eloise looked up and feigned some interest.

"Don't worry about it. You carry on texting your lover."

Eloise cocked her head and stared at her, a guilty expression on her face.

"I'm sorry." Ashleigh groaned. "It's sweet, in a sickly way. You two are sweet together."

"Sickly way? That's not nice."

"I'm sorry. I'm grumpy and miserable, and jaded and old."

Eloise was silent for a while, then, "I know what your

problem is. You need to speak to Ford and tell him how you really feel."

"I've tried but he doesn't seem to want to talk about it."

"You have to make him listen."

"We have other problems to deal with." Ashleigh lowered her head and knew she'd done what she could. She'd lost him. She regretted making him feel as if she hadn't cared, but he should have understood she needed her space. But now that she had it, she didn't want it.

Her space. Or the loneliness that came with it.

She hated being alone and she missed him more than ever.

"Ginny will get better."

"She will be if she takes her pills."

"She has to." Eloise's eyes were still pinned to her phone, and that evergreen smile never left her lips. Then, as if she sensed Ashleigh's disapproving eyes on her, she set her phone to the side and flopped back on the sofa. "It takes a while to heal a broken heart, and Ginny's has been broken so many times. In time she'll see that she has to move on."

"Kayla called and told me that Ginny kept to herself for most of the day. She picked Benjy up once but when he started to cry, she handed him over to her, and disappeared." Ashleigh hoped Kayla wouldn't bail on them. It was a miracle that they'd been able to find someone so quickly, and they trusted Darcie's recommendation. The shop was busy, and it was clear that they needed all hands on the deck especially since they'd neglected the business for so many months.

"She's still recovering from giving birth," Eloise reminded her.

"How much time does she need?" Ashleigh grumbled. "It's been a month."

"She lost a lot of blood. You saw how she was afterwards."

Ashleigh rubbed her forehead. "I know. I know. She's had it

especially tough, and it never seems to stop for her. I must be gentler with her. I'm just a grumpy, sad, lonely old woman."

"You're not old," Eloise shot back.

"All I need is a cat." An old woman and her cat. That was the promise life held for her.

"You can't get a cat, not if you intend to go traveling again. Things will get better, for Ginny, for you."

"You're in love," said Ashleigh getting up. "The whole world looks lovely and happy for you."

Eloise flashed an infuriatingly happy smile.

Ashleigh groaned again. "I'm going to bed."

RYAN

He'd finished washing up the dishes and had overheard most of Kayla's conversation. So he wasn't at all surprised when she hung up the phone and sighed loudly.

He looked at Kayla expectantly.

"They're worried about her," she announced, "and they've put her on anti-depressants."

"They might help her."

Kayla pulled up a chair and sank down on it wearily. "Ashleigh said that when they walked into the house after work, Ginny at the foot of the stairs, staring into space. The baby was howling upstairs."

He pulled up a chair and sat down opposite her. "She just stood there?" He didn't want to believe it but, given what little he knew of her, he could see how that might have happened.

Kayla held her head in her hands.

"Do you regret taking this on?" he asked, mindful of the fact that his sister was recovering. It was bad enough that he was burdening her with his problems—not that she complained

—but this new job she'd taken on didn't seem like a normal childminding or housekeeping job.

There was way much more to it.

The woman, Ginny, looked lost. Ryan was still struggling with what had happened to him, but it was nothing as horrific as what had happened to her. It was only Daisy who kept him going, and he felt sure that in time, Ginny would find strength in her son. "She needs help," he said, simply. "She needs therapy."

"She won't get help. Ashleigh said Ginny didn't like the idea of having anyone help her, but it's obvious that she's incapable of doing much herself."

"She does need you," he said. "She can't look after that baby by herself. Not yet, but she will, in time."

She was grieving and hurt. He understood her helplessness and her desire to want to let go of everything and everyone. He'd felt that way at first. As it was, he sympathized with her; could almost feel her pain which made his own diminish in comparison.

CHAPTER 8

GINNY

"Not everyone is able to breastfeed, and it's not anyone's fault, so don't be hard on yourself," Kayla told her, before handing the baby over.

Ginny recoiled as if Kayla were giving her a cactus instead of a baby. She was about to put the bottle of milk into Benjy's mouth, but paused. He was making funny expressions, moving his lips as if he knew what was coming.

"Just give it to him," cried Kayla clasping her hands, almost as if in prayer.

Ginny plugged the milk into the baby's mouth and he started to suck, then started to guzzle greedily.

"You see?" Kayla clapped her hands together. Ginny stared down at her son, at his little button nose, and his soft little eyes which looked up at her, wide with wonder. Her heart melted. He was so beautiful when he was like this. His shiny, gorgeous soft eyes stared up at her with pure innocence. She hankered for his smile; for a glimmer of recognition that he knew who she was, but then it came. Regular as the next day. He choked, and a trail of milk dribbled out of one side of his mouth. Alarmed, she pulled the bottle out of his mouth and he started to howl.

She jolted, fearing the worst. He didn't like her. And when his cries reached fever pitch, she panicked. "I … I can't …" She angled the baby up and moved him away from her slightly. Kayla was there in an instant, grabbing him and wiping his mouth. "There, there," she soothed.

"He doesn't like me." Her baby's rejection hit like a truck.

"Nonsense! They do that sometimes. He took that down so fast, and it choked him. It happens and it's nothing to worry about." Kayla slipped the bottle back into the baby's mouth, and sat down beside Ginny. "Take him again," she offered, moving the baby towards Ginny.

But Ginny shook her head. "He doesn't want me. He wants you."

Kayla's eyes widened in disbelief. "That's just something you're telling yourself, but it isn't true. Take him, Ginny."

She couldn't. Instead, she scooted away slightly. "He doesn't want me. I told you. He never wanted me."

"He's your son. You're his mother. Of course he wants you. He needs you. He's hungry and agitated because he can't get the milk fast enough."

But the hurt was too deep. The rejection too personal. She was still in pain, still bleeding, still unable to sleep. She was a wretched mess. Broken into too many pieces to put herself back together again. She stood up slowly, holding her stomach because her wound was hurting. "I can't have him. I'm in pain."

It wasn't a lie; she was in pain, both physical and emotional.

～

RYAN

"What are you doing with that?" Kayla's voice cut like a scythe. His sister stared at him with contempt. "Please don't tell me you still miss her?"

"What? No. No, I don't."

"Then why are you caressing that dress?"

Ryan looked down at the layered tulle in his hands. "I'm not." He let go of his ex-wife's wedding dress and it fell back into the box. He tried to dislodge the feelings out of his brain, the memories of how happy he'd been when he'd seen Vanessa walk up the aisle towards him. It seemed like only yesterday.

These days he barely recognized the woman she'd become. He was tidying up, getting rid of his past, things he'd packed up and brought along with him, but which he now needed to sort out and throw away because he didn't want to clutter Kayla's house.

"Why do you even have this?"

He swiped a hand across the back of his neck, feeling guilty. "I packed up everything when we moved. I wasn't thinking. I just took what she'd left behind."

Kayla lifted the dress gingerly. "What do you want to do with it?"

"Do what you want with it. I don't ever want to see it again."

"I know what to do with it."

"What's that?"

"Ashleigh will know someone who could take it. They own a bridal shop. Or did I already tell you that?" Before Ryan could reply, she shoved the dress back into the box.

"Do they sell secondhand clothes?" he asked.

"No. They're an upscale boutique."

He'd been having a clear out this weekend, and was going through his belongings. He'd left all the furniture behind and had sold it to the nice couple who'd bought their family home. A home that he and Vanessa had moved into when Daisy was a toddler. The home where they'd talked about having another baby; a sibling for Daisy.

But she would always be an only child now.

CHAPTER 9

GINNY

Ginny dreaded the time when Kayla slipped out to pick her niece up from school.

It was a strange setup, as far as she could tell. Kayla's brother dropped her off every morning, and then came to pick her up, with his daughter, every evening.

She hadn't seen him since that first day. He hadn't come to the house again, and in the evening Ginny sometimes saw his car parked outside the house. She wondered where Daisy's mom was. One day she'd innocently asked Kayla, only to be told that Daisy's mother was a high-flying career woman who was often away on business trips.

Ginny was often in her room, or watching TV, and she stayed out of the little girl's way. Luckily, Benjy was always down for a nap, so she didn't have to worry about him too much. As for her anti-depressant pills, she wasn't keen on taking them and often purposely didn't. It was only when

Ashleigh asked her that she felt guilt tripped into taking them, but it was random and haphazard.

One day, when Kayla left to do the school run, Ginny went downstairs and her eyes fell once more on the rectangular shaped white box that lay on the floor. Kayla had mentioned that she had something to give to Ashleigh and Eloise but they'd been in a hurry to leave.

Ginny's curiosity got the better of her and she lifted the lid off. There, neatly folded with beautiful beadwork was what looked like a wedding dress.

Her heart sank.

She'd had something like this, once, but she'd never worn it because she'd never had her special day.

An odd tingly feeling fluttered in her chest and she slowly unfolded the dress which was interleaved with layers of tissue paper. Gently, she pulled the dress out. It was long and white and made from satin. With a low neck, it had halter neck style tie at the back. The soft satin flowed through her fingers as she examined it carefully. It reminded her of her own wedding dress, which had taken months to make.

She was so caught up in thinking about the past, her mind going to a faraway place, that she was caught off guard when the door opened and Kayla stepped inside with her niece. The little girl's eyes went to the dress in Ginny's hands, then to Ginny's face. She looked tearful.

Caught red-handed, Ginny didn't know what to say.

Kayla frowned. "What are you doing?" she asked. The little girl let go of her aunt's hand and stepped towards her, making Ginny feel worse. She quickly put the dress back into the box. "I'm sorry I ... I was ... just ... curious." There was no explaining this and coming out of it well.

"That's my Mommy's wedding dress! She showed it to me once."

Ginny swallowed, feeling small and foolish. "I'm sorry. I shouldn't have been looking through it."

Kayla sneezed. "Oh! Excuse me. The dust is getting to my …" She sneezed again, then again and waved her hand in front of her nose. "I should have gotten Ryan to wipe the box down. There's dust all over it." She sneezed again, and in the next moment, a baby's cries pierced through the air.

Ginny froze and stared at Kayla, who got ready to sneeze again.

"Your baby's crying," Daisy told her, stating the obvious. Ginny stared at the floor, wishing it would open up and swallow her. Kayla heaved out a heavy sigh before stomping upstairs, and making Ginny feel even more inadequate than she already did.

"Why don't you like your baby?" the little girl asked her.

Ginny took a step back in shock. "I *do* like him. I-I love him so much—"

"But you never go to him when he's crying."

The accusation cut like a blade.

"Daisy, that's enough!" Kayla appeared with the baby in her arms. He was quiet again. Like he would be with Kayla.

"But she never—" the little girl started to protest.

"Come with me. Into the kitchen now, Daisy. Let get you some milk and cookies." Kayla used her schoolteacher voice. She continued rubbing Benjy's back. He was still, his face resting along Kayla's shoulder and he was probably asleep again.

"You don't have to bring the milk with you, or the cookies," said Ginny, recalling the carton of milk she'd seen in the fridge and some chocolate cookies that clearly didn't belong to any of the sisters.

"They're the ones Daisy likes." Kayla replied.

"But we can get them," Ginny offered. She felt bad for upsetting Daisy and wanted to do something nice for her.

"I feel bad enough as it is, having to leave you and the baby while I go to get my niece from school," said Kayla, in a rare confession.

"Please, don't." She was grateful for Kayla's help.

"When he's a little older, and it's not so cold outside, I'll take him for a walk for some fresh air. Maybe you can come along, too," Kayla suggested.

"Sure."

Daisy stood by her aunt's side, and stared up at Ginny innocently. She hated having been caught looking at the girl's mother's wedding dress, but she hated even more that she'd made her sad.

～

RYAN

Ryan got out of the car when Kayla didn't answer his text, and rang the doorbell.

He didn't like calling her because he was never sure if the baby might be sleeping, but he had to get back home, then get ready to go back out for the management dinner he'd been invited to at the new company.

But no one was answering the door either. Ginny hardly ever came to the door, and Kayla was probably busy. He strained his ears for the sounds of a baby crying, but there was silence. Just as he leaned against the wall, deciding to wait, the door opened.

It was her. The new mother. Ginny. He wasn't sure what to call her, having never been formally introduced, and he also felt it was wrong that he knew so much about her; stuff she probably wouldn't want many people to know.

They looked at one another in silence for a few seconds, enough time for him to see that she seemed more composed than when they'd met last time.

"I was looking for Kayla."

"She's upstairs. With the baby. He made a mess and she's changing his diaper." It was the longest he'd ever heard her speak and he wasn't sure how to respond. "You're probably wondering why I'm not taking care of him," she said, her voice flat. Robotic almost.

He was struck by her directness. "You're still recovering, from what Kayla told me. These things take time." He was trying to be mindful, and not too nosy, trying to be understanding without giving away how much he knew. Trying to not make her blame herself, because he could sense she blamed herself enough.

Daisy ran towards him. "Hey, Dee. How was your day?" His little girl wrapped her hands around his waist. He bent down and kissed the top of her head.

"She wants Mommy's wedding dress." Daisy pointed a finger at Ginny who looked nervous.

"Don't point, sweetie. It's rude." He could sense the woman's discomfort and wanted to put her at ease.

"It's not ... it's not true," Ginny said, her voice barely audible. "I didn't ... I don't want it." She let out a nervous laugh. "I don't want it. I was just ... curious."

"What's going on?" Kayla came downstairs, and he felt relieved to be leaving soon.

"Tell him it's not true," Ginny cried.

"Tell him what?" Kayla looked at him in confusion.

He was conscious of the time, as much as he was aware of Ginny getting worked up. "It's not important. Can we hurry up?

I'm going out to dinner with the management team and I don't want to be late."

"Daisy said I wanted the wedding dress, but it's not true. I was curious, that's all. The dress was here and I was looking through it." Ginny started to wring her hands, and he felt sorry for her.

"But she was holding it like she wanted to wear it!" Daisy protested. Ryan crouched down. This was also clearly upsetting Daisy. "Sweetie, let it go. Please. I'm sure Miss Rose was only curious. I'm sure she doesn't want your mommy's dress." He glanced at his watch again, eager to leave. "We should go. Now."

"I was curious." The woman said to him as he stood up. "I'm sorry. I didn't know what was in the box."

Acutely aware of her discomfort, he tried to reassure her again. "It's okay. Daisy is a kid and sometimes these little people have overactive imaginations. Not that it's a bad thing, huh, sweetie?" He winked at Daisy, wanting her to know that he wasn't angry with her.

"I never got to wear my wedding dress, not for real. I just liked the feel of it in my hand," Ginny told him, making him feel even more sorry for her.

"I meant to give it to Ashleigh this morning but your sisters were in a rush," said Kayla, grabbing her handbag.

"Did you tell them we don't want anything for it?" Ryan asked.

"Why are you giving Mommy's wedding dress away?" Daisy's sad eyes stared back at him.

He bend down again and took her soft small hands in his. "Sweetie, your mom took everything she wanted and she left this behind, so I don't think she wants it."

"But *I* want it."

His breath held in his throat and he didn't know what to say.

"Then you shall have it." Kayla picked up the wedding dress box. He could see by his sister's expression that she wished she'd given it to the women earlier. They'd have to take it back home with them. "I'll see you tomorrow," she said to Ginny.

"'Bye," said Ryan.

He hated that the dress was coming back home with them.

Daisy and her crazy ideas.

One day he'd have to tell her that her mother had chosen her new life, one that didn't include her or him.

"What happened with the dress?" he asked Kayla later that evening as he was about to leave for the team dinner at some fancy upscale restaurant.

Kayla shrugged. "The poor girl. She'd taken it out of the box and was staring at it when Daisy and I returned home."

He frowned. "Staring at it?"

"She canceled the wedding."

"They never got married?"

"She called it off the first time because there were rumors that he had cheated on her."

"Cheated?" He snorted in disgust. The poor woman. No wonder she was so helpless and lost. And having to bring up a child on top of everything could only make things worse. His problems were minor compared to what she was dealing with.

"They assumed it. He never admitted to it, but there were photos from his bachelorette party and the woman in them wasn't Ginny."

"He was such a douchebag."

"But then she found out she was pregnant, and they reconnected again. Ashleigh wasn't here, and Ginny hid it from the middle sister. The sisters didn't like him, they didn't think he was a good man, turns out he wasn't."

"Oh?" He folded his arms in preparation to hear more.

"Don't you have some place you have to be?"

"Only to the management dinner. I don't want to go but it's something they do every so often."

"You need to go and make an impression."

"Make an impression on who?" he asked.

"Your boss, and new people. You need to meet new people. Lots of new people."

"That's the last thing on my mind."

"Are there any nice single young women there?" Kayla asked.

"I don't know, and I won't be looking out for any. Turns out he wasn't, you said." He tried to nudge his sister back towards the original conversation.

"What?"

"The guy, Ginny's cheating fiancé. The sisters didn't like him."

"Oh." Kayla rolled her eyes. "They suspect he was cheating on her again, or was starting to because when he died, there was another woman in the car with him. She survived."

"Does Ginny know about the other woman?"

"She knows. Apparently it came out after he died, and then she had a difficult pregnancy, and had a hard time giving birth. She's had such bad luck. Her life hasn't been easy. Enjoy your dinner." She yawned. "I'm going to have an early night tonight."

GINNY

Ginny felt compelled to fix her reputation. The little girl had called her out and said she didn't love Benjy, but it wasn't true.

She did.

She loved her little boy, but it just wasn't easy to show it. Not when he bawled each time she picked him up and tried to comfort him. She was trying to do more around the house, tried to make herself more useful because she hated the way Kayla looked at her sometimes. The wound from her C-section still hurt a little, and she wasn't completely pain free yet.

Nothing came easy.

Nothing.

She often wondered if things would ever be good again. If she would ever feel happiness again..

As the weeks passed by, she was able to fix a light dinner for when her sisters got home from work. She was also able to do some light cleaning around the house now she was getting better with the pain from her C-section. She wasn't back to her usual self, and she still felt a little down some days, but the days when she was motivated to get out of bed were increasing in number.

"Hey, how are you?" she asked Daisy one day, The little girl was sitting at the kitchen table busy with her coloring book. An array of coloring pencils were spread out all over.

The little girl eyed her with trepidation but said nothing. Ginny was eager to talk. It was nice to have company and children weren't purposely judgmental. She pulled out a chair. "Mind if I sit down?"

The girl said nothing, so Ginny sat down. "Did you have a good day at school?"

Daisy nodded, the crayon still in her hand.

"That's pretty." Ginny jerked her chin at the sunflower Daisy was coloring in.

"My mommy likes flowers."

"Does she? Then she will love your pictures." She coughed lightly, waiting for Daisy to say more, but she didn't. "I didn't mean to make you angry." Ginny was hesitant and worried she might say the wrong thing. Confusion spread over Daisy's face and Ginny wondered if she was doing the right thing in raising the subject. Would there ever be a right time? "When I was looking at your mom's wedding dress. I was ... I was being nosy." She made an apologetic face. "Us grownups can do silly things like that. I'm sorry if I upset you."

But Daisy didn't look amused. Ginny cleared her throat as the little girl gazed at her intently for a few moments. Then she continued with her coloring. After a few moments she stared up at Ginny again. "She's coming back, you know." There was a hint of defiance in her voice.

"Of course she is. She's busy with her work."

"How do you know that?" Daisy asked.

"B-because your aunty told me."

Daisy continued coloring in the flower.

"You must miss her and I'm sure she misses you." Ginny felt a sudden rush of affection seeing Daisy with her head lowered and coloring in, a look of pure concentration on her face. The little girl was adorable. Her eyes were downcast, her lips pressed together in concentration as she colored in.

"You are adorable, did you know that?"

"My mommy loves me."

"Of course she loves you. How could anyone not?" Ginny answered, with a smile.

"But you don't love your baby."

The words punched her in the stomach with full weight.

"I ... I d-do ... " Ginny stammered, feeling a physical blow to her solar plexus.

"Then why does Aunty Kayla have to look after him? Why don't you do it?"

Ginny gulped, feeling a little breathless now. "I ... I'm not well. I'm trying to get better. Your aunt is helping me."

"How?"

"How what?"

"How is Aunty Kayla helping you?"

"She ... she ... she looks after Benjy for me and she helps me around the house."

"But you're always watching TV."

"I'm not always watching TV," Ginny replied, defensively.

"Are you always sleeping, then?"

"What, no?" She was aghast. "Who told you that?" She was starting to feel paranoid.

"Where's Benjy's dad?" Daisy asked.

Ginny blinked.

"I never see him," Daisy said.

Ginny was so taken aback she didn't know what to say to the child, or how much she should tell her. "He …he …" She swallowed. It wasn't her place to talk about death to a child. "He's not around."

"Where is he?"

"He's in a faraway place."

"Doesn't he love Benjy, or you?"

Ginny struggled for composure with the simple and innocent question. "What?" Her voice was a whisper.

"My mommy's coming back 'cause she loves me and I get to speak to her sometimes, and she blows me kisses and smiles at me and tells me how much she loves me." Daisy's pigtails jiggled when she nodded vehemently, her jaw set tight in concentration as she ran her yellow crayon over the sunflower petals.

"That's wonderful. I'm sure you can't wait to see her."

"See who?" Kayla asked walking in. Something buzzed and she pulled out her cell phone. "Your daddy's here, honey."

"Yay!" Daisy squealed as she jumped up from her chair and raced out of the room. Kayla quickly gathered her belongings. "See you tomorrow, Ginny."

"Yes. See you tomorrow."

When they were gone, Ginny hunched back, and let out a breath she didn't know she'd been holding.

Her interrogation by a five-year-old was over.

RYAN

It was a tricky situation.

Not tricky as much as delicate.

He was worried about Dee. As much as he loved his little girl, what she'd told him about Ginny and her conversation had been playing on his mind for days. He'd been looking for the ideal opportunity to have a word with Ginny and to set the record straight but the opportunity hadn't presented itself. He'd tried to explain to Daisy why she couldn't go around telling people that they didn't love their children.

"I'll have a word with her," said Kayla when he recounted what Daisy, in her blissful ignorance, had told him. "I'm sure Ginny didn't realize. I wouldn't worry too much about it because it must have gone completely over her head. That girl seems to be on another planet most of the time."

Ryan gritted his teeth together. He didn't like the way Kayla talked about her sometimes. "I need to apologize, in case it upset her."

Kayla peered at him suspiciously.

He pushed back. "Daisy said some unkind things and I feel responsible."

Kayla's eyes narrowed. "You weren't even there."

He didn't understand what she was implying. "It's irrelevant whether I was there or not. I don't want my child going around accusing mothers of not loving their babies."

"She's not wrong."

"She's not well!" he cried, shocked by Kayla's casual comment.

"Children can be perceptive."

"You said she's suffering from post-natal depression. It's hardly her fault. She's not doing this deliberately, and I am pretty sure she loves her baby."

"Children say things as they see them."

Ryan scratched his cheek. "That's what worries me."

"Do you pity her?" Hands on hips Kayla faced him.

"Pity? No. It's not like that."

"Like what?"

"Whatever it is that you're thinking."

"What am I thinking?" Kayla's eyes fixed on him, making him shift uneasily.

"I don't know, Kayla. I never know what you're thinking, or how you think. You don't sound too fond of her, and I don't have a clue as to what's running through your head right not."

"I don't want you to rescue this so-called damsel in distress."

"She's not asking to be rescued, and I don't see her as a damsel in distress. I see her as a woman who has known great tragedy in her young life and—"

"She's twenty-five. She's young. You're older, and you have your own baggage."

An eight-year age gap. He suspected as much. "I'm not attracted to her."

His sister gave a derisive snort. "Dear God. I hope not. That girl has had so much drama in her life, there's a lot of baggage there. It will take years of therapy for her to heal."

He didn't like Kayla's casual and cruel take and was slightly surprised. "You don't sound very empathetic. Not one bit."

"I feel sorry for her. You'll be making a mistake if you get involved with someone like her."

A knot of anger, like a gnarly, thorny fireball, formed in his gut. "I'm not planning to get involved. With anyone. Ever." He wanted to knock that silly notion out of Kayla's head. She was overprotective, and interfering and he didn't like being constantly watched in his dealings with other people, or being told how to go about his business.

He felt sorry for Ginny, and it was natural for him to feel empathy for her. What shocked him more was Kayla's complete lack of it. "Don't you want to help? Don't you feel bad for her?"

"I do, but I worry about you more. The last thing you need

in your life with everything going on, is further complication. Genevieve Rose is a truckload of trouble."

Ryan balled his hands together into a fist. "Believe me. I have no intention of ever getting involved with anyone ever again. I can relate to her. That's all it is. I can relate in some small way to her pain, and the last thing I want is my daughter accusing an already fragile woman of not loving her son. I'll talk to her tomorrow and sort it out."

CHAPTER 11

GINNY

"Could I ... could I have a word, please?"

Ginny looked up to find Kayla's brother standing in the doorway of the living room.

"With me?" she asked, feeling uneasy and half-expecting Kayla or Daisy to walk in, or the baby to start crying.

"Yes."

She hadn't even heard the doorbell ring. Taking her legs off the couch, she quickly ran her hand through her hair. She hadn't even brushed it today, and was aware that it looked unkempt. Kayla's brother appeared uncertain as he hovered around the doorway, then glanced over his shoulder as if he, too, were expecting to be interrupted.

"Uh … sure. Come in." She gesticulated in the direction of the couch furthest away from her.

Ryan walked in, tall and handsome, smoothing down his tie. It was then that she noticed his suit. Dark blue, tailored and expensive looking. She wondered if he'd always looked this way, and she'd been so deep in her darkness to even notice.

A thought flashed inside her head. This was about the wedding dress. Instantly her hopes deflated like a balloon. She'd made a fool of herself that time. "If this is about the other day, about …" She struggled to find the words to admit to her nosiness.

"It is."

"I'm sorry. I didn't mean to go through your wife's belongings. I didn't know it was a wedding dress and then when I saw what it was, I couldn't help myself and I took it out and I … I wanted to see what it was like." Her voice wavered towards the end, and she hated that she was unraveling so fast. Falling into pieces so easily.

His eyes met hers and she felt a compassion she hadn't experienced in a long time. These days even her sisters were irritated with her. But this man, with his soft gaze and his gentle expression, looked at her with a tenderness she yearned for. He made her feel safe, not stupid or useless. The mere fact that he'd come here to talk to her made her feel valued.

This was new.

"It's okay. I understand," he said.

What did he understand? She frowned, hoping that he hadn't heard the rumors around town and now felt nothing for her but pity.

"But that's not what I wanted to talk to you about."

"Then what?" she asked.

His hands were still in his trouser pockets, as he moved towards her, forcing her to crane her neck upwards to look at him.

"Can you please sit down?" He was so tall. Taller than she had at first noticed. Too tall for her to be staring up at him the whole time. He put her on edge, being here. Dressed like *that*.

Looking at her with kindness, and talking to her in a voice that was kind yet confident. Soft, yet seductive.

He did as she asked. "I want to apologize for what Daisy said to you the other day. She told me, quite innocently, and I was appalled."

"About what?"

"When she said you didn't love your baby. She shouldn't have said that."

Ginny scratched the skin at the back of her head. *That* was what he wanted to talk to her about? "She didn't ... she didn't mean it, I'm sure."

"And I'm sorry she asked you about Benjy's father. That must have hurt. She didn't know."

Ginny fidgeted with her hands. "I didn't know what to say to her. Children shouldn't know about death. I told her that he was far, far away."

He leaned forward, encroaching on her personal space, but she didn't mind. "I'm sorry for your loss. Children ask questions unfiltered. They don't think." A hint of his cologne swept over her and the hairs on her arms jumped to attention.

"Th-that's refreshing. The world would be a better place if people just said what they thought. I wish people—grownups—could be more like that."

"I'm not sure I agree." He fiddled with the knot in his tie, and she noticed that he wasn't wearing his wedding band.

"Why's that?" She was most curious to hear what he had to say.

"Some people need to filter their thoughts."

"Watch what they say, you mean? That's not being honest." She was thinking of Ben and how deceitful he'd been.

"But at least we know where we are with honest people," Ryan countered.

A quiver of electricity shot through her. This was exciting

and new, being so close to him and talking like this. Just the two of them alone in a room. Did he feel it too? This low thrum between them which turned the air electric, alive and potent with promise.

But this wasn't right.

She was no better than Ben or the other women who'd shown an interest in him when he and she were together. She couldn't have any interest in a married man.

She changed the topic. "Your daughter is adorable. She's so excited about her mommy coming back. She can't wait." Something in Ginny's heart felt heavy as she said that. Would Benjy ever feel that way about her? Could he sense that she kept her distance sometimes, that she was scared and wary of him? Did he know?

Ryan stared at her, and she shrank back. "We didn't know what to tell her. At first I said nothing, I was in shock myself."

Ginny tilted her head, not understanding.

Ryan continued. "A few times Daisy said something about mommy being at work, then Kayla said it was better to let her think that. She said in time, as Daisy grew older, we could tell her the truth."

"The truth?" She was afraid of what Ryan might tell her.

"Her mother left us." Ryan's voice lowered to a whisper and he glanced over his shoulder at the doorway. When he turned to face her again, there was a dullness in his gaze, as if the light had gone out. "She fell in love with her boss. She was always working. Working away, working late. Working, working, working. At least, that's what she told us. No wonder Daisy thinks she's busy with her work." He air quoted the last two words.

"Won't she come back?" Ginny was reeling from the revelation. "For Daisy's sake?" The thought crushed her, of the poor little girl waiting for her mother to return; a mother who had walked out on her child for another man. She shuddered in disgust.

Ryan looked wistful. "She's not coming back. She calls her once a week. They have a video call, although lately she'd been quite haphazard with her timing. She's not been good at keeping up with the calls, and she hasn't been to see Daisy for months." His eyes filled with sadness. Ginny couldn't believe her ears. "I've come to terms with it, but I'm still at a loss to understand how a mother can't love her child—" He stopped, and they hung in the air; the words that could have also equally applied to Ginny. "I'm sorry. I didn't mean it like that."

Ginny waved her hand dismissively. "I'm sorry for your news, for Daisy. It must be difficult."

"It is."

"I feel so bad for Daisy. She believes her mommy is coming back."

Ryan shook his head. "She's not. It wouldn't surprise me if they end up getting married. Vanessa knows when she's onto a good thing and she obviously upgraded from me. She won't downgrade after the life she's discovered with him."

"Don't put yourself down like that" Ginny was surprised to hear him talk like that. He looked so smart, so business-like, so handsome and she wondered what sort of woman would give up a man like that.

An uneasy silence mushroomed between them. Their eyes met and in his gaze she could see reflected back the anguished pain she constantly lived with.

"I am trying, with Benjy." She broke the silence, wanting him to know that she wasn't a bad mother. She wasn't cold. She cared, she loved, but she was afraid of rejection.

"I know you are." He looked pensive. She wondered what his ex-wife looked like. What sort of a woman she was. How she could walk away from such a man, and a beautiful little girl. A perfect family. What sort of woman would do that?

"I'm sorry about what happened, to your husband."

"We weren't married."

"Oh, yes. Sorry. I forgot." He rubbed his brow. "I'm sorry for your loss. I can't begin to imagine what you're going through."

"Seems like …" Ginny paused to take in a breath. "Seems like you've had a difficult time of things yourself. I had no idea."

"That's the way I like it. A new town, new people. I figure nobody needs to know my business."

"And yet you told me." She wondered why he had, but now she realized. They were the same. They were hurting, and broken people, struggling to cope.

A cough interrupted the conversation and Kayla appeared, giving Ginny a knowing look which made Ginny's cheeks heat up. Embarrassed, she lowered her head, wishing she could melt into the floor. "Daisy's hungry and we should go."

Ginny stood up and swiped the back of her neck, not quite understanding why her skin had broken out in goosebumps.

CHAPTER 12

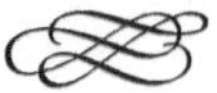

RYAN

The shrill sound of a baby's cries emanated from the house.

Ryan walked towards the door in trepidation. Kayla was busy; no wonder she hadn't read his text. He rang the doorbell, and the crying got louder. Ginny opened the door. She looked flustered, anxious, struggling to carry a wailing baby in her arms. "Kayla's not here," she said, above the noise, then left the door open, and walked away.

He stepped inside and closed the door, feeling apprehensive. "Where is she?" The baby's face was red and it looked as if he'd been crying for a while.

"She went out." Ginny paced around, telling the baby to shush. "He won't hush." Desperation gave her voice a higher than usual pitch. She looked exhausted.

He peered towards the kitchen and looked around, suddenly fearful. "And Daisy?"

76

"Shshhh!" Ginny rocked the baby harder, but it made him scream even more.

"Daisy? Is she here?" Ryan asked.

"She had a rehearsal or something for the play ... at school … Kayla said—" But the baby's wails drowned out the rest of her words.

Relieved, he swiped a hand across his brow as relief set in. The rehearsal for the play. Kayla had mentioned it to him in passing, and he'd completely forgotten. Back-to-back meetings all afternoon had sapped his mind.

"Be quiet!" Ginny hissed at the baby. The woman was an anxious wreck. Her nerves like the frayed edges of the oversized cardigan she wore. She was struggling, her desperate eyes boring into his. "I told you he doesn't like me. He doesn't want me."

"That's not true." He moved towards her, wanting to calm her. "Maybe he's hungry?"

"Hungry." Her brows pushed together. "He must be hungry. I think he's hungry." It was as if a light had gone on in her eyes. She held out the baby for him to take, but he shook his head, remembering that Kayla had talked about Ginny not bonding with her baby. "Maybe if you try putting him on your shoulder. That might soothe him. I'll get his milk."

"Kayla left some in the kitchen."

The baby's cries turned softer. "See," he said, glancing over his shoulder to see that Ginny had adjusted how she was holding him. He grabbed the bottle of milk on the countertop. It was warm. "Here. This might be what the little man needs."

Ginny shook her head, and started to take the baby off her shoulder. "You do it."

"Hey," he said, trying to coax her gently as he pulled a chair out for her. "Sit yourself down, and you feed him." She looked anxious and uncomfortable, and the baby's screeching didn't help. He felt sorry for her.

"I can't." She shook her head, and held the boy out to him. He had no option but to take him. "You can do this, Ginny. He doesn't hate you." He nodded at her to sit, and she complied. "He just wants milk. That's all babies know, hunger and dirty diapers. They don't form opinions or have bias. Here, feed him. He's hungry." He placed the baby gently back in her arms, then held the bottle of baby milk in front of her. Fear flickered in her eyes. "Take it," he urged, his tone sterner than he liked. But it worked. She took the bottle of milk from him and gave it to the baby.

The poor boy was so hungry, he started to gulp it down, maybe a little too fast because he then spluttered and started to cough. Ginny immediately moved him a little upright, but the baby started to cry again. "See. He doesn't like me feeding him." She pulled the bottle out of his mouth while milk trickled down the sides of his mouth. He wailed even louder. "Please take him," she begged.

Ryan had no option but to take him. He wiped Benjy's mouth then settled him on his shoulder and rubbed his back. That's when he heard a little burp. Trapped wind. "Hey, buddy. You had some trapped wind, didn't you?" He continued rubbing the boy's back and saw Ginny starting to leave. "Where are you going?" he asked.

"He likes *you*."

"You're his mother, he loves you. Why don't you sit back down?"

She did. He walked towards her. "He's let out some trapped air. He took the milk down too quickly, that's all. He was uncomfortable, but he's fine now. Aren't you, buddy?" He cradled the baby's head gently in one hand and handed him back to his mother.

"He'll start crying again," Ginny protested.

"No, he won't. Here." He angled the baby in her arms so that his head was slightly lifted. "And maybe try holding the bottle like this, so that the milk doesn't go down so fast when he sucks." He helped her to make the adjustment, and soon the baby started to drink the milk.

Ginny gazed down at her son, her expression softer now.

"What did I tell you?" Ryan was happy to see her finally look relaxed. "He was hungry."

"Kayla told me to hold him like this, but I forget, especially when he screams and yells." She looked up at him.

"It's hard to focus when they holler so loudly. It's as effective as the loudest siren. It gets our attention. Their cries make parents jump up and tend to them."

Ginny's face turned sad. "I don't feel like that. I want to make him quiet, but I can't make him."

"It's easy to think you've failed him, or that you've done something wrong, but you haven't. Babies can be demanding. It's a tough time for parents, especially the first few months." He regretted his words, wished he hadn't mentioned 'parents', knowing she was a single mom. The last thing he wanted was to make her feel bad.

"He's falling asleep," she murmured softly.

"They're sweet when they do that."

"He's not taking any more down. I think he's had enough." She pulled the bottle gently from his lips, but Benjy was quick to notice. His lips wobbled, so she put the bottle back in and he started to drink again. "He's playing with me." She giggled.

Ryan smiled. "Looks like it." That's all it had taken, a little bit of encouragement. Giving her a little belief in herself. "Babies get mad when they're not fed or held, or they have a dirty diaper. That's all it is."

"I had a hard time when he was born, and I think I maybe didn't bond with him as well as I should have."

"And look at you now. He loves you, Ginny. He's safe and comfortable and snug in your arms."

She seemed to mull over his words, before nodding. "You're good with him. I bet you're a great dad."

He sucked in a breath. "I try to be."

"You are. I can see it. You were so good with Benjy now."

"Benjy is a sweet little boy. He loves you."

"Ginny?" It was Kayla's voice.

"In the kitchen," Ryan answered.

"Daddy!" Daisy came running in from the cold, her cheeks red, her eyes shiny. He put a finger to his lips. "Shush, Dee. Benjy's sleeping." Daisy put a finger to her lips, in acknowledgement. Her eyes widened and filled with happiness. "He's so cute! I don't want to wake him," she whispered.

"No, we don't," Ginny replied. "Did you get a good part in the play?"

Daisy started to answer, her voice turning loud, until Ryan put a finger to her lips. "Baby's sleeping. You can tell me at home," he said in a hushed tone.

Kayla appeared then, her gaze darting between Ginny and Ryan. His insides hardened. There was something off whenever his sister caught him talking to Ginny. He didn't like it.

"What's this?" Kayla's tone was filled with disapproval, confirming his opinion.

"Ryan helped me with the baby," Ginny answered.

"You couldn't manage by yourself?" Kayla asked.

He threw his sister a cold stare. "We should go," he said quickly, standing up and placing a hand on Daisy's shoulder.

"See you tomorrow." Kayla barely glanced at Ginny as she rushed out.

"Can we get pizza tonight?" Daisy asked before running on ahead.

"Great idea!" he called out after her. "I forgot about the rehearsal," he said as he and Kayla walked towards his car.

"I didn't mean to be so late but the rehearsal went on longer than the teacher's note said."

"Any reason you have that look on your face?" He wanted to address this issue now. Kayla stopped and turned to him, her eyes searching his face slowly. The muscle along the side of her cheek flexed, and it was obvious that she was fighting to keep quiet about something. "That was a very cozy scene, you and Ginny. Anything I should know?"

He was startled. "She was struggling with the baby, and I encouraged her to feed him. She doesn't trust herself."

"She's a mess of emotions. She's all mixed up inside and that girl is carrying too much baggage for you to be thinking about getting involved."

Indignation spiked in his chest. He held up his hand. "For the hundredth time, that's not what's going on."

"Are you coming?" Daisy shouted. She was standing by the car. "I'm cold!"

"Isn't it?" Then to Daisy she shouted, "Coming, honey!"

"No, it's not," he hissed. "The baby was crying, and she was adamant that he didn't want her."

"She has more baggage than an airport."

"That's not nice." Kayla's words alarmed him. He'd never heard her be so casually nasty about anyone. "You offered to help her," he said, defiantly, "I hope you're not as nasty to her when you're there."

"I am helping her,."

"You seem to be anti-Ginny."

Kayla stopped short of the car. "Anti-Ginny?"

He lowered his voice. "As if you don't like her."

"It's not Ginny. It's not that I don't like her. It's just that she's had such a run of bad luck for years. Her parents died when she was a toddler."

"What?"

"The girls were orphaned a long time ago. It was their aunt and Ashleigh, the older sister, who took care of them."

"I'm cold and I'm hungry!" Daisy shouted.

Ryan raised his arm. "Coming, sweetie." Then, to Kayla. "It's getting cold, we'll talk later."

"There is nothing to say, Ryan. You're dealing with so much emotional trauma yourself and the last thing you need is to fall for someone who is as messed up as Genevieve Rose."

"I'm not falling for anyone."

"Getting involved with then."

"I'm not getting involved. I was trying to help."

"Well, don't."

CHAPTER 13

GINNY

She'd seen the effect on Daisy, of how that child pined for her own mother, and she didn't want that for Benjy.

Ginny was determined to show everyone that she could look after her baby; that she was starting to do better. To *be* better.

So, she forced herself to not give up. To not shy away from her son when he wailed at her and cried so loudly her heartrate would race. She forced herself to go to him and pick him up, and cuddle and hug him and hold him close. She wanted to be a good mom. Not an inadequate mess.

"I made it for Mommy." Daisy held up a pretty little card she had made. A pink love heart, sprinkled with golden glitter. "It's for Valentine's Day, because I love her."

"For Valentine's Day? Wow. It's beautiful! You're such a talented little artist. Your mommy would be so ... happy." A knot formed in her throat. She felt so sorry for the girl. Ever since Ryan had told her about Daisy's mother, Ginny had held a place in her heart for Daisy.

It also made her more determined to prove everyone wrong, and to do as much as she could for Benjy. She didn't want her son to ever feel that his mother didn't care, and she hoped that one day things would be normal, and he would grow up not having known how hard she'd fought against this terrible sadness and misery she was engulfed in. She couldn't shake it off. It stuck to her like toxic mold, keeping her chronically tired and miserable.

She didn't want to take the anti-depressant pills because they fogged up her brain and made her feel like a zombie. But, making herself get up, through sheer will and determination seemed to do the trick sometimes. It also helped that Daisy had called her out on her behavior. That the small child had noticed how she was with her son, made her feel guilty. And of course, there was Ryan. Not married, but single. It helped to have something to look forward to; the possibility that he might come in the house again. He'd been so good to her that day when he'd helped her with Benjy.

The girl turned coy, lowering her head and looking up at her through her eyelashes. "I made one for Daddy, too, but it's at school 'cause the paint didn't dry."

"Your Daddy will love it," Ginny gushed. Daisy's eyes fixed on Benjy, who was in Ginny's arms, staring up at her contentedly while downing his milk. "Benjy's too little to make one for you."

"That's okay. When he's older, I hope he'll make me cards that are as beautiful as the ones you're making."

"My friend at school said people send them to people they love. Daddy will get one from Mommy and she will get one from him."

"That's nice."

"She said you get one if you have a boyfriend, or daddies and mommies give them to each other."

Ginny nodded, not knowing what to say.

"I'm going to make one for you," the little girl declared. "'Cause you don't have anyone to give you a card."

Ginny inhaled a deep breath. "That's okay, it doesn't matter if I don't get one, but that's really sweet of you to make me one."

"What's your favorite color?"

"Blue."

"Mine too!" Daisy's excitement amused Ginny. That something so simple could make this little child so happy, was a testament to the unbridled wonder of childhood. It was tragic how jaded humans became, the older they became. Ginny wished she could find the small things in life as wonderful as this child did. "Do you want to make some cookies?"

"Cookies?" Daisy's eyes turned as round as saucers. She set her crayons down. "Now?"

Ginny shrugged. "Benjy's going to take a nap soon, and I'll have nothing to do, and you're almost done with your coloring." She loved to bake and hadn't done it in a long time. Hadn't done much of anything in a long time, except for sitting around and moping. Thinking about things, dwelling on the past that could not be changed and the future that was scary.

Doing things made time go faster.

Doing and keeping busy made her focus on things outside of herself. She liked it when Daisy came home from school, and she was grateful for the company. Kayla was becoming prickly. Not as easygoing as she'd been in the beginning, and Ginny found a stiffness in their interactions. She couldn't put her finger on it, there was something cold and distant about her lately.

"Can we make them now?!" Daisy jumped up excitedly.

"Let me put Benjy down, and we'll get to it."

Not long after, they set to making cookies, Ginny quickly got out the mixing bowl and spatula, and she and Daisy followed the instructions from her mother's handwritten recipe.

"I'm a caterpillar," Daisy announced as she mixed the dough.

"You're a what?"

"A caterpillar. In the school play."

"Oh. How ... how nice. How interesting." She tried to get a visual on that.

"Can you help me with my lines?"

"Sure."

"It's two sentences."

"Awesome. We can do that tomorrow, if you want."

"Thanks!" She gave Ginny a mischievous grin, before dipping her finger into the dough, scooping some out and plopping it into her mouth. "Ummmm. Tasty."

"They'll be even tastier when they're baked."

Half an hour later two trays of freshly baked cookies were on the countertops. Ginny had given some to Daisy who was happily chomping on them when Kayla walked in. "Your daddy's here," she announced. She sniffed the air, and her gaze fell upon the two trays. "You made cookies?"

"I used to like baking," Ginny explained.

"Daisy, not before dinner time! You'll spoil your appetite."

The little girl giggled in return. "But they're delicious!"

"She'll have an appetite for dinner. Kids can eat anything," said Ginny, not wanting to get Daisy in trouble.

Kayla started to put away Daisy's belongings into her school bag, and saw the Valentine's card. "This is pretty. Who's it for?" She opened the card just as she asked the question and saw the answer for herself. "Your ... mother ..."

There was no hiding her cool glacial demeanor. Ginny

suspected that Kayla didn't like Daisy's mom very much. Maybe Kayla was like this with most people, not just her.

"We should get going. You'll be okay?" Kayla asked.

"I'll be fine. Take some cookies home," she said to Daisy.

"Can I? For Daddy!"

"Yes, of course you—"

Kayla cut in. "It's 'May I' and no, I don't think that's a good idea to take any cookies home."

"But Daddy will like them! And I helped made them," cried Daisy.

"Take some." Ginny was determined not to let Kayla win. She filled a small plastic container with half the cookies they'd made. "You Daddy will like them."

Something flashed across Kayla's eyes. Disapproval. A caution. "If you insist. Thank you. I see you're doing more with Benjy."

"Yes."

"Pretty soon you won't need me at all."

Ginny pondered about that long after the two had left. It was getting a little easier. During the day she took care of Benjy more and was slowly becoming more confident. She was able to soothe him and quieten him when he cried. But the nights were still bad. She couldn't sleep, and when Benjy woke up multiple times during the night, she got up for him, but it meant she was exhausted in the mornings.

Still, it was progress.

CHAPTER 14

ELOISE

"**I** saved some for you," said Ginny, taking a container out of the cupboard.

She took off the lid to reveal golden brown cookies with chocolate chips and macadamia nuts.

"Cookies!" cried Eloise. She'd just finished tidying up after dinner. Ashleigh was stacking the dishwasher. "Cookies?" she echoed, straightening up.

"I made them with Daisy," Ginny announced proudly.

Eloise and Ashleigh glanced at one another. This was encouraging. For weeks Ginny had been a walking ghost. Kayla had often grumbled to Ashleigh that there was a lot more work to do than she'd been led to believe.

Lately though, they'd noticed a change in Ginny, which Kayla confirmed in one of the daily late night phone calls after Ginny went to bed. Their sister had turned a corner. Apparently, she'd started to spend more time with Benjy during the day. She fed him and bathed him, changed his diapers, played with him and talked to him. She'd started to insist on doing it all herself.

She was stepping up to her role as a mother, and the sisters were relieved to see this change finally happening. These days Eloise and Ashleigh had to fight Ginny just to get a chance to hold Benjy.

"Were you hiding these from us?" Ashleigh asked, taking one from the plate and biting into it.

"I saved them until after dinner. I let Daisy take half home for her dad."

"You did, huh?" Eloise draped a dishcloth over the countertop.

"It seemed only fair, seeing that she helped me make them," Ginny retorted. "I'm going to give Benjy a bath."

"Can I?" Ashleigh asked.

"No. I've got it, thanks."

Ashleigh rolled her eyes as Ginny left.

"She seems almost back to normal." Eloise commented. She closed the kitchen door before grabbing a plate of cookies and setting them down on the table. They always had an end of the day appraisal about Ginny because she'd been their biggest worry, but it looked like things were on the mend.

"Making cookies with Daisy?" Ashleigh whispered. "I'd say so."

"She seems much better." Eloise glanced at her watch, not wanting to spend too long here. Liam was waiting for her at the summer house.

Her home.

A home she slept in a few nights a week. A home she'd been trying to move into completely for months, but with one drama after another, it had been impossible. She didn't feel right abandoning Ashleigh and leaving her to deal with Ginny by herself.

She and Ashleigh used to take turns to help with the baby, even after they'd taken Kayla on, but lately Ginny seemed determined to care for her son herself. "I can sleep during the day, you two can't," Ginny had explained.

And boy, was she right.

Having a child was hard work. Eloise had no desire to ever have children, especially at her age but, during their conversations, Liam had hinted on a few occasions that he would like to be a dad. The age gap between them made her self-conscious, even though he reassured her that three years was nothing.

Ashleigh yawned then reached for another cookie. "These are *so* good! Why aren't you having one?"

Eloise was tempted, but declined. "I'm full."

"From what? You barely touched your crab cakes."

"I ate!" She had become more conscious of her figure and so she resisted. While her romance with Liam was moving along nicely, she was worried about having a younger man and keeping him.

Not that Liam had a roving eye.

He didn't, but she'd heard about Kayla's brother from Ashleigh, who had the full story from Darcie, and she didn't want to be like that, in the dark and completely ignorant right up until the end. She'd never get over it if something like that happened to her. If Liam found someone younger, and prettier, and left her; and she never saw it coming.

"Ginny's been so much better lately. Those pills are working."

"They sure are." Eloise stared at the plate of cookies, her mouth starting to salivate. The crunchy nut and choc chips were calling her.

"It's one less problem to think about. I don't want to worry about her. I want Ginny to get on with her life."

"Ditto." Ashleigh wasn't the only one. Eloise needed Ginny to move on, so that she could move on with her own life, with Liam.

"Taking Kayla on was the best suggestion Darcie ever made. She's been a great help," Ashleigh remarked.

"I don't think this change is Kayla's doing." Eloise had a gut feeling about what the cause of it was. Ashleigh tapped her fingers on the table, an expectant expression on her face.

"Ryan," Eloise said. "She lights up whenever Ryan's around. Haven't you noticed?"

"Ryan?" Ashleigh stared back in disbelief. "They've barely know one another."

"They know *of* each other."

"But they've barely met."

"Barely met? Have you been blind? He's come inside a few times when he's come to get Kayla and Daisy."

"And?" Ashleigh peered at her with narrowed eyes, not understanding.

"He and Ginny have talked. They do talk. I'm telling you, Ash, there's something going on."

Ashleigh didn't seem to believe her. "I don't see it. You're seeing things. You're so in love, you think everyone else is, too."

"Don't say I didn't tell you."

Ashleigh shrugged. "These are *soooo* good!" She reached for another cookie. "You sure you don't want one?"

Eloise shook her head.

"Why are you dieting?"

"Who said I was dieting?" She wasn't counting calories, but she had cut down on her portions. Unfortunately, Ashleigh had noticed.

"You went to the diner for lunch and had salad!"

"What's wrong with that. I love beetroot."

"I haven't seen you eat a burger in weeks," Ashleigh protested.

Eloise's mouth salivated at the thought. Ashleigh wiped the crumbs from her mouth. "Liam is crazy about you." Her sister wasn't blind, or stupid.

"He's also younger than me."

"Not by much. What do you hope to achieve by starving yourself?"

"I'm not starving myself. I still eat."

"You're already thin enough, Eloise."

It was a fear she had. A genuine fear. One that often kept her up at night, when Benjy's cries woke her. That was another reason she needed to now make her move to the summer house, for good. She'd had the place renovated months ago but with everything happening, Ginny almost dying while giving birth, and then struggling to raise the baby, she'd had to postpone leaving. Now things seemed to be working out for the better, for everyone.

"Should I have another one?" Ashleigh reached out to take another cookie, but her fingers hovered over the plate and she stared at Eloise with a guilty expression. "I've already had two."

"You can eat the whole plate for all I care. Ford won't mind you putting on a few pounds. He'll always love you."

"Ford doesn't care." Ashleigh grabbed another cookie and ate it heartily.

"He's taking care of his mother."

"She's still recovering from the fall," Ashleigh noted.

"She's not doing very well." Ford had mentioned it to her last week. "He's just busy with her. I wouldn't take him being distant towards you to mean anything more than that." She'd seen the way Ford still looked at Ashleigh sometimes. She'd caught him once or twice. It was the look of a man who was filled with regret. Regret for what had happened between them.

Ashleigh shrugged, but said nothing.

"You hurt him, Ash."

"I said I was sorry."

"He needs time, and he's worried about his mom. It's not always about you."

"I'm not making it be about me!" Ashleigh threw back. "I miss him, and I want to get back together with him but he doesn't ever want to talk about it."

She could hear the fear in her sister's voice. "You have a great guy," Eloise pushed back. "Don't let him walk away without at least trying to get him back."

"*Had* a great guy," Ashleigh mumbled.

"He'll come back to you. Give him time, be there for him. Look, Ginny and I, we haven't had much luck with guys. We seem to attract the cheaters—"

"That curse is now broken, for you at least."

Eloise rolled her eyes. "You have a guy who has a heart of gold. You took him for granted, maybe ..."

"I did *not* take him for granted." Ashleigh scratched at something on her jeans. "Maybe a little."

"He was so excited about surprising you. He missed you, and he was so desperate to see you."

"I know. You keep telling me. Believe me, I know."

"He thought you didn't want to see him. He thought maybe that you were meeting people and he didn't matter."

"I was on vacation! A long-planned trip of a lifetime, for myself. Something I'd been planning for years."

"Years?" Eloise blinked.

Ashleigh shrugged. "The shop had me chained. I didn't get to escape to Hyannis Port like you did."

"I understand why you needed that break." She sighed,

understanding this more than ever. It had been difficult taking care of things back at home, the shop, the house, Ginny and her secret, and then Ben, while Ashleigh had been away. They'd taken her for granted. She'd stepped in and taken responsibility for them after their parents had passed away. No wonder she was desperate to get away. "Give him time. He'll come back. For him it's you, it's only ever been you, Ash."

"It can't have only ever been me. He has an ex-wife."

Eloise suddenly remembered. "Talking of which, Susan's getting married."

"She's what?" Ashleigh coughed, almost choking on her cookie. Eloise wondered whether to move in with the Heimlich maneuver. "He didn't tell you?" She waited for Ashleigh to stop choking.

"He doesn't tell me anything."

Eloise was puzzled that he'd told her at all. The man wasn't only hurting, he was angry at Ashleigh and he was purposely blocking her out of his life and letting her know.

She stared at the fast-dwindling plate of cookies and watched Ashleigh take another one.

Her sister sighed with contentment. "She used mom's recipe."

"Mom's recipe," Eloise whispered and reached for a cookie. Her parents had been gone so long now that the memory of them—in the tattered old photo taken outside the bridal shop—was fading, though deeply cherished.

How different their lives would have been were it not for that fateful day of the accident.

CHAPTER 15

RYAN

He was ironing his shirts for work when he heard her.

"Mommy, did you get my card?"

Panic pinched Ryan's heart and his next breath stopped. Daisy had picked up his phone and was calling her mother. He rushed to her side and almost had a coronary when he saw Vanessa's face.

"Card?" Vanessa asked. "What card?"

"Daddy said he was going to send it."

"No I didn't."

"When are you coming home, Mommy?"

He tried to snatch the phone out of his daughter's hand, but Daisy was quick and snuck under the table, clutching the phone to her chest. He ducked down, crouching on the floor and saw her lower lip start to wobble. "I haven't checked my post yet, baby," he heard Vanessa say.

"Did you send it, Daddy?" Daisy asked him.

He'd posted the damn thing a few days ago. "I sure did."

"I didn't get anything, pumpkin." Vanessa was adamant and Daisy looked as if she was about to cry.

"It will get to Mommy in a few days' time, Dee." He tried to reassure his daughter. The card would have arrived, he was sure of it, but Vanessa was on vacation. Something his ex-wife hadn't yet told their daughter.

"I miss you, Mommy."

"I miss you too, baby," Vanessa said.

"Daisy, give me the phone, please," he begged, swiping his arm out to try and grab it.

"Babe, another top-up?" The sound of a man's voice turned his stomach to steel. Daisy brought the phone closer to her face and examined the screen. "Who's that?"

Ryan knew exactly who it was. He tried to scramble under the table, but hit his head on it, then he grabbed the phone, and banged his head again when he tried to get up.

"I want to talk to Mommy!" Daisy screamed.

"How could you let that happen?" His ex-wife snarled as he quickly went into another room and barricaded himself against the door so that Daisy couldn't get in. Vanessa was on a recliner, sitting up now, wearing a bright orange bikini, as far as he could make out. Palm trees and the azure blue water glittered behind her. Something hard twisted in his gut.

Was this woman for real? Had she forgotten she was a mother? That she had a daughter? Had she forgotten everything about them?

"Gimme the phone! I wanna talk to mommy!" Daisy cried from the other side of the door.

"Mommy's busy, Dee."

"Open the door, Daddy. Lemme in!" Daisy wailed.

Fire flashed in Vanessa's eyes. "Can't you lock your phone

and warn me before you call? I told you we were going away this week."

"She's been wanting to talk to you for a week now. You're the one who's not been free to talk. I didn't call you. Daisy did."

"Mommy!" Daisy burst out crying. Ryan's stomach twisted, sadness and anger knotted in his gut.

"You need to speak to her. *Just* you," he snarled, hating his ex-wife more than ever. This selfish, fickle woman who didn't have a maternal bone in her body, was enjoying her life on some exotic island. He'd seen Avery, the bare-chested man, Vanessa's boss, a man he'd met an many occasions in the past, lurking in the background, trying to stay out of sight.

"You should have warned me," his ex-wife hissed.

"Talk to her, quickly," he hissed back. He opened the door, to find Daisy sitting on the floor, leaning up against it, her knees folded and her face buried in her hands. "Here you go, sweetie. It's Mommy." He handed Daisy the phone.

"Who's that man?" Daisy asked.

"Which man?" Vanessa could lie like the best.

"That man who was behind you. He wasn't wearing any clothes. Where are you, Mommy?"

"I'm at work, pumpkin." Vanessa flashed a lying smile.

"But there are palm trees there."

"My workplace is a lovely place, pumpkin."

"I made you a pretty Valentine's Day card. Can you check your mail again?" Daisy asked. Ryan heart splintered into pieces as he listened to his daughter being fed lies by her deceitful mother. "Pumpkin, I told you. It hasn't come yet."

"You're sure you sent it, Daddy?" Daisy's large eyes bore into him.

"Yes, Dee. I told you I did. I sent it a few days ago."

"Baby, I have to go, but when I get back ..."

"Are you coming home?" Daisy's face lit up like a lamp at the hint of her mother returning.

"I meant ... I mean when I ... uh ... pumpkin, I have to go now but I'll check my mail. I'm sure it's a beautiful card. Thank you, baby. I'll let you know as soon as I get it. I love you."

"I love you, Mommy."

Ryan took the phone from his daughter, then scooped her up in his arms and held her. Daisy's arms went around his neck and she was silent.

He stayed like that with her for the longest time.

CHAPTER 16

RYAN

"What're you making there, Dee?"

"I'm making a Valentine's Day card for Ginny." Ryan's heart took a funny little turn at the mention of Ginny's name. "Oh ... that's ... that's nice of you."

Kayla, who was peeling potatoes over by the sink, walked over wiping her hands on a dishcloth. "For Benjy's mommy? Why?"

"Because she doesn't have anyone to give her a card," Daisy replied, as if it were the most obvious, most natural thing in the world. Ryan held back a chortle, listening to his daughter schooling his sister on the subtle art of being nice. He braced himself for Kayla's disapproval.

"That's sweet of you, Dee," he said, jumping into the conversation. "That's kind and nice of you."

"Ginny's gonna love it," Daisy proclaimed. "She said I'm really, really, really, *really* good at coloring."

Ryan toned down his smile, given that Kayla was standing next to him. "She said that?"

Daisy nodded. "She said she loved my drawings, and that I'm the best colorer-iner she's ever met."

Kayla coughed and returned to peeling vegetables, and even though she had her back to them, he could tell she was displeased. He patted Daisy's head absentmindedly, trying to get a grasp on his emotions. He felt something when he thought of Ginny; what exactly, he wasn't sure, and he still struggled to find the words to describe it. It was a lightness, a lifting of the weight on his chest, a sliver of light entering the grimy, bleak, darkness which had enveloped him ever since he'd caught a sniff of Vanessa's infidelity.

For the first time in a long time, he hadn't thought much about his ex, or the life they'd all had, of how she'd broken their family, how she'd walked away from her young daughter who doted on her and who was still waiting for her.

He'd gone from trying to pick up the pieces of their tattered lives and wondering if he'd ever be happy again, to someone who now looked forward to the promise of every new day.

Not yet.

Life was harder for Ginny. The thought of her made his heart jump again. He shook his head, not understanding his reaction. It's not like he was looking for someone to help him bring up his daughter. He was more than capable of doing that himself. It would be a while before he trusted someone enough to truly let them in.

He decided that it was pity and concern. That's what he felt for Ginny. Nothing more.

"Well, it was sweet of her to make cookies with you." They'd been pretty darn tasty, too.

"It was so much fun!" The wide grin on Daisy's face filled his heart. Vanessa had loved her and no doubt still did. She was her mother, but she was a selfish, self-serving woman, too, and she no longer seemed to care as much. She had no plans to ever be a part of her daughter's life again, and he couldn't sleep at night sometimes trying to figure out how and when he would tell Daisy the truth. Not for years, he hoped. But seeing his little angel getting close to Ginny, and baking and having fun, that dulled the ache in his heart, and he was thankful for that.

Kayla remained silent. She hadn't had any of the cookies; and he hadn't been too bothered about it because it meant more for him and Daisy.

"I want her to come to the school play," Daisy declared. Something hard clanked into the sink. Kayla turned around. "You want to do what?"

"I want Ginny to come and see me in the school play. She's helping me with my part."

Ryan folded his arms. "That's nice of her."

Daisy nodded. "She's cool."

"You're a caterpillar with two lines," Kayla's retorted. "How much is there to remember?"

His mouth twisted. "I'm sure Daisy is a wonderful caterpillar, and she reads her lines magnificently." He placed his hand on his daughter's shoulder. "I'm proud of you, Dee, and I can't wait to see you perform." He raised an eyebrow at Kayla and gave her a we'll-discuss-this-later look.

"Please, Daddy! *Please* can Ginny come?" Daisy begged. Ryan scratched his cheek. "I don't know. Maybe you should ask her." The woman never left the house, as far as he could tell, and this might be something good for her.

It would be good for him, too.

Of course there was no attraction.

None whatsoever.

Ginny was dealing with a lot, as was he.

But together, they seemed to get on and click.

"Can we go see Mommy? I made her another Valentine's card."

"Another one?"

"She didn't get the first one." Daisy held it out to show him. Ryan swiped a hand over his face. "Okay, then. I'll post this for her as well."

"Can't we go see her?"

He looked inside the card, his heart breaking at the words Daisy had scribbled.

I love you lost, Mommy. Come home we miss you x x x x x x x x x x x x x x x x

He suppressed a chuckle at the typo, but his heart was bleeding. Ignorance was bliss, especially in Daisy's world, but he hated deceiving her. "We can't go yet. I'll mail this in the post as well."

"But what if she doesn't get it, like the last one?" Daisy's voice rose, her tiny lips wobbling.

"She'll get it. I promise you she'll get both of them." He could feel the muscles in his face tighten. It wasn't fair. Vanessa was enjoying herself somewhere faraway, and he was having to lie for her. Worse, he had to watch his daughter long to see her.

"I haven't seen mommy for a long time." Daisy wouldn't let it rest.

"Hey." Ryan bent down, lowering his face to her level. He tapped her on the nose gently. "We will see her, soon. We will. But Mommy's busy now, and it's not a good time." He would have to make the trip to go and see her, because it didn't look like Vanessa planned to take time out to come to her daughter.

"Can we call her now?"

"Maybe not now. How about you finish the card you're doing for Ginny? She's going to love it."

And, just like that, Daisy got on with her coloring in.

～

"You shouldn't encourage her," Kayla said, when he was deep in an action thriller, long after Daisy had gone to sleep.

"With what?" But he knew what his sister was referring to.

"It doesn't look right for Ginny to come to Daisy's school play."

Ryan lifted his shoulders, not understanding. "Look right to who?"

"She's grieving, and struggling and depressed."

"She seems a lot better to me, lately."

Kayla pressed her lips together. "I wonder why."

Ryan shut his book. "Nothing is going on. I don't talk to anyone except for you and Daisy and my work colleagues. I like talking to Ginny. We can relate to each other. We've both experienced hurt. We've both lost a lot. We're both struggling to find ourselves."

"I don't want you to get hurt."

"How would she hurt me?"

Kayla's lips twitched, as if she were fighting to contain her words. "She's bad luck."

"It's wrong of you, and cruel, to say something as silly as that."

"Don't put Daisy through another hell, and don't say I didn't warn you," Kayla threatened.

He let out a slow breath, and only then realized that he'd fisted his hands. Kayla's disapproval was something he didn't need right now, especially when he was starting to find his bearings in a new life, in a new town, and doing well at work.

His stomach churned at the idea of Daisy still missing her mother so much, but Daisy seemed happier now, and that was the most important thing of all. His little girl, who had no idea that her mother no longer wanted to be a part of her life, had something in her life that made her smile.

The next evening, when he went to pick Kayla up, he marched up to the house and rang the doorbell. This time he hadn't even bothered to text Kayla to say he was waiting for her.

Kayla opened the door, surprise making her eyebrows shoot north. "You didn't text."

He walked in with the empty plastic container in his hand, and caught sight of Ginny sitting in the living room,. The baby was lying on a playmat on the floor, a musical baby gym hanging above him with soft fluffy zoo animals out of his reach.

Ginny turned and saw him, and her cheeks flushed. "Oh, hi," she said, sounding breathless, as if caught off guard. Her hand went to her hair and she smoothed it back.

He raised the plastic container in response. "I came to give this back. The cookies you made were delicious. Thank you."

"Daisy made them, too."

"Thank you for doing that, making cookies with her. We wolfed them down."

"I'm glad you liked them. I used my mom's recipe."

He nodded, thinking about her past and how much loss she'd known for someone so young; about how she was still suffering and how unfair her life was. Up until now he'd only been focused on his own misery. Ginny made him see how much worse things could be. His gaze went to the baby on the floor. "He's a happy little boy." The baby was kicking his legs in the air, while a musical tune played and the mobile spun around gently with various animals out of his reach.

"He's making funny noises now." Ginny smoothed down her sweatshirt. "Come in."

"I don't want to impose."

"I'll get Daisy, and then we should go," Kayla said, behind him.

"Daddy!" Daisy rushed in and put her arms around his waist. "Ginny loved my Valentine's Day card."

Ginny stood up. "It was lovely. She's such a gifted little girl." Daisy giggled, her arms encircling his waist. "Did you want to ask Ginny something," he said softly, "about the school play …"

"I already did! She said she will!"

"Shall we go? I'm ready," Kayla announced.

"I didn't say I would." Ginny appeared nervous, her eyes fluttering anxiously to Kayla then back to Daisy, and finally landing on him.

"Please come, Ginny! You helped me with my lines," said Daisy.

"Thank you for doing that," said Ryan, "and you should come, if you can." He was bolstered by his daughter's enthusiasm. He hadn't seen Daisy so animated in a long time, and this meant a lot to him, that she had found someone she liked so much, enough to want her at her school performance.

With her mother walking away, Ginny was the best thing to have happened.

"I … I mean, I don't know if I should …" Ginny's voice dropped lower, as if she were speaking to him, "but it was very sweet of Daisy to ask me."

"It's only two lines, for heaven's sake," Kayla muttered under her breath, but loud enough for them all to hear.

Silence fell and an icy chill spread out. Then, a laugh and a giggle sounded before the door opened and Eloise and Liam walked in.

"What's wrong?" Eloise asked, surveying them all as Liam stood behind her.

"Ginny's coming to my school play!" Daisy cried.

"Oh, she is, huh?" Eloise's reply was a slow drawl.

"We should go." Ryan touched Ginny's arm and she jolted. "Think about it. If you can make it, Daisy would love for you to be there."

Ginny blushed, and he was convinced.

It wasn't just him, then.

Something electric simmered below the surface between them.

She could feel it, too.

CHAPTER 17

GINNY

"I'm going because Daisy asked me to," Ginny said, crossly.

"It's got nothing to do with that good-looking father of hers?" Eloise asked, grinning.

"No."

"But you're also making cookies for him. Sounds like romance to me." Eloise folded her arms and surveyed her.

"Stop harassing her," Ashleigh chided in the background. Ginny let out a groan and wished Eloise would stop making fun of her. This was real. Delicate. Fragile. She didn't want her sisters to mock her or to talk about it. "I've fed Benjy and he's asleep. Will you be okay with him? I should be back before his ten o'clock feed."

Eloise twirled a lock of hair around her finger coquettishly. "You might be later, you never know."

"I'm coming straight home!" Ginny protested.

"His sister's with them," Ashleigh reminded them.

"Ooof." Eloise made a face.

Ashleigh blinked. "You get the same vibe from her too?" she asked Eloise. Ginny nodded to herself. It wasn't just her imagination. Her sisters were thinking what she herself had sensed.

Kayla didn't like her.

"Maybe I shouldn't go." She set her handbag on the table.

"You should go!" her sisters cried in unison.

She'd been jittery all day about going. After Daisy had asked her last week, she'd hoped the girl would forget, but then Ryan told her he'd put her name down on the list of people coming to the school, and Daisy reminded her almost daily about the play.

And now, here she was. All dressed up. Trying to fit into something decent. Nothing fit. Nothing looked nice. She felt extremely self-conscious. This was the first time she was going to a social event. She hadn't left the house since Benjy had been born, and she feared so many things. She was scared of leaving him, scared of being seen, scared of being around people and scared of being talked about.

Eloise picked up her handbag and handed it to her, and while Ashleigh ushered her towards the door. "Are you sure you're okay to drive?"

"I'm sure."

"You haven't driven since—" Eloise started, then stopped. *Since Ben's car accident.*

"I'll be fine." She was determined to be fine. She wasn't going to have an accident. She was more afraid of walking into a school hall filled with people who would whisper about her.

But she couldn't *not* go. She couldn't disappoint Daisy, and it would be nice to see her, and Ryan, but the thought of Kayla being there sent chills down her spine.

Kayla was different when it was just the two of them at home. She still helped Ginny around the house; even though these days, Ginny was able to do a lot more herself, but she'd noticed that whenever Ryan was nearby—something happened a lot more these days— Kayla turned into a different person.

She and Ryan managed to talk a little, and have snatched conversations about Benjy, and Daisy, mostly. Ginny looked forward to seeing him and when he didn't come inside the house she felt let down, a wave of disappointment ruining her mood.

She started the car and looked ahead. She could do this.

A short while later, she walked into the school hall. Paranoia swirled thick and fast around her because she was sure people were talking about her. They looked away when she walked past, some smiled, awkwardly. While she didn't know these people intimately, they knew of her. The Rose sisters were known because of the bridal shop and because of their tragic history, and now with Ben's death, she expected more rumors to fly.

She'd come early. Partly because she didn't want to walk in late and face a school hall full of people she barely knew. But mostly because Eloise hadn't stopped ribbing her about Ryan. She found some empty seats near the back. Her mouth was dry, her heart beating like a steel drum. She felt out of place being here, surrounded by people she didn't know. She felt strange not being near her baby. She also had never been to a school play, and now she was going to see one for a child that wasn't hers.

These things made her jittery, and she had already worked up a sweat which was made worse when she had to tell people who wanted to sit in the empty seats beside her that she was saving those places.

The air buzzed with the cheery chatter of anxious parents, and as she looked around surveying the hall, she saw Ryan walk in. He was tall and striking and he stood out. He wore his suit well, and that was something different because most of the people around here wore mostly casual clothes.

He was different too. There was no boyishness. He seemed older. She tried to guess his age, but couldn't. He was calm and strong, and steady. Nothing like Ben.

She noticed that women's heads turned, and they gave him the side eye when he walked past. Her heart was already thundering in her chest, as he walked over to her. A few awkward seconds passed.

"Hey." Ryan glanced at the two empty seats next to her, and still looked unsure about where to sit.

"Hey." She tried to keep her eyes on his face, and fought the urge to check him out in his suit now that he was so close.

"You're here early," Kayla came out of nowhere and sat down beside her, which prompted Ryan to take the seat beside his sister.

Ginny shifted in her chair. "I didn't want to be late."

"It's only a school play, Ginny. It's not the army."

Ginny racked her brains trying to think of what to say, to make conversation. It would have been so much easier if Ryan were next to her but talking to him was now impossible unless she leaned forward and across Kayla, and she didn't want to do that.

A glance in his direction showed that he was busy talking to some parents already; someone behind him and a couple in front. Kayla waved at a lot of people. As a teacher here, she obviously knew all the teachers and a lot of the parents.

Ginny felt more alone than ever. But soon the lights dimmed and the curtains parted, and the children filled the stage in their cute and funny little costumes. There, on one side, was Daisy, in her green caterpillar costume, lying on the floor, on her side, with her face propped up by her hand. She was so busy scanning the crowd trying to find her dad, that she almost missed her lines. Thankfully, they were only a little delayed, and her face lit up like a lamp when she saw Ryan. She almost waved to him, but remembered in time where she was and what she had to say.

Ginny watched, rapt, and found herself laughing and enjoying the show. She savored Daisy's time on stage, holding onto the edge of her seat, hoping that the little girl wouldn't mess up.

And she didn't.

When the play ended, Ginny clapped enthusiastically.

CHAPTER 18

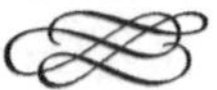

RYAN

The play ended and parents were told to wait outside in the parking lot while the children got dressed into their normal clothes.

Ryan wanted to talk to Ginny, since Kayla had prevented this by planting herself strategically between them. Other parents from Daisy's class were friendly and chatty, and a few sought him out and introduced themselves. He was conscious of Ginny being left on her own, especially with Kayla being approached by many. His sister seemed to know everyone.

After the play, when Kayla moved away, he was about to go over to Ginny when he was interrupted by another couple from Daisy's class. To his dismay he saw Ginny leaving the hall by herself. It had been like this ever since he'd been trying to leave. He'd be approached by parents, and each time he tried to leave, another parent or two would come by.

When, at last, he managed to get out of the school hall and

saw Ginny waiting alone in the parking lot. A tiny sliver of hope lit up inside him, that maybe her sisters had dropped her off and therefore he'd get the opportunity to give her a ride home. He headed towards her when another mom approached him and introduced herself. Mild irritation swept across him as he forced himself to make small talk.

"Daddy!" A small hand tugged at his jacket. Daisy's exuberant face stared up at him.

"Hey, Dee! You were amazing!" He almost scooped her up in his arms but remembered where he was and that she would not like it. Instead he squeezed her hand. "I'm so proud of you!"

"I didn't forget my lines."

"No, you didn't." He excused himself from the mom he was talking to, and led Daisy out to his escape. "You were the most interesting caterpillar in the world. I couldn't take my eyes off you."

"Did Ginny like it? Has she gone?"

"No, she's here. Over there." He pointed in her direction. "Shall we go and—" Before he could suggest they go and talk to her, Daisy had let go of his hand and ran towards Ginny, throwing her arms around her waist. By the time he reached them, Ginny was lavishing praise on Daisy's performance and his little girl was beaming from ear to ear. "There you are," he said. "I tried to get to you earlier."

Ginny's cheeks turned pink and she chewed her lower lip. "I saw, I did wait but then you were always getting accosted it seemed like. Daisy was amazing."

Ryan smiled proudly at his daughter. "Yes, she was."

Their eyes met and held. She looked pretty, prettier than usual. She'd done something to her eyes because they looked bigger, and more defined, her lashes long and thick. "Are you leaving?"

She nodded. "I didn't want to leave without seeing Daisy, and now that I have, I'd better be on my way."

His hopes deflated like a lead balloon. This would have been such a great opportunity to talk to her. He was also ready to leave. "I'm sorry I didn't make it to you sooner."

"You were busy with other parents," she commented.

"I tried to get away."

"You're obviously very popular."

"New parent syndrome," he answered, sensing something in her tone.

"Kayla seems to know all the teachers and parents here," she remarked.

"She used to work here, and she's planning to come back soon, when she's ready." He wasn't sure how long Kayla planned on working for Ginny, and what her plans were to return to work.

"So there's a possibility that she might be Benjy's teacher one day?" Ginny asked.

"Could be. That day might seem far away to you, but it will come by so fast." It had for him. He still cherished and remembered the day Daisy was born, how it felt when he'd held her for the first time. How much he wanted to protect her, and provide for her. How the outpouring of his love for her was beyond anything he had ever known, different to what he felt for Vanessa.

"You must be Daisy's mother." Ryan groaned inwardly. The same woman who had hounded him earlier now stood between them, flashing a wide and toothy smile at him, her gaze volleying between him and Ginny. Ginny's mouth opened and it looked like she was about to say something, only, she seemed to freeze.

"We're friends. Ginny is a friend," he said, his voice low, conscious that Daisy was nearby and talking to the woman's daughter. The woman had asked him earlier where his wife was and, luckily, he'd been interrupted and hadn't been able to give an answer. She'd wanted to know why they never saw her. He couldn't tell her the truth without Daisy overhearing.

"Oh. Who's your child?" the woman asked Ginny.

Ginny shifted uneasily from foot to foot. "My son is … just a baby."

A knot tightened inside Ryan's stomach. It was easier to talk to Ginny at the house because Kayla was a lesser problem compared to these parents. "Ginny's a family friend, and Daisy was excited for her to come."

"Your wife didn't come at all?" The woman looked around; her expression filled with questions.

"She's busy at work," he answered easily. He'd had forgotten about the gossip. The same gossip that had swirled around him when Vanessa walked out and left him to bring Daisy up alone. He'd found a way, with the help of a few friends he trusted to keep his secret, to help him do the school pickups. But he was all too aware of the gossip mill.

Gossip was what Ginny also likely dreaded and in this small town, it was insidious. It was therefore all the braver of her to turn up tonight. He admired her quiet strength.

"Could you excuse us? We need to get home." He walked towards his car which was parked at the far end of the parking lot, and grabbed Daisy along the way. He hoped that Ginny had followed him. When he was far from the main crowd, he turned around, and was relieved to see Ginny. "Sorry about that."

"It wasn't your fault."

"Daddy, I want to talk to my friend over there. Can I?" Daisy pointed two cars along where a group of girls had congregated.

"Go on. But stay where I can see you." Daisy rushed off,

but was within his sight. "Thank you for coming," he said to Ginny.

She laughed. "You don't have to keep thanking me. It was a pleasure. It was wonderful. They're so funny at that age. So innocent and unaware of their little mannerisms."

He nodded. "They're wonderful. I'm blessed that I get to see all of this." He was thinking of Vanessa and how much she had missed of her daughter's life, how much she would miss as Daisy grew up into a teenager and then a woman. How absent she would be from her daughter's life. For this reason he was even more grateful that Ginny had come along, so that Daisy might not feel her mom's absence as much. He wanted to talk, to say something, only, words failed him. He wasn't sure what to say, or how Ginny felt.

"I should go," Ginny said, when the silence stretched out like old worn out elastic. "My car's at the front, near the school." She made a face as if she didn't want to brave going back through the crowd. He glanced in that direction, his heart sinking because he didn't want her to go just yet, especially not now when he'd finally gotten a moment alone with her. Perhaps it was for the better. "I wouldn't do that yet, because I see that nosy woman still there. She'll be in your path and she'll interrogate you."

Ginny glanced over. "Was she alone? I didn't see her husband."

"She doesn't have one. She's a single mom, and she made sure to let me know a few times. She suspects that something isn't quite right with my situation. I obviously didn't tell her that I'm divorced."

"Why not?"

"Because Daisy doesn't know. She's so young and she adores her mom. You saw how she was with the Valentine's

Day card. She made her another one, because she told Daisy she hadn't received the first one."

"Poor Daisy," Ginny said softly, looking over at his daughter. "I didn't know you were divorced. I thought maybe you were separated." She seemed a little flustered and looked away when his eyes met hers.

"The divorce only came through recently, and that's when I moved here. Now it's time to make a new start."

"I see."

"Some situations are so final that a new beginning is the only option. I dwelt on the past too much, at the start, when it all happened. I thought maybe I misunderstood."

"Misunderstood?"

"That she had feelings for this man, and that's all it was. I wanted to believe that nothing had happened; that it was a flirtation that became all consuming."

"And was it?"

"No. It was more than that."

He lowered his head, thinking back to that painful, heart breaking, gut-wrenching time when he found out that truth. It wasn't just an emotional affair. It had moved way beyond that. Vanessa had lost her mind. She was talking about being with this other man forever.

It had shaken Ryan to the core. As if an earthquake had uprooted everything solid, everything he had taken for granted in his life, and reduced his world to shattered debris. Only Daisy remained. His little girl, and the one he would protect and love with an intensity that grew in proportion to the anger he felt towards Vanessa.

"I'm so sorry, Ryan."

He looked up. "And I'm sorry too, for you, for your loss, and for everything you've gone through."

She let out a heavy breath, her shoulders rising and sinking. "I should go." But she didn't move. She didn't even turn to look at the crowd she was dreading passing through. He wished she wouldn't leave, but there would be interruptions, and it was time to go. It was late and Daisy was tired. This wasn't the time or place to talk to Ginny, and yet there were things he wanted to say, things he wanted to talk about, about her situation and his. "Thank you for coming. It really meant a lot to Daisy, to have you come."

"I'm so glad Daisy invited me."

"I appreciate you coming. It means a lot to me there especially because Daisy's mother isn't going to be present at most of these things. I also know it's a lot to ask of you, leaving Benjy at home."

"It's the first time I've left him."

"It must have felt strange, coming here, especially, what with gossip mongers among us."

"I was scared, I admit, and I was half tempted not to come, but I didn't want to let Daisy down. Besides, I was glad for an excuse to leave the house."

He suspected it would be a good break for her. It was also nice for him. And for Daisy. Because Vanessa wasn't maternal and didn't seem to care too much. "I'm glad you're here."

"You must be Daisy's mom! So nice to meet you." Another couple appeared. Ryan frowned, more for the interruption than anything else.

"We're Shelby's parents. Our girls have been playing together a lot," the woman explained with a friendly smile. Her husband and Ryan shook hands.

"I … I'm … not Daisy's mom," Ginny looked flustered again, and Ryan hated that he'd put her in such an awkward position again. "Ginny's a friend, and Daisy's mom couldn't make it," he explained, testily.

"I see." The woman's gaze ping-ponged between them both and a prickly silence fell.

Thankfully the woman's husband intervened. "It was good to meet you. Maybe we can get Daisy over for a play date soon?" he said to his wife who was still checking Ginny out, no doubt running through various permutations of who Ginny was, why she was here, and who she was in relation to Ryan, and, most pressing and mysterious of all, where Daisy's mother was.

"Sure. We'll sort something out," she said vaguely. Ryan was sure she hadn't even heard the question properly.

When they were clear out of sight, Ryan breathed deeply. "I'm sorry about that. I hate to subject you to all of these small-town rumors and gossip."

"I hate rumors and gossip." Ginny didn't meet his gaze and seemed faraway.

"Hey." He tapped her arm gently, sensing that something had shifted inside her, that this was something about her past, about her story, something that hurt, and he had unwillingly participated in bringing that hurt to the forefront.

"People talk about me. I can feel it. I can sense it. The way they look at me, or pretend not to. People know about me because of the bridal shop, but also because of what happened between me and Ben and with me canceling the wedding. And then with the accident … it's more gossip for them." Her lips pressed together and she looked lost and lonely. He stepped towards her, and touched her arm but resisted the urge to put his arm around her. He wanted to comfort her, as he would any friend, any stranger in discomfort, only, he couldn't do that with her because … oh because there were so many reasons why he couldn't.

He hated to see this fragile woman look so sad, and now he blamed himself.

"They'll think I'm a homewrecker—"

He hated that for her. She'd come for Daisy's sake and she was suffering for it. "You're not. You shouldn't care what people think, but I know that's easy to say. I just want to thank you again, from the bottom of my heart for coming tonight. I'm sorry that it's been such an awful experience for you."

She shook her head vehemently. "It hasn't been that bad." She cast a dismissive glance at the people around them. "Because I barely leave the house this was a good opportunity for me to get out of my comfort zone and to see a budding actress on her first night."

He chortled, then glanced over to where Daisy was playing with her friend. "It would be good for you to get out and about, maybe not for school events with the town gossips, but for yourself, for your mental health and ... I mean, when life sucks so much you want to crawl under a stone and stay there. It can make you spiral, take you down to the depths of the darkness and leave you there."

"You feel it too?" she asked, sounding surprised.

"I've been sinking all year," he confessed.

Her lips parted as if his words had shocked her. "You understand," she murmured quietly, a look of relief coming over her face. "I could never get Ashleigh and Eloise to understand. They think I should be able to get on with it. Like it's easy to get out of bed and function like a normal human being."

"It's impossible to function, but I do it because of Daisy. There were days when I couldn't get out of bed but I made myself. What happened with my marriage, with my wife ... ex-wife, it hit me like a freight train. I didn't see it coming. I was broken. In pieces. It hit me like a juggernaut. I hadn't seen it coming. I hadn't read the signs which, now that I look back, were glaring. But I loved her and trusted her. I didn't think that anything like this would happen. Not to us. We were in love.

We had Daisy. Our lives were complete. I never guessed she'd ever do anything like that to me. To Daisy. I decided to move and start again."

Ginny's eyes shone under the lights of the lamp. "It's nice to know I'm not alone in my misery."

"You're most definitely not alone."

A small smile threatened to form on her lips. "It's good to know. Being lonely and feeling alone is the worst thing in the world."

"You're not alone, Ginny. I promise you that. You and I are swimming in our misery, but it's in the same ocean."

"I want to reach the shore."

"We'll get there," he assured her, because meeting her and hearing her story had helped him to dwell less on his problems and to empathize more with hers. "How's Benjy doing?"

"He's good. He's great." Her face beamed with happiness. "I might start taking him out now that he's a couple of months. I … I haven't ventured out much with him, and I feel so guilty. The most I've done is take him out in the yard."

"You did what you could."

"If I wrap him up and all, I can take him for walks. This was nice, getting out tonight, and I need to do more of it, with my son."

"You should take him for walks. Maybe go to the park or something."

"Do you take Daisy to the park?"

"I have a few times. It's cold, so we wrap up, but it's nice and we're slowly getting to know the area."

"You should go. I mean, *come*, you should come with us one time. It would be … nice."

He loved the idea of that, "I would love to. *We* would love to. Daisy would love to." He sounded like a rambling fool.

"Then bring her one day. Benjy's too little to go on any of the swings and things."

An odd feeling stirred inside him. "I will. It would be good for you. You must look after yourself, Ginny. You must be strong, for Benjy's sake. It's not easy, but you have to make yourself be strong."

He quite liked the idea of seeing her outside of this school parking lot and the confines of her home where their snatched conversations were usually interrupted or in full view of others.

Not that he had underhanded motives for wanting to get her alone.

"Then, maybe we should … maybe we should … I don't know, um…" She twirled a lock of hair in her fingers.

His heart started to thump. "Say it."

"Maybe we could exchange phone numbers?"

And that was when his heart did a somersault inside his chest.

CHAPTER 19

GINNY

"Someone's here to see you."

Ryan?

Ginny's insides lit up. She'd been replaying the night of the school play over and over in her mind, thinking about Ryan and the conversation they'd had. She'd felt heard, and understood, because he'd listened and given her advice as well as sharing his own pain.

It felt good.

It felt as if she'd met someone who was like her. Hurt and broken. Someone who was trying to put themselves back together while going through the daily motions of life. She felt as if she'd found a like-minded soul. She saw Ryan as a welcome intrusion in her life and she felt better for having him around. She tried not to rush to the door.

"I'll be right here," Ashleigh said, as she walked away.

Ginny opened the door wider and found herself staring at a woman she didn't recognize. She blinked and narrowed her eyes.

"Hi. We haven't met before, but I've wanted to come and see you for the longest time."

Ginny cocked her head. She'd never seen this woman and had no idea why she was here or what she wanted. "I'm sorry, I don't know you."

"I'm … I'm Rhonda. Rhonda Moore."

The words hit her like a sledgehammer, sucking the air right out of her lungs as she clasped a hand to her heart. She tried to say something, but only a gasp came out.

"I was in the car with Ben when he had the accident. I'm sorry for showing up like this, but I didn't have the courage to do it before."

The words fell like bullets. The taste of bile crept up Ginny's throat and she placed a hand on the door, trying to stay standing.

She knew her.

Rhonda Moore.

The woman who had been with Ben. The woman who Ben had chosen to be with, instead of her. Words failed her.

"I'm so sorry," the woman continued. She had the audacity to carry flowers which she now shoved at Ginny. "I didn't know what to bring."

At first Ginny didn't know what to say or whether to take them. She was frozen. Her body shutting down like a robot whose battery had died. She would rather have never crossed paths with this woman, though there had been times soon after the accident that she'd wondered what she'd do if she ever saw her. And now here she was, on her doorstep. "You didn't have to come, let alone bring anything."

"Please take them," the woman begged when Ginny didn't move. "*Please*."

Ginny took the flowers, holding them awkwardly, as if they were a ticking timer for a bomb.

"May I come in?"

Ginny blinked at the request. A myriad of images flashed through her mind, of the crash, of Ben with this woman, a montage of the bachelor night photos and then of happier times with her and Ben as they planned the wedding. It was a livestream that played in her mind, suddenly fast forwarding to this woman and Ben on that fatal night. Ginny imagined them laughing and talking.

Where were they going? What was playing on the radio? Were they laughing at her, poor pregnant Ginny, as they drove?

"I would just like a few moments of your time," the woman said.

Courage found its way to Ginny. "You have no right to be here."

"I know. I'm so sorry. This must be a shock."

"Huge."

"I'm sorry."

"Apology accepted." Ginny tried to close the door, but the woman halted it with her hand. "Please. I've been wanting to come and see you for a while. I never plucked up the courage."

"You don't need to see me. I don't want to see you."

"I'm so, so sorry for what happened. I feel awful. I can't sleep. I can't eat. I can't do anything."

"I don't care about any of it, of what you feel, and what you can't do. I don't care." Ginny held the flowers like a shield between them.

"I didn't know you and Ben were back together. He never said a thing."

Ginny's heart missed a beat. There was a story behind that sentence. A story she'd been trying to piece together lying awake at night wondering, just as she had with the photo taken at his bachelor party, what had happened.

With Ben gone, she'd would never know the truth because only the two people involved in a relationship ever really knew the truth. And her cheating ex-fiancé was dead. If he hadn't died, would she ever have known the truth? When had he planned on telling her? Before or after she'd given birth?

"It was new," the woman continued, selfish and ignorantly unaware of the trauma she was unleashing in Ginny. "It was early days and we were getting to know one another."

Early days?

Ginny felt as if a boulder crashed into her. A force so hard, so huge, the blunt force of which made her feel faint. If she wasn't careful, she'd fall, crashing to the floor. She had no way of verifying whether this woman was telling the truth, though her words hinted that *something* had taken place. What did she have to gain by lying, especially now, when everything was dead and buried and in the past?

Rhonda Moore was cleansing her guilt, and it could only mean one thing: she and Ben had started something. "I don't want to know." Her voice sounded strangled in her throat.

"Please," the cheater begged. "I felt awful as soon as I found out about you and the baby. I've had Ben's parents yelling and screaming at me."

Ginny was so shocked, she couldn't help but utter, "They *knew?*"

"They must have figured it out, like you must have. It was new. We were on our second date."

Ginny's hand flew to her chest and her shoulders hunched, as if she'd felt a physical pain.

Second date.

"I was in the car with him, so … They lost it with me when they came to the hospital. His mother was furious. She was crying and shouting and calling me all sorts of things."

Ginny felt a tiny bit better.

"I just wanted to tell you," the woman continued. "I want you to know how sorry I am, and that I didn't know you two were together. I'm not a cheat."

Rhonda Moore had obviously stepped off her broomstick to come here and clear her guilt, but her words sent Ginny into a tailspin. They confirmed the worst. Ben *had* cheated on her. He and Rhonda had been together, in *some* capacity. All this woman wanted was to say her piece and walk away, but for Ginny she'd ripped open a scabbed over wound and left it exposed and bleeding. All the progress she'd made in healing was now reversed.

There didn't need to be a kiss involved, or physical intimacy, for it to be labeled as cheating. It hurt like a hot steel knife through her skin to know that Ben had been interested in someone else, that he hadn't cared about her, even when she carried his child.

"Stop!" Ginny rasped. Her gut twisted and she fought the urge to throw up.

"I'm s-s-s-sorry."

"Get out! Go! Leave me alone!"

Ashleigh was at the door in an instant.

"I'm sorry. Tell her I'm sorry," the woman pleaded with Ashleigh. "I didn't know. If I had, I would never have gotten involved with him."

Ginny threw the flowers in Rhonda Moore's face and stumbled back inside.

"You've said enough. Please leave my sister in peace."

Ashleigh slammed the door. Ginny leaned against the wall, trying to breathe, but her lungs felt like they'd filled up with sand.

"Gin." Ashleigh's hands framed her face. "Gin!"

CHAPTER 20

RYAN

"*W*here are you going?" Kayla asked.

He set down the vertical support he was putting up for the new shelving unit and read the text message on his phone. It was from Ginny.

"Ryan?"

"Hmmmm." He looked up. "Out. I need to get something. "

"If it's extra screws you need they're somewhere in the basement."

"No, it's not screws." Ginny's frantic texts worried him and now he was desperate to talk to her, to hear her voice and find out what had happened. "Do you want to come with me, Dee?" he asked his daughter.

"Yeah! Where are we going?" He loved that she didn't care where, and was happy enough to just accompany him. "I need to get something." He felt bad doing this, lying to his sister. He shouldn't have to be wary of a grown woman's opinions, but if he told Kayla the truth, she wouldn't like it.

He drove away, rushing to get to the park, and only when he was on the road did he realize that in leaving so fast he'd have a lot of explaining to do to when he returned. There would be hell to pay, and he couldn't ask Daisy to lie for him. He'd cross that bridge when he came to it.

"We're going to the park!" Daisy cried as the familiar surroundings came into view. "Daddy! We're going to have fun!" She giggled, happiness gurgling out of her like water from a fountain.

But his mind was on Ginny, and he was anxious to speak to her face to face. As he parked up and glanced around the park, he saw her, sitting on a bench near the play area and pushing the pram to and fro. She was looking at her phone.

"Ginny's here!" Daisy yelled. "With Benjy!" She raced towards them. Ginny stood up then reached out with her arms as Daisy went careening into them. Then his and Ginny's gazes met, and he scanned her expression trying to gauge what might have gone wrong enough for her reach out to him.

As he walked towards them, Daisy staring adoringly at a sleeping Benjy.

"Hey." This was a different Ginny to the one he'd seen recently on the night of the school play.

"Hey," she whispered, taking a deep breath. Her shoulders sagged as if burdened with the weight of worry.

"You okay?" It was a futile question, given how she looked.

"Rhonda Moore came to the house."

"Who?" he whispered.

"Can I go on the swings, Daddy?" Ginny yelled, and a second later Benjy started to cry.

"Dee you woke him up!" Ryan wanted undisturbed time to get to the bottom of whatever this was.

"It's okay. I'll see if I can put him back to sleep again." Ginny lifted the baby out and put him to her shoulder. He was dressed in warm winter clothes and a cute navy blue hat.

Daisy was on the swings, her legs flailing as she tried to swing higher. Ginny walked around, patting Benjy gently on his back, trying to quieten him. "He fell asleep as soon as I started to drive."

She hushed the baby with soft murmurings and in time his cries slowly quietened.

"Daddy!" Daisy yelled, and Benjy started to cry again. Ryan rolled his eyes, and Ginny started to pace around again, rubbing his back.

It was like Groundhog Day.

He remembered it well when Daisy had been a baby. Luckily the park was mostly deserted, and the few children and parents who were there, were relatively quiet.

"You take care of him, and I'll take care of her." He marched over and started to push Daisy on the swings, telling her to be quiet, because of Benjy.

"But Daddy, Benjy will have more fun if we put him in the baby swings."

He explained why they couldn't do that, and kept an eye on Ginny. He was itching to know what had happened. She looked anxious and worried and all things in between. And he had no idea who Rhonda Moore was.

A short while passed, before he saw Ginny put the baby back into the pram.

"Be quiet now, Dee. Benjy's asleep again, and we want him to stay asleep if you want to play here for a long time."

"Okay, Daddy. I wanna play on the slide. Can I?"

"May I?" he corrected.

"Yes," she answered.

He suppressed a laugh. "Go on." At least the slide didn't

require a manual intervention from him. He walked towards Ginny who put her fingers to her lips and beckoned him to walk away from the pram.

"Who's Rhonda Moore?" he whispered.

"She's ... she was in the car with Ben when he ... on the night of the accident." Ginny's words trailed to a whisper, and she was quiet. He waited, watching and giving her time to tell things when she was ready. Then she told him how the woman had turned up on her doorstep earlier with flowers, and apologized, and told her that she didn't know about her and Ben being together. "I was blissfully ignorant until she told me. I didn't know for sure whether he was cheating or not, but she confirmed it, and now I'm in pieces all over again. She raked up a bed of dirt, everything I'd pushed out of my mind because I couldn't bear to analyze it, and now she's gone and brought everything back to the surface again."

It was insanely selfish of that woman to turn up like that, to force Ginny's past into her present, to shove it into her face all in the name of wanting to absolve herself from guilt. People could be selfish like that. Thinking only of themselves. Vanessa had. Now, seeing Ginny's face, he could feel her pain. "I'm sorry. You didn't deserve this. You didn't need this muckraking. I'm sorry she did that to you."

"I wish I'd never seen her." Her eyes were filled with tears that threatened to spill. She recounted the conversation, how the woman had wanted to come in, how Ginny had been frozen and in shock. He listened, and nodded, letting her know he was here for her, letting her vent her rage, and unleash her fury. "People can be selfish. They want to unburden themselves and that's all they care about, making themselves feel lighter."

"But I feel sick," she cried, then snapped her head in the direction of the pram in case she'd woken Benjy.

"It's not fair." He spoke in a hushed tone.

"I feel like I'm back where I was when the accident happened. I was starting to get better. I was starting to make progress. I was starting to put that behind me, and she's gone and shoved it down my throat. She's put it front and center and shown it to me all over again." She held out her hands, palms upwards. "I don't want to be reminded of my past, Ryan. I want to move on."

"You *are* moving on," he reminded her gently. "This is progress." He beckoned at the pram. "You made it to the park. First time, right?"

She was too in her head to reply. Too spaced out, in a far away place. He stepped towards her and placed a hand on her shoulder. "You are making progress, in leaps and bounds. You've gone to a school play filled with nosy, gossipy moms, you've had a confrontation forced upon you by someone you'd rather not have seen, and now you've come to the park with Benjy. Ginny, look how far you've come. You've done things you couldn't have done a few months ago."

"When I used to lie in bed, wishing I were dead?"

His stomach lurched at the thought. He'd had those feelings himself. Glimpses of darkness taunting him, making him think there was a way to end the pain. He shook his head, not wanting to let those demons back into his head, but he worried about Ginny, and in that moment, he vowed to do whatever he could, to make her life better. Her sisters were busy, that had been the whole point of taking Kayla on, but Ginny was a new mother, still recovering from a birth, and grieving, and coming to terms with a man who had cheated on her. This fragile woman who had made time for Daisy and who was trying so hard to get by, deserved someone to help her out of the dark place she'd fallen into.

His hand went to her elbow, and he was almost tempted to take her hand but resisted. "You're not that person now, Ginny.

When I look at you, I see a woman who is battling her demons and winning."

"Is that what you really see?" She didn't sound as if she believed him.

"I do. I look at you and I feel like a wimp for the way I dealt with things. I wasn't physically frail, and Daisy wasn't a baby. And Vanessa is still very much alive. But you, you've dealt with all the worst things, and despite it all, you still have time to come to the park with Benjy."

"I can talk to you," she said, looking thoughtful.

"It's nice talking to you."

"We have a lot in common." When she looked up at him, her eyes were filled with sorrow. He wished he could make it vanish.

"We have collective trauma, you and I," he told her.

"A truckload of it."

"Boatloads," he agreed.

"I knew you'd understand. Ashleigh is sad and busy, and Eloise is happy and busy with Liam. I don't want to take up their time, and I don't want them to worry about me."

"I'm here for you. Whenever you need me. Night or day, whatever the hour. Call me. Okay?"

"Are you sure?"

"I've never been more sure." He waved to Daisy who waved at him as she sailed down the slide. His little girl was so good. Usually she would be squealing and making noises, but she was mindful of Benjy.

He had a good daughter.

A *great* daughter.

"I feel like I take one step forward and ten steps back."

"It might feel like that, but it feels to me as if you're taking three steps forward and only two steps back. You're making more progress than you think."

She seemed to ponder this. "Maybe."

"From what you've told me, I know you have. And you texted me." He was grateful that she'd been the first one to do it. He'd thought about contacting her plenty of times since they'd exchanged numbers, but he'd stopped himself, not wanting to encroach, and hoping that she would reach out first.

She had.

They smiled at one another. He thought he heard a cry, then looked over to the slide. Daisy wasn't there. In a panic, he scanned the play area, and was relieved to find her bopping up and down on a springy horse. Benjy's cry caught his ears and he saw Ginny trying to soothe the baby. She'd picked him up and brought him over.

"He needs milk, and I forgot to bring it." Ginny made an apologetic face. "I've never left home with a baby before. I didn't realize there was so much to carry."

"Did you drive here?"

"No. I wanted to go for a long walk."

"I'll take you back." He beckoned Daisy over.

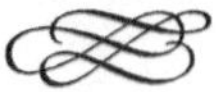

CHAPTER 21

GINNY

Ginny took Benjy upstairs to change his diaper while Ryan said he'd get the milk ready.

The baby hollered so loudly she had no choice but to tend to him first. Thank goodness Ryan was on hand to get his milk. As she changed Benjy to a clean diaper, she imagined, for a split second, that this was real. That this was her home, and her family, and she and Benjy were no longer alone, living with the tattered memories of the past.

"Shhhuuuush." She lifted her son up and rocked him in her arms. "Hush, baby." His cries turned to whimpers. He was hungry. She cradled him gently in her arms, wanting to savor the moment for a little longer. To feel how it could be, to not be a single mother.

Benjy's lips wobbled and in the next few seconds he let out a high-pitched shriek.

"You almost fooled me, Benjy," she said, tenderly, stroking

his soft peachy cheek. As she went downstairs, she heard voices, even over the baby's cries. She walked into the kitchen, her stomach hardening when she saw who it was.

"There you are!" Eloise's face was a big cheeky grin as Ginny walked into the kitchen. The sweet and buttery scent of freshly baked cookies wafted over her.

"Here, it's the right temperature." Ryan handed her the bottle of milk.

"Thank you." She sat down in the chair he'd pulled out for her, the thought crossing her mind to go into the other room, away from Eloise's and Liam's inquisitive stares, but Benjy was howling so much, she had to give him the milk immediately.

He quietened straightaway, and she kept the bottle lowered, so that he didn't guzzle it too quickly.

"So?" Eloise leaned against the countertop; her arms folded, waiting expectantly. "*This* is nice. You look dressed up. Go anywhere nice?"

Ginny wanted to put a Ziplock on her sister's mouth.

"We went to the park," Ryan replied.

"The park?" Eloise cried, as shocked as if he'd said she'd been on a motorcycle ride with the Hell's Angels.

"Yes, the park," Ginny replied, stiffly. She wished Liam would make an excuse and physically remove her sister from the kitchen. She stared down at Benjy, at the way his cheeks hollowed in when he sucked, at his beautiful shiny eyes as he stared up at her, and her heart blossomed with more love than she thought was possible to hold.

"I smell cookies." Liam, the savior, sniffed the air.

Ginny looked up. "Ashleigh was baking some. They must be here somewhere." She now desperately wanted one. Eloise started looking around for them. "What made you *all* decide to go to the park today?" she asked, not one to hold back.

Ginny tried to keep calm. What should have been a fitting

end to a lovely day was now being ruined by her nosy sister. She didn't want to give her sister more ammunition and tried to think of something to say but Ryan beat her to it. "It seemed like the perfect day for it. Daisy had a great time."

Eloise peered at him. "Where is she?"

"Watching TV inside," answered Ryan as he sat back in his chair. Ginny could feel him watching her feed the baby. Her cheeks flushed with heat and she prayed he wouldn't notice. It would reveal more about her than any words ever could.

"We should go," Liam stated, reading the room a lot better than his girlfriend.

"Should we?" Eloise's face wore a grin.

"Yeah, you should," Ginny replied.

"It was nice seeing you, Ryan. We're having a housewarming party, Liam and I, at my new place." Eloise waved ambiguously in the direction of her house. "And you are all invited."

"Uh … thank you." He stared at Ginny unsure. "*All* of us?"

"Kayla, Daisy … it's a small informal housewarming now that I'm officially sort of moved in."

When Ryan looked puzzled, Ginny explained. "Now that she doesn't have to get up in the middle of the night to help out when Benjy gets up. Not that she got up much."

"Hey!" Eloise swatted her gently. "I got up a few times.

"Few being the operative word," mumbled Ginny, and was grateful to see her sister leave.

The kitchen was silent after they left, and she and Ryan were alone. Benjy had finished his feed and she propped him gently on her shoulder and rubbed his back. "Babies have such a great life, don't they? Eating, sleeping, pooping."

"Yes. Things get much harder the older you get."

She heard the gentle escape of air. "He seems content, given that his sleep was interrupted a few times."

"We should go and let you rest." Ryan stood up.

"No, stay a while."

She couldn't let him leave. Didn't want him to leave, but she was also worried that he might go into the living room with Daisy, and that would make it impossible for them to talk. Though it seemed that he was content to stay, judging by the fact that he wasn't moving. Every conversation they had was snatched, or interrupted. At last, they'd reached a place where Benjy was content, Daisy was happily watching TV, and Eloise had left and Ashleigh was out.

"Could I hold him?" he asked.

"Sure." She handed him over carefully, then sat back, watching Ryan with her baby in his arms, making funny faces and talking in a funny voice to him. Her heart was full. She wished this could be real. A normal day in her life. "You're so good with him."

"I've had practice."

Of course he had. The thought of his wife was like a pinch in her arm. A tiny, painful prick that left a stinging feeling.

"It's funny, well, not so funny, but freaky, you telling me about that woman turning up on your doorstep. The thing is, we can't control much of anything. We can try, but life has a way of unfolding." His gaze swept over her face, and she sat up, sensing he was on the verge of telling her something.

"I don't follow."

"Do you remember when Daisy made that Valentine's Day card for her mom?"

"Yes."

"Daisy picked up my phone and video called her mom because she wanted to ask her if she'd received the card."

"Had she?"

"No, she was away, on vacation, with her lover."

Ginny gasped, imagining the worst. "They weren't …
indecent, where they?"

"They were in their swimwear, and he was bare chested, but
Daisy doesn't even know about the other man." Ryan lowered
his voice, his gaze darting to the door.

"Daisy saw?"

"She saw. She asked her mom who he was, and why he
wasn't wearing anything and why there was sunshine and palm
trees."

"Oh, poor Daisy." The thought of what that child had
witnessed made Ginny feel sick.

"You never know when things will go belly up."

"Don't you think you should tell her the truth, before she
finds out, before someone lets it slip?"

"I'm being careful. I don't want to hurt her unnecessarily."

"You can't control that, that's what you said. Look what
happened to me. The woman turned up on my doorstep." Ginny
felt a heaviness inside her.

"I don't know." Ryan appeared lost in thought. It was much
harder for him. Daisy was old enough to hear things and make
sense of them. Benjy was just a baby. It was easier for her. She
felt a pang of sadness for Ryan, which was ironic because he
probably felt the same for her.

"That was the day she asked if you could come to the
school play, and that's why I was so relieved when you said
yes."

Hearing this made her happy. Plucking up the courage to go
had been a good thing. "I'm glad you asked, and I'm glad I said
yes."

"Me too. We could do this again, sometime, maybe?" he
asked.

Do what?

Sit in the kitchen and talk?

Or go to the park and talk?

She was so thrown by his offer that her mind turned to mush. Whatever he meant, she was ready for it. "I would like that."

His cell phone started to ring and he pulled it out of his pocket, his face turning somber.

"What's wrong?" she asked, always fearful of bad news.

"It's my sister. She's wondering how long we're going to be."

"Didn't you tell her where you went?"

"Not exactly."

Ginny blinked. "What exactly, then?"

"I didn't say anything. I just left."

Ginny closed her eyes. "Kayla's going to hate me even more." She instinctively knew that Kayla would resent her taking up her brother's time.

"I meant what I said." Ryan hooked his thumbs into the belt loops of his jeans. "Whenever you need to talk, or you're feeling down, just call me."

Ginny had every intention of doing that.

CHAPTER 22

ASHLEIGH

ord looked surprised to see her. Ashleigh held out a tin. "I baked cookies for ... for your mom."

Surprise flickered in his eyes as he took it from her. "Thank you, but she's not eating much at the moment." He motioned for her to come inside.

"Then you can have them." She knew he liked them, which was partly why she'd baked them in the first place. She followed him into the kitchen, already feeling as if she were pushing a boulder uphill in trying to reach this man.

He still lived with his mother. It was a temporary arrangement until he figured things out. He was still setting up an accountancy practice here.

He didn't reply to her, but placed the cookie tin on the kitchen table. "Did you want to say 'hello' to my mom?" he asked, facing her across the room.

"It's one of the reasons I came, yes." She wanted to see him, but also his mother, because it had been a while and because she was so sick.

"I'll take you to her. We had to bring her bed downstairs because she can't really walk up the stairs now."

"Oh, really?" She was shocked to hear this. She'd come to the house on a few occasions after they'd started dating again, and even on her first visit back after a long time, nothing much had changed. The interior was as she remembered it from when they were first dating, all those decades ago. Looking around, surveying the hallway and casting her gaze over the stairs as she followed Ford, the wallpaper was faded, the carpet and floors were worn in, and there was a musty smell about the place.

She almost gasped when she saw Ford's mother lying in the bed, her eyes closed, sleeping. Her skin was deathly pale, her hair white. She looked a shadow of her former self, so thin and delicate.

Ford took her hand gently and bent down. "Mom," he whispered softly. "Mom, Ashleigh's come to see you."

"Don't wake her, Ford." Ashleigh was in a state of quiet shock. Ford's mother had gone downhill fast since she'd last come here before she'd left for her trip.

"She's never fully awake. This is how she is pretty much for most of the day now, ever since that fall."

She looked peaceful, though, and her mouth was slightly open, her breathing labored. Fear crawled over Ashleigh. Is this what happened to people in their twilight years? Is this how it would be for her, twenty, thirty, forty years down the line? "She looks so fragile."

"She is."

"Let her sleep."

"She sleeps all day. It's not really sleep, it's like she's wasting away," he whispered. "The way I see it, a little interaction is good for her." He stroked his mother's hand. "Hey, Mom, Ashleigh is here. You remember? From the wedding dress shop?"

His mother's eyes fluttered open, and she looked at Ashleigh, then blinked a few times. There was no recognition in those grey ringed eyes. She mumbled something and Ashleigh moved closer. "Hey, Mrs. Montgomery." She smiled, her gaze taking in the woman's leathery face, her deep wrinkles that mapped out lines across her skin. Ford's mother seemed to look right through her. She mumbled something else.

"Yes, from the bridal shop," Ford answered.

Ashleigh was startled. "You understood that?"

"It's a skill I'm learning very quickly."

"I'm Ashleigh Rose, Mrs. Montgomery. Do you remember me?"

"You used to call her Patricia," Ford reminded her.

"Patricia ... it's me, Ashleigh." She took Patricia's other hand and held it. It was warm and leathery and much softer than she expected. "It's so good to see you. How are you?"

Patricia blinked a few times, and in her eyes was a far off distant expression, as if she were looking right through her instead of at her. Then she opened her mouth but the words which came out were mumbles, nothing coherent.

"What was that?" Ashleigh strained to hear, then glanced at Ford when again she couldn't decipher what his mother was saying.

"She looks different, eh, Mom?" he chuckled, and Ashleigh marveled that he was able to understand that much.

The woman mumbled again, this time a longer sentence. Ford lowered his head. "No, Mom."

"What did she say?" Ashleigh could sense his reticence, and when he shook his head again, she asked him again.

"She thinks you're Susan."

"But she thought I was Ashleigh a few seconds ago."

"She gets confused easily. It's like she slips in and out of different timelines. She remembers things differently, and confuses people and places."

His mother's eyes closed her eyes again, and her breathing sounded labored. She'd slipped into sleep again, surprising Ashleigh with the speed of it. "Is she asleep again?"

"She drifts in and out of sleep. That's mostly how she is now."

"I'm so sorry. I didn't realize she was so bad."

"I didn't expect her to be so weak. I expected her to be mobile, still in the wheelchair or using her Zimmer frame."

Ford shook his head. "That stopped a while ago. Her dementia has gotten worse. I hate seeing her like this. She's wasting away before my eyes."

"I'm sorry, Ford. I'm so sorry. I wish I'd been here for you more than I have—"

"You shouldn't feel sorry, and, for the record, I don't expect you to be here for me."

There it was again, the touch of harshness, pushing her away before she'd had a chance to get anywhere close to him.

He walked away, but instead of going back into the kitchen, he led her to the front door. She glared at him, silent rage simmering inside her. "Are you really so eager to see me off? Don't you even want to talk to me anymore?"

"You came to see my mom."

"I came to see you, too."

Ford shrugged, and she could now clearly see the dark circles under his eyes, the gauntness in his expression.

She touched his arm. "You're angry and hurting, and I completely understand that you hate the sight of me. You're going through a lot. I'm sorry about your mom, but I'm here for you. Please let me in. Don't punish me any longer."

"Punish you? It's nothing to do with punishment or you."

"Then what is it?" She didn't understand why he wouldn't relent, why, even with the little she was giving him, her support as a friend, for that seemed to be all he wanted, he still pushed her away.

It seemed futile to protest.

Whatever she said, he took it the wrong way. "I miss you." Her hand trailed up his arm slowly, her heart beating as she dared herself to keep her hand there, hoping he wouldn't flinch. Hoping he still cared for her, and wanted her, and that he was being cold towards her just because he wanted to teach her a lesson. "I'm sorry. How many times do I have to apologize for not saying 'yes' when you wanted to surprise me on vacation?"

He moved a few steps away from her. "How many times do I have to tell you that I understand your position? I feel I rushed you into something you weren't ready for."

"I'm ready now. And that trip wasn't about you. It was about me. About a dream I had, it was about me feeling tied down and wanting to escape."

He breathed in loudly. "Obviously I presumed too much. I thought I could walk back into your life and everything would be like it used to be, but we've changed. We're not who we were in our early twenties. What you want is different to what I want."

"How do you know what I want?"

"Because you told me. You want freedom and independence and you want to be left alone."

She ground down on her teeth. Men behaved like little children sometimes. He was taking this as a full on rejection, because she'd wanted her space. Could he not understand that in the time he'd left this small town, married and had a family, and lived a full life, she'd been holding down the fort, running the business, taking care of her sisters, and dreaming of an escape?

That she'd planned her escape long before he'd walked back into her life. That she'd wanted to stick to her guns and travel alone, as she'd planned, and it didn't mean she didn't want to be a part of his life.

He felt rejected, bitter and angry beyond reason. She'd done all she could to try to make up for it. When was he going to give her a break and let her back in?

"I hear that your ex-wife is getting married again. Eloise told me. Why didn't you tell me?" She was annoyed with him. More than annoyed. *Furious*. Furious that he'd told Eloise but had ignored her completely.

He let out a sigh, looking more like a defeated man than ever, and she was worried that he was so much less the Ford she knew and more a man who was battling some sort of inner demons.

"She's a remarkable woman and she deserves all the happiness."

Ashleigh's insides turned to stone.

She saw it clear as day.

Ford wasn't distant with her to teach her a lesson; he was still in love with his ex-wife.

It wasn't that he was punishing Ashleigh. It was more that he was no longer interested in her.

CHAPTER 23

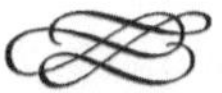

RYAN

"I had so much fun, Daddy! Can we go to the park with Ginny and Benjy again?"

"Sure, Dee." He'd been thinking the very same thing as they drove home. He'd had a good time, too, and he hoped he'd been of some help to Ginny in her time of need. He'd come to this town to start over, and meeting someone hadn't been on the cards, yet here he was.

He opened the door to Kayla's house and he braced himself for the military level interrogation. "Why don't you run upstairs and get ready for school, Dee? It's getting late."

"Can we go again next week?" Daisy asked.

"I said we could, didn't I?"

Kayla stood in the hallway and looked oddly at him. "You obviously didn't go to the hardware store."

"No. We went to the park with Ginny and the baby! It was so much fun!" Daisy answered, excitement oozing out of every cell in her body. Then she raced up the stairs, leaving him to face his sister's wrath.

Kayla's arms were folded across her chest. Her brows knotted. "You went to ... *The. Park*?" If he'd been a lesser man he'd have shrunk under the weight of her glare. "I assumed, wrongly, that you'd rushed off to get something for the shelves you were supposed to be putting up. Why didn't you say, instead of hiding it?"

Ryan scratched his nose, feeling sheepish. "Sorry about that. I should have said something."

"But you didn't."

"No." He knew why he hadn't. He'd been so worried by Ginny's text, that he was eager to get to her. It had occurred to him to explain to his sister, but it would have caused more problems, and so he'd gone without an explanation. In that moment, Ginny had been the priority.

"So, you're seeing her, despite my warning?"

He walked into the kitchen, wanting to make sure he was out of Daisy's earshot. "I am not seeing her. She's a friend. She needed me."

"Needed you? How does she even have your number? *Why* does she have your number?"

"Are we really having this conversation, Kayla? I'm a grown man, I can make decisions about who my friends are."

"That woman is trouble."

"That's cruel and opinionated and unkind."

"It's the truth. You've only got to hear about what's happened to her in the last few years to know that."

"Her fiancé cheating on her wasn't her fault."

"No, it wasn't. Just like your wife cheating on you isn't your fault."

"My *ex*-wife." He huffed out a breath, trying to rein in the temper that was threatening to unleash. "What point are you trying to make?"

"You don't need more drama in your life. You've already had so much upheaval. Daisy doesn't need more volatility. She needs a stable life. God knows Vanessa leaving has upended that poor girl's life enough."

"What's your point?" he hissed, then walked out of the kitchen again, desperate to get away from her. She followed him. "Ginny is grieving. She's not thinking straight."

"That's not what you meant. You've said in the past that she's bad luck. What does that even mean?"

"I love you, Ryan. You're my baby brother, but some of the choices you make sometimes—"

"I'm a grown man."

"You will always be my younger brother, and I've always felt responsible for you. I watched Vanessa wrap you around her fingers, and I've had to shut my mouth through the years."

"Jeez ..." His insides were on fire. He swept a hand through his hair, trying to dispel the energy building up inside him. "The two of you never got on because you're so different."

"I'm a good judge of character."

"I'm not so sure you are."

"I wasn't wrong about Vanessa, was I? I had a feeling that woman was fickle. "

"Please don't disparage her. She's still Daisy's mother."

"But I was right about her, wasn't I? And you watch, I'll be right about Ginny, too, should you decide to make another mistake."

Kayla was like a pit bull. Once she'd grabbed hold of something, she wouldn't easily let it go. "I'm sure you're feeling pretty smug and satisfied about it now," he said through gritted teeth.

Kayla threw her hands in the air in exasperation. "I'm not

feeling that at all. I care about you, Ryan, and I don't want to see you get hurt again, or do something stupid!"

"What stupid thing are you alluding to?" he snapped.

"You've come here to make a fresh start in a new place. This is supposed to be a new beginning for you and Daisy. You've already made the mistake of being with a woman who has no interest in raising her child. Vanessa doesn't care about her daughter, because if she did, she wouldn't have left her like she did."

He still didn't understand the point she was trying to make. "What does any of this have to do with Vanessa?"

Kayla pressed her lips together as if it were struggling to contain herself.

"We had a day out, for goodness sake. Why are you blowing it out of proportion?" he growled.

"It always starts with a day out, or a date! There's no getting through to you." Kayla stormed off in a huff, and he breathed easier for it.

CHAPTER 24

ELOISE

$\mathcal{E}$loise was at work early on Monday morning. She'd jumped out of bed, happy with her lot, with life, with Liam.

There wasn't a thing in the world she wanted. He'd come over last night, and helped her move some furniture around in one of the bedrooms. Then he'd left some of his clothes in her closet, though he was eager to point out that he wasn't moving in. He asked her a few times if she minded, and whether she felt he was imposing or intruding on her privacy by leaving two pairs of pants and three shirts at her place.

No, she didn't mind.

Not at all.

In fact, she welcomed it. Relished it.

Before Liam had come along she'd been sullen, moody, and unhappy a lot of the time; always wanting to escape from Whisper Falls.

Her friend Beth had been her escape. Through her Eloise had partied and met people, and had lots of fun, but she'd never experienced the type of security and belonging that she now did. It was only because of Liam.

It mattered to have someone to share her life with because life was more meaningful when shared with someone else.

Only this morning Liam had made her coffee and left her one of the artisan protein bars she'd recently discovered. She'd only mentioned it to him the one time. He listened. He took it all in. He made her feel that she mattered.

Life was good. So good that she was positively bouncing as she got to work, but her mood soon dampened when she saw Ashleigh at the counter, her shoulders hunched together as she stared down at her hands.

"Good morning," Eloise said, warily.

Ashleigh looked up, her face somber. "You're early."

"You're earlier," Eloise retorted.

"I couldn't sleep."

"Benjy?"

"No. He was a good boy. I didn't hear him or Ginny last night."

"Anyone else?" Eloise winked, and wondered how long Ryan might have stayed.

Ashleigh's forehead creased. "What?"

Eloise grinned. It was about time that Ginny found some happiness, and Ryan seemed like a good guy. "Was Ryan there, when you got back?"

Ashleigh "Ryan? No. Had he been there?"

"Oh, yes." Eloise nodded vehemently. "Oh, yes, he'd been there. Don't say I didn't tell you."

Ashleigh looked more puzzled than ever. "Whatever for? Kayla doesn't work on the weekend."

"Ginny took Benjy to the park where she met Ryan and his daughter."

"She did what?"

"You heard, and I called it. I told you something was going on."

"How does she even know him to talk to?"

"You completely missed this budding romance that took place under your nose."

"Maybe they're just friends?" Ashleigh countered, though judging by the expression on her face, she didn't look convinced.

Eloise smiled smugly. "I'm not so sure they'll stay as just friends."

"Ginny has a lot to deal with right now. She's not ready to get into anything."

"How did you not know this? Where were you, and where were the cookies, because we couldn't find them?"

"I went to see Darcie. We had wine and pizza and watched a movie, and by the time I came back it was late." Ashleigh swiped her hand across the back of her neck. "Ginny was upset when I left her. I didn't *want* to leave her. Maybe I shouldn't have, but I managed to calm her down a little and she told me to go."

"Calm her down? Why?" Eloise was starting to get worried.

"You don't know?"

"Know what?"

"Rhonda Moore turned up at our door yesterday."

"Rhonda Moore?" Eloise parroted.

"The woman who was in the car with Ben when he had the car crash. From what she said, it seems like she and Ben were at the start of something."

Eloise pulled her bag off her shoulder. She'd been walking on sunshine coming into work, and now Ashleigh had dampened her enthusiasm by telling her about Ginny's woes. "This is what happens when I sleep over at my place for one night," she grumbled, pulling up a chair.

"It's not been just *one* night," Ashleigh muttered.

"I have been trying to move into my own place for months," Eloise countered. "And now I can. Ginny seems to be coping and we don't have to get up at night times because she's adamant that she wants to do it all. Therefore, it makes sense for me to slowly start moving myself out of the main house and into my place. Talking of which ..." She decided to hold off on the announcement, given that Ashleigh looked stressed. "What's this about Rhonda Moore?"

Ashleigh told her everything that had happened, about that woman having the audacity to come to the house, and demanding to see Ginny. About how she seemed to want to make herself feel better and, Ashleigh concluded that it was highly likely that Ben had started to see her.

"That ... that ..." Eloise groaned, stopping herself from calling Ben names. That cheating, lying, loser of a man. Rage coursed through her veins. She felt bad for Ginny. It wasn't good to speak ill of the dead, but that man was a perfect candidate for it. "Why would he do that to Ginny. *Again?* Ginny must have been so upset."

"She was. She yelled at the woman to go. Then I came to the door and told her to leave. Then I slammed the door in her face."

"Poor Ginny." Eloise's heart ached for her sister. "After everything she's been through, she didn't deserve this."

"No, she didn't."

"She was just starting to come out of her depression. Things were looking good. She was getting better with the baby. Having Daisy and Ryan has helped."

Ashleigh let out a sigh. "They really were here? In the kitchen?"

Eloise described the scene to her sister, pointing out that they seemed cozy and comfortable together. She didn't want to jinx it or say too much, but she truly believed that Ryan was good for her sister. Maybe it was too early for romance to blossom, but the two of them seemed to share heartache, and surely that had to help? "It's good that she has Ryan to talk to," she said, finally. "Ginny needs something good in her life, and we can't always be there for her."

"She's trying," said Ashleigh softly. "It's been a terrible few years for her. Just awful."

"But she has to learn to move on." As far as Eloise was concerned, she and Ashleigh had supported Ginny as much as they could, and they would always be here for her, but finding someone of her own, in time, and having a life and family of her own was a good thing. It was time for the sisters to not be bound together forever. She looked at Ashleigh, wanting to say these things, but was wary of coming across as selfish. She was simply stating a fact. Ashleigh herself had longed for independence and freedom, though she now seemed the unhappiest of them all. "You must have come back really late from Darcie's if Ginny was asleep when you got back."

Ashleigh looked at her guiltily. "I needed the wine and pizza and a good chat."

"Why's that?"

"Because before that, I went to see Ford."

Eloise sat up straighter. "So *that's* who you made the cookies for?"

"I made them for his mom."

Eloise chortled. "She's not well. I doubt she'd even be able to chew one of your cookies. She's bed bound."

Ashleigh gaped at her. "How do you know all that?"

"Ford told me."

"He tells you everything."

"No, he doesn't. What's going on?" Eloise leaned forward, and listened while Ashleigh recounted the details of her visit.

"He's secretly pining for Susan again," Ashleigh said. "I just know it."

Eloise pooh-pahhed that. "I don't believe that for one moment."

"They have a child together. They have history. They have twenty years of marriage. He and I have nothing compared to that."

"You were his first love and he was yours," Eloise retorted.

"He was my only." Ashleigh's voice wavered and Eloise was fearful that she would burst into tears.

"Oh, Ash." Eloise leaned across and hugged her. She now felt guilty for being so in love and happy with her own life, and then she'd gone and gone on about Ryan and Ginny, too. No wonder Ashleigh looked so down. Up until a few months ago, she'd been the one to escape and go on her travels, and this just after her first love had come back into her life. Now Ashleigh's world was in shambles. It had unraveled so quickly. Life could be such a rollercoaster of highs and lows. "I don't believe for one moment that Ford has feelings for his ex-wife."

"You didn't hear the way he spoke about her, or see the look on his face. Ashleigh took a steadying inhale. "I'm fine. I'll be fine," she said with a determination that didn't match her body language. "I'll still be here for him because his mother is so frail and I don't think she's got long left."

"He's not in love with Susan."

"You weren't there, Eloise. He's been so distant for months. I just need to heed the message."

"You wait. Just you wait. You two were made for one another—" But Ashleigh put up her hand, halting further conversation. "I don't want to hear it. Please." Her eyes were shiny as if she were on the brink of tears, but she held strong, the way she always did. "I don't want to talk about it anymore. What about you?"

Eloise tried not to smile, at all, but it was difficult especially when memories of last night's candlelit dinner and the movie and Liam staying over, were still so fresh in her mind. "What about me?" she asked, soberly.

Ashleigh sniffed. "Is marriage on the cards?"

"What? No! It's too soon!"

"But you've thought about it?"

"We've never talked about it."

"You might not have *talked* about it but you've *thought* about it."

"Well, maaaybe." Eloise stifled a giggle sitting at the base of her throat. She *had* thought about it.

Often.

Liam hadn't mentioned it at all, but they were so happy together. So good together. It was perfect. Her life had changed so much, and for the better. There was more to it than working at the bridal shop, or dealing with Ginny's latest drama, or looking forward to another fun break with Beth.

Liam understood her and was there for her. He was the support she'd never had, the shoulder she'd wanted to cry on, the listening ear she'd needed in troubled times.

That feeling, to have someone to go home to, to have someone on the other end of the phone to share good and bad moments with, that feeling was priceless.

It had been like having therapy, talking to him about her past, about her failed marriage and her cheating husband. He always listened intently. He helped assuage her fears about this new relationship, her worries about being the older woman, her insecurities about him being young and gorgeous.

When she started to flounder, to doubt and worry, he always reminded her that he'd had a crush on her at school, when she barely knew he existed. He told her that finding her again, and being with her was the stuff of dreams and some days he couldn't believe that he'd finally ended up with her.

She'd met his friends, and their partners. He hadn't yet met Beth, and she wasn't sure when they'd get a chance to. She wasn't sure Liam would enjoy Beth's decadent world of parties and old money, and these days, she cared less about it herself.

These days she didn't need to escape to Hyannis Port to see Beth. She'd found paradise here.

"You have thought about it!" Ashleigh cried. "Oh, dear God. You, too."

"Me, too? What do you mean?" Eloise retorted, feeling her cheeks turn hot.

"You, too, will sail off into the sunset, and I'll be left here alone."

"Don't be so dramatic," Eloise implored. "Nobody is going to sail off anywhere. I don't want to rush into anything. Things are perfect as they are."

"Lucky you," Ashleigh said grumpily. "And Ginny, too." She groaned. "I sound like a complete witch, but I don't really mean it. I'm happy for you. I want my sisters to be happy and have great lives. I'm destined to be the spinster who'll run this shop until the day I die."

Eloise rolled her eyes. "Enough with the drama. We have work to do, and I'm finishing early on Friday to prepare for the party."

"The party." Ashleigh heaved a sigh as if this were a great burden. "It's really going ahead?"

"Yes, it's going ahead." Eloise stared at her sister as if she'd grown a third arm. "We're having a housewarming because I am finally moving into my house. It'll be fun! Darcie will be there with her family and you'll get to meet some of Liam's friends, and I've asked Ryan, Kayla and Daisy to come along."

"What about Beth?"

Eloise snorted. "It's a housewarming more than a party, and I don't think it's worth Beth coming all this way for it." She felt as if she and Beth were worlds apart. Liam was a down-to-earth rough and rugged kind of guy, and she doubted that he'd have much in common with Beth's husband and friends. "She's getting ready to go to Fiji for another vacation, but even if she were free, I doubt something like this would be worth her while."

"I thought she was your friend."

"She is."

"Your good friend."

"Liam's replaced her." She placed her hand on Ashleigh's shoulder. "You'll come to my party, won't you?"

"I'll be there."

"Good, because I invited Ford."

Ashleigh groaned. "What did you have to go and do that for?"

CHAPTER 25

GINNY

"Do you want to do some coloring?" Ginny asked, carefully examining Daisy's face.

She enjoyed the little girl's company and looked forward to her return from school. She was often able to get some time with Daisy alone because Kayla would be busy.

But lately, ever since they'd gone to the park, she'd noticed lately that Daisy was different. She was subdued, and noticeably quiet in recent days.

Ginny was paranoid that it was something to do with her; that maybe Kayla had said something to Daisy about her.

A steely determination was set on the child's face as she focused on a list of spellings. She was carefully writing them into her notebook. "Daisy?" Ginny said, when she got no reply. Daisy looked up. "After you've finished your spellings, do you want to do some coloring?"

"Can I do it now?" She didn't sound as enthusiastic as

Ginny expected. "I've finished my spellings." She shut the notebook so fast that Ginny didn't have time to check whether she had or not.

"Sure."

Daisy reached for her pencil case.

"Wait! I've got something for you." Ginny went over to the drawer where she'd been storing the gifts she'd bought. "I got you a few things. Ta-da!" From behind her back Ginny whipped out a packet of coloring pencils and felt-tips and two new coloring books. "This one is about animals, and this one about places, like towns, cities and beaches."

Daisy's mouth turned into a big 'O.' "For me?"

"Yes, for you."

"Thanks, Ginny!" She got up and flung her arms around Ginny's neck and held onto her for a while.

"Why don't you get started?" Ginny asked, examining her face for tell-tale signs. Daisy sat down and looked through both coloring books before selecting one. She opened the first page and started coloring with her new felt-tips but there seemed to be an air of sadness lingering about her.

"My mommy went on a vacation." Her eyes were on the coloring and she didn't look up. Ginny's insides turned rigid. Ryan had mentioned this. "She did?"

"She went without me."

"Oh." Ginny scrambled to think of something to say, something kind and reassuring. "She probably went there from work."

"She went with a friend. She doesn't love me anymore." Daisy's lower lip wobbled and she looked seconds away from bursting into tears. Ginny scooted closer to her and put her arms around her. "That's not true, Daisy. Your mommy loves you very much." She tried to pull away a little, to look into Daisy's eyes and to see if she'd gotten through to her, but the little girl held onto her tightly.

"It's true. She doesn't call me anymore."

Ginny hugged Daisy even more tightly, and then the little girl's body started to shake and she began to sob uncontrollably. Ginny felt wretched. "M-my mommy d-doesn't want me," Daisy snifled.

"No, sweetie. No, no, no. That's not true." Gently, Ginny peeled herself away. "I promise you, that's not true."

Daisy's eyes were red, but it was the lost look in them that made Ginny's heart ache. She now understood why Ryan wasn't ready to break the news about their divorce to Daisy.

"It's true. I heard Daddy and Aunt Kayla shouting."

"Shouting? What about?"

"About my mommy. And you."

"About me?" Ginny's insides froze.

"Aunt Kayla said you were greeking."

Ginny frowned. "*Greeking?*"

"What does that mean?" Daisy asked.

"I have no idea." Ginny rattled her brain trying to make sense of the word but couldn't. She was tempted to ask Daisy what else she'd heard, but resisted the urge.

"Aunt Kayla was angry about my mommy."

"Oh." This made her feel a little better.

"She said my dad was stupid," Daisy continued.

Ouch. "That's not nice."

"She said he was her baby brother and he made a mistake, and my mom doesn't care about me."

Ginny stifled the gasp. She needed to tell Ryan that Daisy had overheard and that it was adversely affecting her. Words could do irreparable damage to an already fragile heart. "Maybe … Maybe you didn't hear it all properly. You just said a word I didn't understand, so maybe you heard the rest of it wrong?"

She wanted to gut out the nasty words that were imprinted on Daisy's mind and heart. "I promise you, Daisy. I promise you, your mommy loves you very, very much."

"Then why doesn't she live with me? You're always with Benjy, even when he cries. My mommy doesn't want to be with me."

She held Daisy's hands and tried to think of something to say; something that the child would believe. "Maybe your mommy is busy with her work, and she needs to focus on that for a while. I can't get much done with Benjy around, you know that."

"But Benjy's always sleeping."

"Yes, he is. He's a baby and babies sleep a lot." She wasn't sure where this was going.

"But I'm at school. Mommy can go to work when I'm at school, like Daddy does. Why doesn't she live with us? Why do we have to live with Aunt Kayla? She makes Daddy sad sometimes."

"She does?" That must be so hard on Ryan. Ginny wondered what else was being said at the house. "But, let's not talk about that for now. Look at me. Look at me, Daisy," she urged when the little girl looked away. Ginny plucked a tissue from the box, then dried Daisy's eyes and wiped her cheeks gently. With her finger under the girl's chin, she tilted her face up, forcing her to look at her. "Your mommy loves you in her own way. I promise you that's the truth. Do you remember a long time ago you asked me why I don't love Benjy? Do you remember?"

Daisy nodded.

"I wasn't feeling well. I had some horrible things happen to me and I was very sad."

"What horrible things?"

"Really horrible things that I don't want to talk about

because it makes me sad thinking about it."

"Because Benjy's daddy isn't here, like mommy isn't here?"

Ginny felt as if someone had punched her in the stomach and kept their hand there.

"Is Benjy's daddy busy at work? Is that why you don't see him?"

"Uh …" She felt as if she'd been slapped. Children were so inquisitive. She wondered how Ryan coped with all the questions Daisy asked. The poor child needed answers, and it wasn't her fault so much was being kept away from her. Ryan had to deal with so much that she didn't. Benjy was too young to even know what was going on and she was thankful for that.

"Do you feel sad now?" Daisy stared at her with glassy eyes and looked like she was on the verge of tears. "'Cause I don't want you to be sad."

"I'm not sad when you're around."

It was the truth, but instead of this making Daisy feel better, the little girl burst into tears.

"Aw, sweetie. Sweetie. Let it all out." Ginny hugged her closer, sensing that Daisy had been holding all of this inside her. Ginny didn't want her to hold onto the hurt any longer.

She had to tell Ryan, and quickly, but when she heard Kayla coming down the stairs, she gently prized herself apart, sensing that Daisy wouldn't want her aunt to know. She'd obviously picked a time when Kayla wasn't around to tell Ginny of what was troubling her.

Ginny could hardly blame her. Kayla had been a little cold towards her today. Colder than usual. Things had changed since they'd first taken her on and as the weeks passed, Ginny wondered if it was time to let her go. She was able to cope on her own now, and she felt better, physically and mentally.

But her heart sank when the consequences of Kayla leaving dawned on her. She wouldn't see Daisy anymore, nor Ryan. It wasn't as if she and Ryan were firm friends or anything, but there would be no chance for her to be able to speak with him if Kayla left.

"Your daddy's here, Daisy!" Kayla shouted from the hallway. Ginny's heart started to thump. Her insides heated. She shook her head, not understanding why she reverted to being a teenager with a crush as soon as Ryan was nearby.

"Let's get all your things together," said Ginny, and she helped Daisy pack everything away. Bending over to face level, she told her, "Be brave, and don't be sad, okay? Hopefully you'll see your mommy soon and then you'll see that she loves you very much." She prayed that this would be the case. Daisy's mother couldn't be that evil, could she?

She tried to slow down her steps as she headed into the hallway, expecting to see Ryan, but when he wasn't there, a wave of disappointment dulled her mood further. Kayla hurried Daisy up, and told her that her daddy was waiting in the car. They quickly bade goodbye and left.

It left Ginny feeling very puzzled. She'd thought about Ryan and their park visit most nights, and she'd been looking forward to seeing him. But this was the second day since then, and still he kept away.

Maybe he was in a rush. Or maybe that row with Kayla had resulted in him wanting to keep his distance from her.

When he didn't come into the house for the rest of the week, Ginny was convinced the row had something to do with it.

She couldn't prove it, and she would never have known were it not for Daisy, but now she worried that she'd made a mistake by opening up to him at the park.

Just because she was starting to move on, didn't mean that Ryan was. From what she could tell, the poor man hadn't seen it coming, his wife having an affair with her boss. Maybe he was so broken, he was shut off from the idea of getting close to anyone. How silly and presumptuous of her to think their suffering was the same and that they shared a bond?

She'd always had a sneaky suspicion that Ben was hiding something, and, in a way, she'd been prepared for it. But poor Ryan. The guy hadn't had an inkling about his wife's infidelity and the shock must have hit him like a hurricane. Clearly, he was still recovering from the damage. On top of that his daughter blamed herself for her mother staying away.

It was so much harder for him and the last thing he needed was a weak woman offloading her problems onto him.

CHAPTER 26

GINNY

She'd tried on three different dresses, not liking the way each of them made her look bigger than she normally was.

The baby fat was still there. Ginny's was a curvaceous body, but after having a baby the curves were a little too generous, a little too soft. She felt conscious of herself, especially given that Ryan was tall, and slim. And given the many pairs of admiring eyes that had settled over him that day at the school play.

Not that she was going to think of him like that. She was trying not to. It had been radio silence between them. She hadn't seen or heard from him since the day at the park. So much for him being there for her night or day.

Whenever you need me. Whatever the hour. Call me.

She felt silly for having delusional and romantic thoughts about him, and now she wished she could have wormed her way out of attending Eloise's housewarming, but she couldn't. She had to go; she needed to show Ryan that she didn't care. His cold shoulder treatment of her didn't matter.

Settling for capri pants and a loose-fitting top, she threw on a long thick jacket over the baby carrier strapped to her chest, in which she carried Benjy. He was also wearing his warm winter clothes. Together, they set off for Eloise's house, with Ashleigh pushing the pram. It would come in handy for when Benjy fell asleep but for now it helped to transport the food they were providing for the party.

Having Benjy strapped to her chest and facing outward, Ginny couldn't see his expression but she could tell from the way he kicked his legs that he was happy.

"Who are these people?" she asked as they approached Eloise's place. Unfamiliar faces milled around outside, many with drinks and plates of food in their hands. The patio heater provided some warmth on a chilly day.

"You tell me," Ashleigh mumbled. She was in a sour mood, and seemed to think the party was a chore instead of a social event. As they walked into the house, it was full of more people. So much for a 'small' housewarming. Ashleigh parked the pram discreetly in one corner.

They couldn't help but notice the gargantuan feast spread out on the table inside. Eloise had obviously been cooking for days. She'd declined their offer of help, but Ginny and Ashleigh had baked a few quiches and made some coleslaw and potato salad.

"I don't know any of these people," Ginny murmured, casting a hurried glance around the room, scouring for Ryan. He wasn't there.

"They're mostly Liam's friends, I believe," Ashleigh said. "Eloise is mixing in new circles these days."

"Is Beth here?"

"No, but Darcie's here and … oh, there's Ford and … Kayla," Ashleigh muttered. They were leaning against the countertop in the kitchen, talking. "Come and help me take the food into the kitchen," Ashleigh said, lifting out the food containers from the pram.

"I've got Benjy!"

"Just come with me," Ashleigh hissed.

"I can't carry anything." Not with her coat and the baby.

"Just. Come." It sounded as if Ashleigh wanted to avoid Ford as much as Ginny hoped to avoid Ryan. Daisy came running up and hugged her around the waist before grabbing Benjy's legs. "When did you get here?" Ginny asked her.

"A little while ago." Daisy giggled as she moved Benjy's legs up and down.

"Careful, Daisy. Don't pull Benjy's legs off, the poor boy needs them." It was Kayla, and if this was her attempt at a joke, Ginny found it odd. She didn't know quite how to respond to it, and she felt apprehensive because of what Daisy had told her.

"Hey, Kayla." She couldn't think of anything else to say, but when she saw Ashleigh go into the kitchen, she had her getaway. "I need to help Ashleigh with something—"

"Hi!" Eloise and Liam piled over and greetings and hugs followed. Eloise thanked them for the food and gestured to her banquet on the table. "We made all that yesterday." She pointed to the large table up along the wall.

"I saw. We made some food. Ash was going to put it in the kitchen."

"Ash already put it in the kitchen," said Ashleigh, grouchily. "Thanks for helping me," she moaned to Ginny.

"I had Benjy!" Ginny protested.

"I've taken care of it," Ashleigh replied. "You made that all yourself?" she asked the hosts.

Liam stood behind Eloise, his arms around her shoulders. "I helped." Looking at the food made Ginny hungry. "It looks delicious. Were you guys cooking all night?

"It was two days, but we had fun cooking," Eloise replied, stroking Liam's cheek lovingly as they stared at one another. Ginny had a feeling their fun probably had less to do with culinary skills, and more to do with how besotted they were with one another. It was sickening to see sometimes.

"We offered to help," Ashleigh retorted.

"I had it covered and we wanted you both to enjoy yourselves," replied Eloise. "Oh, by the way, Ford's in the kitchen," she said to Ashleigh.

"I saw," was her sister's steely reply.

Ginny's gaze darted around the room again, and while she was glad she didn't see Ryan, a part of her was disappointed. He was obviously staying out of her way and avoiding her, and it made her feel horrible because she'd gotten it all so wrong, *again.*

A different guy and still the same bad luck when it came to romance.

Up until now she'd been thinking of Ryan most of the time, going back over their conversations, remembering the way he looked at her, the advice he'd given her and his own troubles he'd shared with her.

But now the man didn't want anything to do with her.

"Would you excuse me. I need to put out more beers," said Liam.

"I don't recognize most of your guests," said Ashleigh.

"We'll fix that. Let me introduce you to everyone. Some are Liam's friends that I've gotten to know really well. They're nice. Follow me." Eloise motioned for her sisters to follow, but Ginny didn't want to meet people. She wanted to eat. Ashleigh didn't look eager to mingle. "Uh, no. Maybe later."

"Well, go and eat then, and let me have this gorgeous little man!" Eloise kissed Benjy again and waggled her fingers as if itching to hold him. "Give him to me. I want to introduce him to everyone."

Ginny wasn't sure about handing him over yet. "Let him get used to everyone and being in a new place, and I promise I'll give him to you." For now she needed the security of Benjy. She needed him to keep her busy in a room full mostly of strangers. He was her shield should Ryan miraculously turn up.

Daisy had run off but soon returned with a friend. "Lara goes to my school," she said. "This is Benjy!" she told her friend, and she made a funny face at him. He laughed and this made the two girls giggle. Then her friend Lara made a face and Benjy laughed again.

It was non-stop.

"Okay. I see how today is going to go." Ginny sat down and let the two girls entertain themselves with Benjy for a while.

"Want me to get you something to drink, or eat?" Ashleigh asked.

"You go ahead. I'll get mine later." For now she was content to let Benjy be entertained by Daisy and her friend, but the girls played with him for about five more minutes then left. Sitting alone with Benjy on her lap, she started to feel a little self-conscious. Eloise's laughter could be heard above the noise of the chatter, and she was a most gracious hostess, happily talking to her guests. When had she made all these friends? Ashleigh was talking to Darcie and her husband, and Ginny felt isolated and alone in a room full of people. She raised a hand when she caught Darcie's attention, and in the next instance they all came over to her and started to fuss over the baby.

"Let me have him, please." Darcie begged. "I get broody each time I see a baby."

"Ewww, gross mom." Matt, Darcie's teenage son, wrinkled his nose in disgust and walked away.

Darcie helped her to get Benjy out of the baby carrier and then she held him, but not before hugging him, and sniffing him, and sighing appreciatively. "I miss babies. I miss their smell, their softness, their funny faces." She hugged him as if he were the most precious thing to her. Her husband rolled his eyes. "I hope she doesn't go getting any crazy ideas."

"You won't miss sleepless nights, or having to get up every few hours," Ginny told her. She would get up as soon as she heard Benjy start to cry in the night, but her favorite times were the quiet times when the world was sleeping and her baby was content in her arms as she fed him. Almost three months old, he was no longer a fragile bundle of bones she'd once been afraid of hurting.

He was starting to hold his head up by himself now, and he was doing more, kicking his legs and waving his arms and making silly little noises. He was filling out and she loved nothing more than to put him in a clean, fresh baby suit and bounce him on her lap, making him laugh every time she did something to catch his attention.

She no longer resented her broken sleep, and would often stare at him in wonder when he was back in the cot, snug and sound and fast asleep. At times like this she would experience an outpouring of love for her child. These were the moments that told her she was slowly getting better. Getting over the hurt and starting to move on. Even the shock of Rhonda Moore's appearance had subsided, although Ryan had helped her with that.

Ryan.

A rush of adrenaline coursed through her at the thought of him. And then she remembered, and looked away, only to catch him staring at her. He was across the room, near the window, and the unexpectedness of seeing him gave her heart a jolt. She didn't know whether to be happy or angry.

Then, he smiled and she almost turned to look on either side of her, wondering if that had been for her.

Ford came over, and stood in front of her, partly shielding her view. He and Darcie were playfighting over holding Benjy. She was now surrounded by people standing around her and trying to make Benjy laugh. He was such a good baby these days, so pleasant and sociable.

So happy.

Ashleigh walked away when Ford appeared, and when Ford couldn't get the baby from Darcie he moved to talk to Liam. She could now see Ryan again. He was standing with a beer in one hand and he looked at her, then motioned for her to join him.

She wasn't sure what to make of that, given his avoidance of her recently, but she was curious, nevertheless, so she got up, stroked Benjy's cheek as Darcie held him, and told her that she'd be back to get him.

Darcie laughed. "You're not getting him back. He's mine for the rest of the evening."

Insecurities, like skittish butterflies, fluttered inside Ginny's belly as she crossed the room to Ryan. He looked devilishly sexy in his navy-colored jeans and casual dark shirt. She hoped her thighs didn't look too big, or that the loose blouse didn't hang like a sack. She was about to smooth down her hair when she stopped herself. All this preening and for what? hurt. "Hey."

"Hey. Where have you been hiding?" he asked. She tried to act nonchalantly, to hide her feeling and not give away that she thought of him more than was right, or good, or necessary. "I wasn't hiding. Benjy has a fan club in case you hadn't noticed."

"I noticed." He sounded cheerful, and he looked happy to see her. Nothing like the drama she'd manufactured in her head.

"I could ask the same of you," she said, wondering where he'd been the entire time.

"I was keeping an eye on the kids in the yard."

"I wasn't sure you'd come."

He raised an eyebrow. "And miss the chance to see you?" His words danced inside her, light and fluttery.

"Oh," was all she could manage in reply. So, maybe he was genuinely happy to see her. Maybe he hadn't been avoiding her but had been busy? He searched her face, maybe sensing her aloofness. "Everything okay?"

"I haven't seen you lately and I was starting to think you might be avoiding me." She'd gone and said it now. His brow furrowed and his gaze dropped to the bottle of beer in his hand. He avoided eye contact. Maybe she had been right. "Why would you think that?"

"You didn't come to the house. You used to before … sometimes. I sort of thought I might see you more now because …" Because things were different, because of what he'd told her at the park, because of what she felt. She'd talked herself into a corner and stopped before she rambled on and became the trusting and needy Ginny of before. "It doesn't matter."

When he looked up there was a sadness in his eyes, but his gaze moved over her shoulder, and his face turned somber. "Kayla's coming. Brace yourself."

Before she could respond, she felt a tug at the hem of her blouse. It was Daisy. "Ashleigh says can she have Benjy's milk bottle? He's hungry."

"He's hungry, is he? Sure, I'll get it." She turned to leave but Ryan grabbed her hand.

"I want to explain."

"I have to go." She wrestled her hand away just as Kayla joined them and made a hasty escape.

She made up a new bottle of milk for Benjy, then took him upstairs into one of the bedrooms where it would be quieter. Here, away from everyone and the noise and commotion, she thought about her conversation with Ryan and was curious once again. "Hey, Benjy," she cooed, staring adoringly at her beautiful boy. Benjy's lips turned upwards, and he sucked on the teat, looking very content. His stared up at her, watching her carefully, curiously, his expression changing when she made silly baby-talk. She watched in awe as his facial expressions changed from serious, to pensive, to smiling one after another.

After a while his eyelids started to get heavy and, halfway through drinking his milk, his eyes closed and he fell asleep. "I guess the noise and too many people overloaded your senses, huh?" she whispered. She would have liked to change his diaper, but didn't want to risk waking him. Putting him on her shoulder she rubbed his back gently, trying to burp him.

"There you are." Ryan's voice made her feel like she'd taken a huge dip on a fast-moving rollercoaster. She put a finger to her lips to silence him. He nodded in understanding and waited by the door. Now that he'd come upstairs looking for her, she needed to hear what he had to say, because he clearly was waiting for her. "I don't know whether to put him on the bed or put him in the pram," she whispered.

"Maybe just let him sleep on the bed."

She set him down carefully while Ryan put pillows and extra cushions around him so that he wouldn't roll over. Ginny surveyed the makeshift baby guardrails with amusement. "That's a good idea."

"We used to do that with Daisy when she was a baby and we didn't have her cot with us."

"I should stay with him." She didn't want to leave her baby in a strange room, with no baby monitor to track him.

"I'll stay with you," Ryan offered.

"You don't have to."

"I'd like to."

"Won't everyone wonder where you are?"

"Only Kayla. Daisy's far too busy having fun, and no one else cares."

She moved over to the window, away from the bed, and he followed. They faced one another. "You were going to tell me something," she prompted. "About why you were avoiding me."

He winced. "Okay. I admit I was, but it's because of my sister that I'm being careful."

"Careful?"

"About hanging around with you too much."

So, it was just as Daisy had told her. "She doesn't like me much."

Ryan's lips twisted as if he were trying to keep his words in. "She's protective about me, and she says she's looking out for me because of everything that's happened to me."

Ginny sighed. "Big sisters are like that. I should know. I have two of them."

"She means well, even though her tongue can be barbed sometimes. Kayla's not a bad person. She's just looking out for me."

"Do you need her to look out for you when it comes to someone like me?"

"No. It's none of her business." Something flashed across his eyes, something she couldn't make out.

"What does your sister think I'm going to do? Jinx your life?" She was desperate to know more of what Kayla had said about her, because Daisy hadn't told her much. When Ryan made an apologetic face, she realized she'd come closer to the truth. "These small-town rumors," she said, rolling her eyes.

"It's not the rumors. It's not any of that stuff."

"Then?"

"She thinks I don't need to complicate my life."

"How am I complicating your life? We only went to the park!" If she thought her sisters were nosy, Ryan's sister sounded much worse.

"That's what I told her. Kayla's always had a thing about being the older bossy sister." His fingers lightly brushed her hand. "Don't worry about it."

"But you did," she countered. "I thought you were avoiding me, and that's why I didn't see you all week. I thought maybe that ... that I was being needy, that maybe I shouldn't have texted you that day about Rhonda Moore."

He looked perplexed. "I'm glad you did. I wanted you to."

"Wanted me to?" Her heart missed a beat.

"I'm glad I could help, even if all I did was listen. You've helped me more."

"How have I helped you?" The notion of her helping anyone came as a surprise.

"By making me see that I'm not the only one who's suffering. That my problems, my experiences, my trials aren't as bad as yours."

"Don't say that. Don't trivialize your problems like that and elevate mine."

"That's not what I meant. My ex-wife left me, but she's still alive. Also, Daisy is older. She's not a baby. Your situation is different." He moved closer, or maybe she did, but his fingers traced over her sleeve ever so lightly, his electric touch causing her to breath to hitch.

She needed to tell him; about Daisy, and what she'd overheard, but the way Ryan's hand trailed down her sleeve, the way it almost touched her skin made her brain fog over. She struggled with coherent thought. In this moment she could only feel, and was conscious of the loud beating of her heart. She hoped Ryan couldn't hear the thud, thud, thud, thud.

She cleared her throat, trying to get herself ready to talk but her insides were churning. He liked her. The intensity of his gaze, the closeness of their bodies. She felt excited and nervous all at once.

"I meant what I said, Ginny. I'm always here if you need to talk."

"I … I wasn't sure. I thought you were staying out of my way because … maybe you didn't … maybe it was different for you. I feel silly now." She'd really gone and talked herself into a corner now.

He cupped the side of her face. "You, feeling silly?" He shook his head, his eyes twinkling as he gazed at her. He seemed to see inside her. "Never."

The door creaked and they both snapped their heads in that direction. Ginny's insides braced for Kayla's wrath and as she was about to move away, Daisy walked in, her eyes slowly lowering to their loosely touching hands. Their hands sprang apart as if they'd touched a live wire, but it was too late.

Daisy had seen and she now stared at them. "What are you doing?"

Ginny's cheeks grew hot and thankfully Ryan answered. "We were just talking, Dee."

"You're holding hands." She made an 'ew' face. Ginny's stomach hardened and neither she nor Ryan had an answer. "Why are you holding hands?" the little girl asked.

"How about we go for a walk along the beach?" Ryan suggested, ignoring the question. His distraction worked because Daisy jumped up and down with excitement. "Yay! Can my friend come?"

"Of course she can."

Benjy made a noise and stirred. Ginny held her breath. Daisy and Ryan turned silent, but Benjy stirred some more. And then he woke up, his piercing cries screeching through the quietness.

Ginny went to him. "Now would be the perfect time to go."

CHAPTER 27

RYAN

"I can carry him," he offered, seeing Ginny putting Benjy into the baby sling.

"Do we really need to give people more reason to gossip about us?" she whispered. She had a point.

Ryan glanced at all the party guests who were mingling together. There were more people here than he'd expected, and while it had been nice to get to know lots of new faces, the highlight for him had been talking to Ginny. "They look like they're all having a great time. I don't think they'll notice us leaving." But Kayla had, and she'd looked most displeased. Luckily, she hadn't confronted him in a room full of people.

"Then, sure. Why don't you carry him?" Ginny took the baby carrier off, and then helped him put it on, before adjusting the straps. Then she slowly lowered Benjy into it.

"Hey, little man. I've got you," he said. Benjy was in a hat and warm outer clothes, facing outwards, his back snug against Ryan's chest. He kicked his legs excitedly.

This felt familiar. They'd had a similar baby carrier for Daisy, but theirs had been more like a sling. Ryan used to love walking around with her in it. He loved seeing the world as she would have seen it. Far better than being placed horizontally in a pram.

"Can we go now?" Daisy whined, as if she'd been waiting a year for them. She and her friend were in their coats and all wrapped up for the cold. They'd opened the door and were racing to get outside.

"Yes, we're ready now," Ginny replied cheerfully.

They managed to leave the house without an interrogation or an interruption and walked away, looking like a family going for a stroll by the beach. He liked Eloise's cozy little house, so near to her sisters' place that they could see one another's houses from their windows, and yet far enough to give her privacy.

That's what he longed for. It was becoming difficult living with his sister, not just because of Ginny, but because he increasingly felt hemmed in. Kayla was like a strict parent who needed to know where he was and who he was with. While he understood her need to protect him, it wasn't her place to decide who he should talk to or not.

Away from the house, from everyone, from all the interruptions, he felt freer. Like he could breathe and talk without judgement or interruption. He liked that he could just be, and he didn't relish the thought of Kayla's questions when he got home.

"Ahh. This is nice and refreshing. I'm so glad we came out for a walk." Ginny closed her eyes and breathed deeply. The wind ruffled her hair, turning her hair into a wild mane that she had to continually keep moving away from her face.

"I'm glad, too. There are so many people inside, it was starting to get a bit stuffy." He let Benjy grab his fingers. "You're happy, too, aren't you, buddy?"

Ginny leaned over and stroked her baby's face. "You like it out here, don't you, Benjy?" she said in her baby voice. The little boy kicked his legs again and grabbed onto his fingers harder.

Ryan laughed. "He likes it. That's a strong grip you've got there, buddy." The girls had raced on ahead and were shrieking with excitement as they collected seashells.

"It was starting to feel claustrophobic in there," Ginny agreed. "I like this better."

So did he.

"We wouldn't have been able to talk," he said.

Ginny turned to him, her hand moving her wind-swept locks away from her face. "It's like they don't want us to."

"Who?"

"People. The universe. They all conspire against us." She chuckled lightly. Their hands brushed together as they walked, and neither of them moved to widen the distance between them. Soon he'd be tempted to take her hand in his again.

Further ahead, the girls had bent and were looking at something.

"You mean when Daisy walked in?" He hoped to draw it out of her, a hint as to how she felt. He'd made a brave move up there in the bedroom, perhaps it had been a foolish move, but there was something that drew him to Ginny, and in that moment he'd acted on impulse. He would have said something had his daughter not interrupted and now that moment was gone.

"Yes." He thought he heard a slight chuckle from her. "Collecting shells?" she asked because they'd caught up with the girls. They nodded, then proudly showed off their collection.

"Nice," said Ginny. "I used to love doing that when I was your age." Daisy held up a pale pink fan shaped shell.

"That's pretty, Dee," he said, taking the shell from her and examining it as if it were a flawless diamond. He liked that his daughter was having fun, and seemed to be settling in at her new school. He liked most of all that she'd made friends because that had been his biggest worry. He felt bad about uprooting her from everything she'd known in her life, and bringing her here, but she seemed to have adapted fine. But as time passed he blamed Vanessa for not making any effort to come and see her own daughter.

"Can you hold these, Ginny?" The girls heaped a dozen shells into Ginny's hands before running off. Ryan chuckled as Ginny blew the sand off the shells and put them into her pockets.

"You're going to have sand in your clothes," he said.

"Next time we should bring a bucket."

Next time. He liked the sound of that. "That's a good idea. We will." In the summer, this would be a great walk. A great place to be. Coming to Whisper Falls was working out well.

"Ryan, there's something I need to tell you."

He didn't like the way her voice turned serious, and braced himself for the rejection. He shouldn't have presumed too much. He shouldn't have held her hand.

"I wanted to speak to you about it last week, but I didn't see you. It's about Daisy."

"Daisy?" The relief he felt was replaced by fear.

"She's upset. She confided in me about an argument she overheard between you and Kayla. She was really upset, Ryan. She was sobbing."

He felt as if he'd been kicked between his legs. The idea of his daughter sobbing was bad enough, but to discover that he hadn't known, hit hard.

"She thinks her mom doesn't love her," Ginny continued. "She thinks she's to blame for her leaving."

He watched his daughter in the distance, laughing and playing with her friend, and his heart broke. She'd hidden it from him. Her hurt, her worries. While it was some relief that she'd confided in Ginny, it broke his heart to know that she'd put up a brave face in front of him. He'd noticed that she'd been quieter last week but when he'd asked her about it, she said she was tired and had lots to do at school.

He rubbed his forehead, going over the last few days, recounting his conversations with Daisy, trying to see how he'd missed something. He hated that she had been wrestling with guilt and that she felt responsible for her mother going away. He hated that he'd missed all of it.

More than that he hated that he and Kayla had discussed any of it. "I wish I'd kept my mouth shut when Kayla was worked up." He shouldn't have entered the row. "Daisy was sobbing?" A knot of anger balled in his throat at the image of his daughter crying.

"She was heartbroken. I hugged her and held her and told her that her mommy loved her so much. I told her it wasn't her fault."

"What exactly did she say she'd overheard?" He tried to think back to the conversation, tried to remember the words, to pinpoint what damage he had inadvertently inflicted on his young daughter. He listened as Ginny recounted the conversation and told him that Daisy believed her mother didn't love her anymore, and because her mother hadn't called her much, that she didn't want her. His heart cracked like ice under a skater's blade.

Daisy was hurting real bad and didn't understand why her

mother didn't live with her. If there was one good thing to come out of this gut-wrenching story, it was that Ginny had been there to comfort his daughter. He was so grateful that Daisy felt comfortable enough with Ginny to confide in her. "I feel sick to my stomach." He'd failed her. He'd wanted to protect her, and wanted the best for her, and yet, one slip, one silly, needless row with Kayla and it had led to this.

"Then she wanted to know about Benjy's father, and where he was. She has this idea that he's also busy at work, like your wife, I mean, Daisy's mom, is."

"What did you say to that?"

"I couldn't bring myself to tell her what happened, so I said I didn't want to talk about it because it made me sad. I didn't know what to say." She made an apologetic face and he wanted to hold her.

"You handled it really well, Ginny. I owe you so much."

"You don't owe me anything!" She swatted his arm playfully and his gaze drifted to her luscious lips which were a deeper shade of red than usual, maybe because it was chilly out here. He hadn't felt the stirring of attraction, the scary and exhilarating feeling of wondering if the other person felt what he did, for so long now that he wasn't sure if what he felt with Ginny was something he was just making up in his head.

"You've helped me and Daisy so much. I'm sorry she's so inquisitive, but I'm also deeply grateful that she opened up to you, because she hasn't said any of this to me."

"I like it when she comes back from school. I look forward to it. Being stuck inside the house most of the time gets hard, and Benjy isn't making much conversation yet."

"But once he starts, it will be wonderful. I also wanted to thank you for the coloring things you bought Daisy. That was so kind of you. Thank you."

Ginny moved an errant lock of hair away from her eyes.

"You don't have to thank me. I love Daisy's company. I like her innocence, believe me, after having no one but my sisters to contend with, Daisy is so funny and refreshing. I had no idea what fun young kids could be. She brightens up my day."

He smiled, feeling happier to learn that Ginny was getting something back, but what he'd learned worried him. "I had no idea she'd heard us, and I hate myself for it, but you being with her, it's been good for her. You're wonderful with her. You're like ..." He almost said it.

You're like the mother she hasn't got.

But he didn't want to say something so weighted, even if it was true. Ginny had stepped up, unknowingly, perhaps, but it meant a lot to him that his daughter could go to her. "It's good that she has you in her life."

He put his hands a few inches from Benjy's face, trying to protect him from the wind and the cold. He had to sit Daisy down and tell her the truth. Until she knew that, she would always mistakenly believe that she had something to do with Vanessa leaving. It pained him the way she was still waiting for her mother to come back. It was such a rare thing, that a mother would leave her child, and then be so terrible about keeping in touch.

They'd been here for months and Vanessa hadn't once mentioned coming to visit. She knew he was staying with Kayla until he got his own place, but she was obviously too busy globe-trotting with her rich CEO lover to care or find time for Daisy.

His daughter was only going to get older and he didn't want her to ever feel a shred of guilt on account of what Vanessa had done. "I need to tell her. I *will* tell her." He paused, unsure of whether to ask Ginny. "Would you mind being there?"

"Me?"

"She likes you."

"You want the three of us to talk about it? Shouldn't you maybe do that with Kayla?"

He guessed at Ginny' reluctance. "This doesn't involve Kayla. You said Daisy wanted to know about Benjy's dad. If it's okay with you, maybe you telling her what happened might help her to see her own situation in not such a bad light." He winced. "That sounds bad. I'm sorry." But it had worked for him. Focusing on Ginny's situation had enabled him to not be as fixated with his own problems. It had helped. He hadn't dwelt on his own misery as much.

"I sort of understand what you mean," Ginny said.

"If you'd rather not say anything, you don't have to. I'll tell Daisy the truth about her mother, that she's not coming back, and that she and I aren't together anymore. I don't know." He shrugged because it was difficult, whatever he said. It was like opening a can of crawling worms. "You being there might help, Ginny," he said, knowing deep in his gut that having Ginny there would soften the blow for his daughter. He groaned. It didn't seem ethical to use Ginny's tragedy to lessen the hurt for Daisy, but he didn't see any easier way of doing it. But, at the same time, he didn't want Ginny to sink into sadness all over again by talking about her past. "Maybe I should do this alone. I *can* do this alone. I'm sorry. I can't ask you to do such a thing. It's painful and I would hate for it to trigger anything."

"You can ask me, Ryan, and if I can help in any way, I would like to." They'd stopped walking and let the girls run on further along the beach. Ginny faced him. "Why are you holding your hands in front of Benjy's face?" she asked.

"I'm protecting him from the wind."

This made her laugh. She touched Benjy's face before swooping down and kissing him on the cheek. "Are you a whittle bit cold, Benjy?" she asked in that baby voice of hers.

"Do you want to head back?" He didn't want the baby to

catch a cold, but as Ginny talked gibberish to him, Benjy kicked his legs in excitement.

"Benjy says he wants to stay out here," said Ginny, straightening to standing. "He's all wrapped up and with your windshield hands in front of his face, he'll be fine for a while."

"Okay. Whatever Benjy wants."

Ginny stared at him pensively. "Don't worry about triggering me, about my past. I'm starting to move on, and I feel good. I'm learning to deal with it and a part of that is talking about it, and if it helps Daisy, I most definitely want to do what I can."

"Are you sure?"

She nodded. "It's important for Daisy to know what happened to Benjy's dad. I don't want to upset her, but I also don't want to keep lying to her. She doesn't know who Benjy's father is, but dotes on Benjy and maybe knowing that he is fatherless might help her deal with what you're going to tell her."

"I appreciate your help. I was going to tell you about the row I had with Kayla. It was after we got back from the park that day with you. It's why I didn't come into the house. It's not easy living with my sister. I should have called you, or texted, especially after we'd talked, and especially after I told you I'd be here for you. You probably won't believe a word I say anymore."

She flashed a smile that lit him up inside. "I'll still believe you," she said slowly. "In a world of cheating, lying men, you're someone I trust." He smiled back. There was an understanding in her eyes, a softness about her when she said this, and he was compelled to delve deeper, to get to know her better now that they finally had a chance. "Sisters can be difficult to live with," she said, taking his attention away from her lips, "but they often mean well. I understand your dilemma,

Ryan. Daisy is older and curious and I imagine she asks you lots of questions. And then you have Kayla who, from the sounds of it, is super protective. You're staying in her house and I'm sure it's not easy, not having your privacy and all that. I just didn't know what to make of it when I didn't see you for days, and I really did want to speak to you about Daisy. I just wasn't sure how to."

He frowned because she suddenly seemed nervous. "You can always tell me anything."

"I wasn't sure I could. You see, I'm …" She took a deep breath in. "I'm no good at reading people or situations, so I started to doubt myself."

A strong gush of wind swept Ginny's hair over her eyes. "Doubt yourself?" he asked, moving it away so casually, as if it were the most natural thing in the world for him to do. His fingers lingered a hair's breadth away from her face, and he was tempted, so very tempted, to cup her face again, like he'd done earlier before Daisy walked in.

"As in … us being friends," Ginny said.

"*Just* friends?" It was a risky move, letting his guard down.

They stared at one another, a quiet understanding blossoming between them, and without either of them answering the question, they continued to walk, letting the silence fall effortlessly between them.

"Don't doubt yourself, Ginny," he said, finally. There was something more than words sparking between them. He cared about this woman, had feelings for her, and he thought about her all the time. He hadn't expected to feel that way about anyone for a long time. This last week it had been difficult to stay away from her. A couple of times as he'd waited outside in the car for Kayla, he came out and almost knocked on the door knowing that Ginny was inside, but the strain of having another row with his sister later when they got home stopped him.

And now he didn't want to risk having any more arguments knowing how adversely they affected Daisy.

"It's easier to not doubt myself now. It helps talking to someone. Talking to you. This is nice."

He hadn't expected that from her. "This is nice," he agreed.

"It's just better to have someone outside the family. I have a friend, Talia, but I've not been a good friend to her, and I miss her. I should reconnect with her, but I've had you to talk to, and it's helped me."

"Likewise."

"We don't seem to care about being seen together today." She glanced at the house. "I'm sure your sister, and both of mine too, would be staring out of the windows with binoculars if they had them."

He recoiled at the idea of Kayla having binoculars. "I, for one, don't care anymore."

"No?"

No, he didn't. He wanted to be with Ginny and Benjy. He wanted to spend more time with them because it made him feel good about a future he was only now starting to glimpse.

A future which no longer had to be grey and bleak.

He could be more than just a single father trying to do his best for his daughter. With Ginny, he dared to envisage something warm and welcoming. A happy place.

With his heart leapfrogging into his throat, he dared to tell her. "I like you, Ginny. I like you a lot. You make my life have meaning again. At this uncertain time in my life, Daisy is my center and my world, but you, you take away the painful past and make me feel like I can breathe again. You make me feel that it's okay to step out into the world and to dare to think of having something good in my life."

Her cheeks colored, and her eyes turned shiny. "I don't want to upset you," he said, thinking she was about to cry. He took her hand. It was soft and warm, slender and delicate.

"I'm not upset. I'm ... I'm not upset." Her smile was slow to spread, as if she didn't believe what she was hearing.

In the distance the girls were standing with their backs to them, and they couldn't see him holding Ginny's hand.

"Good, because I never want to upset you. I want to make you happy, Ginny. You make me happy."

She looked surprised. A little shy, her cheeks blushing pink. "Yeah?"

He nodded. "Yeah." He needed her to know. "This year has been hard for me, and coming here and meeting you, it's been the best thing. I can think about the future instead of dwelling in the past."

She shook her head. "You don't want to live in the past. I've tried it, and it's a horrible place to be, for people like us who've suffered tragedy." She would know because she'd been through it. They understood one another because of their trauma. That's why this fit, him and her, why it felt right. He'd tried to fight it, his attraction to this woman; it had started with nothing but curiosity in the beginning, but as he'd come to know her, he'd felt her pain, and wanted nothing more than to make her feel better.

"What if you and I went out, without Daisy, to talk first, about what we'll say to her?"

"You and me?" she asked, quietly and without shock. It was possible that she'd also been thinking about it, about the chance for them to be together without interruptions and prying eyes.

"You and me. Doesn't have to be a date, but ... it *could* be." He examined her reaction. She seemed calm. As if he'd asked her a normal question.

"Are you asking me out on a date?"

"Possibly."

"Then how about you ask me, properly?" She raised a brow.

"Would you like to go on a date with me, Ginny?" His gut turned hard as steel, bracing for the rejection. What was he thinking? Just because his feelings for her were strong, didn't mean she felt the same.

The surprised look in her eyes was replaced by something more cautious. "I sure would," she answered slowly, with a smile.

"Really?" he asked, sounding like a ten years' younger Ryan.

"Daddy! I found another shell!" He let go of Ginny's hand when the girls came running up to them, then he and Ginny expressed wonder when they proudly showed them their handful of shells.

"I like Ginny," Daisy said happily as he tucked her into bed.

"I like her, too." He plopped a kiss on Daisy's cheek. Ryan sat down on his daughter's bed feeling content. They'd come back from the party an hour ago, and after a bath, and some reading, it was time for Daisy to go to bed. She hadn't wanted to leave Eloise's party, but she'd been yawning, and she'd been running around and playing all day.

They'd drawn some inquisitive looks when arrived back to the house after their walk. Benjy had a dirty diaper that needed changing, and Ford had collared him into having another beer.

Kayla had been quiet on the drive home and he prepared himself for an interrogation later when Daisy was asleep. He was determined to say nothing. He would handle whatever accusations Kayla hurled at him, but he would never get involved in another shouting match.

Also, the thought that he and Ginny were going on their first date soon made everything right in his world.

"You like her a lot, Daddy. You were holding hands."

She saw that?

"We were?" He pretended to be shocked.

"When Benjy was sleeping."

He breathed in with relief. She hadn't seen them at the beach, then. "We weren't holding hands," he said indignantly. "Our hands kept bumping."

This made her giggle. "Your hands were bumping?"

He shrugged and tried to think of a distraction. "It happens. Did you have fun today?"

"I had lots of fun. I like Lara. Can we have her over one day for a play date?"

"We sure can."

"And can we go to the park with Ginny and Benjy again?"

"We can do that."

"Daaaaaaaaaddy ..."

"Yes, sweetie."

Daisy looked serious. "Is Benjy's daddy like mommy?"

The air slowly leaked out of his lungs. He'd been dreading this. "How do you mean?"

"Is Benjy's daddy at work all the time, like mommy?"

"It's ... it's not quite the same."

"Why doesn't he live with them?"

"Maybe we can get Ginny to tell you, Dee."

"She said it makes her sad."

"Listen, Dee." He stroked her face gently, before tucking her hair behind her ear. "I want you to know that mommy being busy at work is nothing to do with you."

"Aunty Kayla said mommy doesn't care about me." Something hard sliced into his heart as his daughter's sad eyes stared up at him.

"Aunt Kayla gets angry sometimes. She doesn't think about what she's saying."

"Did she tell lies?"

"She got angry. Sometimes, when grownups are angry, they say silly things."

"They lie?" Daisy repeated.

He wished he'd kept his mouth shut, and that he and Kayla had never had that argument. He'd caused Daisy so much hurt, had maybe even damaged her, because of it. He vowed to never have an exchange like that again. "They sometimes say things they don't mean."

She seemed to be pondering his words, her lips pressing and twisting, as if she couldn't decide on what to say. Then, "But it didn't look like mommy was at work. It looked like when we went to the beach, remember Daddy? Remember the t-shirt you got me with our picture on it?"

Tears started in his eyes when he recalled the happy memories from their Florida vacation. It wasn't long after that when Vanessa broke the news to him. It was their last family vacation.

"Mommy was … uh …" This was difficult. Daisy was more mature than any five-year-old ought to be. Mature in a way that made his life difficult, because he still wanted to cushion her with bubble wrap and keep her from the harsh realities of the truth. "These days people can work from anywhere. They don't have to go to the office, like I do. They can work from anywhere."

"Mommy was working at the beach?"

He scratched his ear. ""Maybe she was."

"Why don't you work at the beach, then I can come and so can Lara and we can collect more shells?"

He chuckled. "How would I get any work done?" When she

looked downcast he said, "How about you, me and Ginny go out one day, and we can all spend time together?"

"Can Benjy come?" The unbridled cheeriness in her voice told him that the distraction worked.

"We can ask Ginny to bring Benjy," he replied. It was time to tell Daisy the truth, the whole truth, and nothing but the truth. And before that, he had the chance to see Ginny, just the two of them.

On a date.

His life was no longer filled with harsh moments. He had a glimmer of some good moments on the horizon.

CHAPTER 28

GINNY

*H*er stomach was in knots.

It didn't help that her sisters knew. She'd had to tell them, because she wanted them to look after Benjy while she went out for a few hours on a Friday evening. She and Ryan had agreed it would be better to meet one evening during the weekdays as weekends would be difficult.

"Nice. Give us a twirl." Eloise surveyed her, like a mother surveying a daughter wearing her prom dress for the first time.

"I'm not giving you a twirl! I am not a child."

"Lord knows you're not." Ashleigh stood before her, folding her arms, her gaze raking over Ginny from top to toe.

She wore a loose buttoned top, with slim fitting pants which had an elasticated waist. The ensemble gave the semblance of her being slimmer than she was. She felt good in it and had confidence which, given the occasion, she needed in truckloads.

"How late will you be?" Eloise asked, a mischievous glint in her eyes.

"We'll stay up until you return," Ashleigh added.

Ginny glared at them both. "I'm not fourteen, and if you two are going to carry on like this, I'm not going." She wondered if the pain her sisters were putting her through was worth a date with Ryan.

"We're just messing with you!" Ashleigh retorted.

"Why did you have to go and give it up so soon?" Eloise wailed to her sister. "This was fun."

"Fun?" Ginny snapped. "I've been miserable, and low and feeling down for months, and I've finally met someone who's nice to me. Someone I get on with. He understands me in a way no one else does because no one else has had their life turned upside down like I have. You don't know what it's like to have your beliefs shaken so badly that you vow to never let anyone in again. Ryan makes me feel like I can, and you two are —"

Her sisters rushed towards her, looking shamefaced.

"Ginny, Ginny." Ashleigh's arms wrapped around her.

"Gin. We didn't mean it." Eloise's fingers smoothed back Ginny's hair.

"We're sorry. We were trying to boost your mood. You seem a little nervous."

"*This* is your idea of boosting my mood?"

Ashleigh gently prized herself apart, and folded her arms defensively across her chest. "Nothing makes us happier than to see you starting to enjoy life again. It's so good to have the Ginny we used to know come back."

"Exactly! We're so happy for you," Eloise chimed in, resting her hand on Ginny's arm. "You're so radiant, and enthused. Your eyes sparkle whenever Ryan's around."

Ginny rolled her eyes. "They do not." She slipped on a long jacket.

"Liam and I watched you at the house party, during the limited time we saw you, when the two of you weren't hiding from everyone."

"We weren't hiding. I was taking care of Benjy!"

"That was a lovely little walk the four of you took—"

"The five of them. Daisy's friend was with them," Eloise reminded her. "Small world, huh? Who would have thought Liam would know the girl's parents?"

"Is there anyone Liam doesn't know?" Ashleigh remarked.

Eloise grinned with pride. "He's a popular guy. He's done lots of little jobs for many people around here."

Ginny gritted her teeth together. "Okay. Enough. I'm leaving. Call me if Benjy plays up. I don't plan on being out for too long. A couple of hours at most."

"Don't rush back!" Eloise cried, at the same time as Ashleigh said,

"Take your time."

"But be home by the stroke of midnight," Eloise told her. "Or maybe don't."

Ashleigh opened the door for her. "But don't be too late, or you might turn into a pumpkin."

"Cinderella didn't turn into a pumpkin, her carriage did," Eloise retorted.

"That's right." Ashleigh nodded, as if she'd only remembered.

"That means Ryan must be Prince Charming," Eloise said, looking proud of herself. Ginny fought the urge to scream and waved at Ryan who was mercifully still sitting in his car. She'd warned him not to come to the house.

"If he's Prince Charming, and I'm Cinderella, that means the both of you must be the ugly sisters," said Ginny, rushing away. Ryan came out of the car when he saw her racing down the path. She couldn't leave fast enough, so much so that she tripped and went headfirst into him. Two strong arms cushioned her fall and she cringed, hoping her sisters hadn't seen.

"You okay?" Ryan shifted her to standing.

"These pesky heels," she muttered, smoothing down her top. Ryan walked over to the passenger side door and opened it. No one had ever held the door open for her before.

"Is she okay?"

"Are you okay, Gin?"

Her sisters voices were a chorus in the inky blue darkness. He gave them a thumbs up.

"You don't have to open the door for me, Ryan. But thank you." She quickly climbed in.

""You're welcome. What's the rush?" he asked when he got in.

"My sisters are stressing me out," she groaned.

"Drive, fast. Please," she begged, dreading that her sisters would turn up at the car to make sure she hadn't broken her ribs or anything. He did as she asked, and soon they were away from the house. She asked him if Kayla had given him a hard time.

"She gave me the icy treatment."

"She knew you were seeing me?"

Shivers ghosted down Ginny's spine at the sentence. It felt sexy and intimate and nice, in a weird way. Romance was so far down the list of things she wanted and needed, that it might as well have not been there. Yet, here she was, going on a date with a guy who was so good to her. If she didn't know any better, this could all be just a dream. But she knew better. This was real, and going out tonight with Ryan pushed all of the terrible past away.

"She knew."

"Ouch." Ginny felt for him. Compared to Kayla, her sisters were a breeze. "I'm sorry."

"I'm sorry for the stress your sisters are giving you."

"That's another thing we have in common," she said. The look he gave her made her pulse quicken and her heart flap as if it had wings. She could get used to this; being together, in one another's orbit, instead of skating around at home on thin ice with interruptions and disapproval all around them.

"But Daisy approves. She wanted me to say 'hi' to you."

"Say 'hi' back to her." Ginny's insides warmed at the mention of Daisy's name, and thinking of her reminded her of Benjy. She wondered if he was looking for her.

"How do you feeling about leaving Benjy?"

"Okay, I guess. I did it for the school play, so I'm getting used to it."

"You won't have any gossipy school moms to contend with tonight."

"I'm looking forward to having a meal with a grown up, in a place outside out my house."

He drove her to an authentic little Italian restaurant near where he worked. It was better to be away from Whisper falls, away from inquisitive eyes. The restaurant had a lovely ambiance and she felt happy, and comfortable, and confident, walking in with a handsome man who had a good heart. Sitting across the table from him, just the two of them like a couple, made this evening even more special. He was so attentive and funny, and knowledgeable about so many things. They talked a lot, about technology and world issues, about the bridal shop, and his new place of work, that time flew. Her heart was already thumping and when the food arrived she was conscious —in a way she'd never been before—of how she ate. She prayed she didn't make a mess or have crumbs on her lips or food stuck between her teeth. Being away from their children and inquisitive adults put them at ease and the conversation flowed. It also helped that they were able to talk without interruption. It was mostly safe talk, carefully omitting mention of his ex or Ben.

After dinner they went for a walk along the parade of shops nearby. Warmly lit lamps cast a golden hue in the dark night, and the street was quiet. She didn't know when it happened, when Ryan slipped his hand into hers, but it was natural, and like the most normal thing in the world. It made her feel wanted, and cared for, and no longer alone.

"Daisy asked me about Benjy's dad again." He squeezed her hand gently as if to comfort her. "I'm sorry for bringing this up again."

"Weren't we supposed to discuss this tonight?" Yet she was glad that they hadn't.

"I don't want to dredge up the past, but Daisy has asked and I don't want her to worry. I hate that she wrongly thought she was to blame for Vanessa not calling, and I don't want her to get any more wrong ideas. Young minds have powerful imaginations."

They came to a park bench and sat down. "I agree. I don't want her to worry, and you do need to tell her," Ginny said. "Daisy's trying to make meaning of her shifting world. Benjy has no father and she doesn't have a ..." She stopped herself just in time. "Sorry, I don't mean to say she doesn't have a mother. She obviously does."

"She might as well not have a mother, because that's how Vanessa has behaved. She's been selfish. She thinks only about herself and she doesn't care for Daisy. She used to care, but she's changed. She loves Daisy—I don't doubt that—but she loves her new lifestyle more. It's the type of lifestyle I could never give her, and she loves the freedom of not having to be responsible for a child. She walked out on my daughter. She chose money and something shiny and new. She didn't think things through when she tossed away years of marriage and a family." He sat forward, his shoulders hunched and she wanted to comfort him. Leaning forward, she hooked her arm through his. "We don't have to talk about this now. I feel so bad for Daisy, and I can see how hard it is for you trying to hold it all together."

Pain-filled eyes stared back at her. "Things are better now, since coming here, since meeting you. You make everything good again, Ginny."

"Do you really mean that?" It shook her to her core, in a good way, to hear him say those words.

"I really mean that."

They'd moved closer, and his gaze dropped to her lips, then to her eyes, then back to her lips again. He looked unsure, and like most people she knew he thought she was fragile, and when he backed away, she'd had enough. She licked her lower lip. "Kiss me, Ryan."

His brows lifted a little, as if he wasn't sure he'd heard correctly, but then he moved closer, the scent of his cologne once more wafting around her. His hands gingerly touched her arms, and he dipped his head towards her. Her insides were in free fall. The gentle press of his lips sent shockwaves down her back, and his electric touch made her skin tingle. He took her to a place of blue skies and lush green grass. Flowers and birdsong. Their bodies tilted more towards one another, their arms wrapped more firmly around each other, and he deepened their kiss.

It felt like *more*.

He was more.

More confident, more sure, more experienced. This wasn't the frenzied kiss of a desperate man. Or one who fumbled. Or a man who wanted to take more than she was ready to give. When Ryan kissed her, it felt like she was floating. His masterful mouth elicited whispered moans from her. This was too much, but in a good way. She'd never been kissed like that before.

Up until now she'd only had little boy kisses. Ben was a boy compared to Ryan. Ryan's kisses, his touch, the way he looked at her, and spoke to her, the way he made her feel, it was all so very different to what she'd known before. His hands now on her hips were steady, assured and going no further.

When they parted, it took a while for her senses to steady, for her to come back to planet earth instead of drifting into the stratosphere.

He held her hand and kissed it, and that motion made the goosebumps on her skin do another Mexican wave.

"Wow." She immediately regretted her syllable.

"I've never been kissed like that before."

His eyes twinkled in amusement.

"How old are you?" she asked, unable to stop herself. She had often wondered about this, had assumed that he was older because of the way he carried himself.

"Thirty-three. Is that a problem?"

"No. No." She shook her head. "Not a problem." That kiss was imprinted on her lips, her mind, her heart. She wanted more moments like this.

"Because I'm twenty-five. Is that a problem?"

He chuckled. "No."

She smiled.

He cupped her face, the way he always did, but this time his thumb rolled over her lower lip.

"It's Kayla's last week next week."

"I know. She's planning on returning to the school soon."

"Not immediately?"

"I expect she'll take a break, do some more cross-stitch and knitting and crocheting."

"Those are her hobbies?"

"I think her hobby is keeping an eye on me."

She chuckled. "You must not be looking forward to going back home?"

"I'm going to start looking for a place to rent, for now, for a little while. It's time I moved out."

"It's time I started taking care of Benjy and the house. I can't go back to work just yet. I miss that and I will return one day, hopefully in the not too distant future."

"You want to go back so soon?"

"I liked being with people, and seeing new brides trying to find a dress for their big day."

He grimaced. "You don't find it difficult?"

"I'm not as fragile as most people think. I'm okay talking about weddings and wedding dresses. I am now." Because of him, because of Benjy. Because the past was where it belonged and it did no good thinking about it.

"You're the best thing to happen to me since Benjy was born. I'm so glad I found you." She meant to hold back, to not open her heart so freely, but she was so overcome with so much feeling for him.

"And you, Ginny, are the best thing to happen to me this past year. I'm so glad my sister took on this job." Their faces were so close that she could feel his sweet breath against her face. He smelled clean and minty, and this time she leaned in and kissed him. It was short, quick and sweet.

"It might not have happened. I argued with my sisters when they told me they'd found someone to help me. I wanted to be left alone. Obviously, I couldn't see what a state I was in back then. I didn't want anyone or anything. I was a bad mom."

He gently caressed her cheek. "I have firsthand experience of a bad mom, and you're not it. Kayla says things were tough for you because you'd had a difficult birth, and you were depressed, and you were still grieving the death of your fiancé."

"My *cheating* fiancé. Back then I was filled with grief and anger. I resented everything, and I also felt humiliated. I hadn't known until later, on both occasions."

"You were blind to it, like I was. Things happened to you and you did your best to deal with it. We didn't instigate these things, Ginny. They *happened* to us, and we were helpless, not knowing how to deal with them. We did the best we could."

"We're survivors."

"Something like that." Ryan scoffed. "Vanessa was so smug, so vicious when I begged her to come back, when I told her that we could try again and that I could be different—"

"You could be different? Why you? She's the one who had the affair."

"I thought it was a phase. I thought she might realize her mistake and come to her senses. I wanted to keep us together. Our family, I didn't want things to change for Daisy, she was so happy. I told Vanessa that I'd try and get a better job so I could have more money, so that I could give her the type of life she wanted, but I was a desperate man. I could never compete with her boss. I was delusional for even saying that."

"You were hurt," she said, quietly. "You would have said and done anything to keep her, to have your family be together." Ginny had done the same with Ben. She'd taken him back for the baby's sake.

Ryan wanted to know more about her past, so she told him, all of it, and why she'd cancelled the wedding, and why she'd gotten back together with him again.

"We do stupid things when we're desperate, and we do them most of all for the ones we love." The entire time they'd held hands and he'd listened patiently. "You got back with him because of your baby."

"Yes, I did."

"Some things aren't meant to be," he said.

"I needed this evening. Just the two of us," she said, after a while, when they'd been sitting silently, holding hands and contemplating this new state of being.

"We would never have gotten to talk so much," he agreed. "Are you okay to tell Daisy about Benjy's dad?"

"I'll break it to her gently."

"She saw us holding hands, and asked me about it."

"I thought we were being discreet."

"Little eyes don't miss a thing. I don't want to keep this a secret from anyone. I don't want to have to duck and dive and dodge when I'm with you, Ginny. I want the world to know that we're together."

Her heart warmed at his words. This evening had been everything she'd hoped for and so much more. "I don't want to hide anymore, either.

She glanced at her watch, and yelped, "It's so late!" It was an hour after when she'd said she'd be back. Begrudgingly, she released her hand from his. It was time for their idyllic evening to end, even though she wasn't ready for it. "I don't want to go."

"I wish we could stay like this forever, or for a few more hours at least."

"Thank you for tonight, Ryan. No interruptions, you and me talking, it was …" She paused to think of the perfect word.

"Bliss," he finished for her.

"It was bliss."

"I hope it's the first time of many."

CHAPTER 29

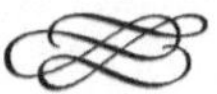

RYAN

He'd been waiting for Kayla to make a nasty comment about his date with Ginny.

She knew about it because he'd told her; he didn't see any point in hiding it but, much to his surprise, she hadn't asked him anything

She'd been almost pleasant, and that threw him off kilter. Kayla was preoccupied right now, what with leaving the Rose sisters' employ and returning to school a few weeks after that. When she'd gone to Daisy's school play, it seemed to remind her of what she was missing and she'd made an appointment to see the school principal next week.

Ryan couldn't wait for Kayla to stop working for Ginny and return to school where, hopefully, she'd be too busy to meddle in his affairs.

His life was starting to fall into place, especially now that he and Ginny were together. He wanted everything to be perfect for Daisy. She worried him, and all he wanted was for her to be happy and content. He had Ginny to thank for some of that. In Ginny Daisy had found someone to look up to, someone who cared about her, someone she was fond of.

Things couldn't be any better.

He was eager to find a place to rent; a small home for him and Daisy. It was time for him to get out of his sister's hair because living together was starting to cause more problems in their relationship. It hadn't been like this before, and that was the only reason he'd even considered moving in with her. He also thought it might help after her illness, but now he needed to move on before their relationship was irreparably ruined.

He'd already prewarned Ginny that he wasn't going to come to the house if he could help it. There was no reason to give Kayla something to be grumpy about. They spoke several time a day, and now that they were dating, they could see one another whenever they wanted; it didn't have to be in her house, under Kayla's nose. And once Kayla left, it wouldn't be a problem at all.

GINNY

She'd been on a high since their first date, and it was enough to sustain her for the rest of the week when she didn't see Ryan. It helped that Ashleigh and Eloise had stopped teasing her too much.

She and Ryan spoke often, many times during the day, and always at night, once Daisy was asleep.

Ginny liked this the most—their deep and intimate conversations. It was easier to open up over the phone, and she shared parts of herself that she might have taken longer to share had they been face to face. Listening to his rich and comforting voice in the darkness made her feel as if she were special. His words reverberated deep in her chest and she would clutch her phone to her ear and close her eyes. There, in the dark, talking quietly so that Benjy wouldn't awaken, she fell deeper in love with the man.

The day soon arrived for Kayla to leave. If Ginny was relieved to see the last of Kayla, she was saddened at losing her time with Daisy.

"I'm going to miss you. I won't see you anymore." Daisy's sad face pricked at Ginny's heart strings.

"Yes you will," Ginny assured her, even though she'd been feeling sad herself.

"But I won't be coming here no more." Her expression was so somber that Ginny couldn't help but put her arms around her. "You are *so* adorable. I can't not have you in my life anymore. We're going to see one another, and it won't just be for a few hours after your school. We can see each other for longer. We'll have days at the park and picnics and maybe do other things you like. We'll be able to have fun!"

"You promise?" Daisy cried.

"I promise."

"I always have fun with you."

"You're so sweet." She gave Daisy another hug.

"And you are," Daisy replied promptly. "I love you Ginny. I love you and Benjy and I wish we all lived together."

Ginny held her breath, feeling fearful that Kayla might have heard. "Oh, sweetie … that would be … that would be … fun." Ginny struggled to reply, thrown off guard by Daisy's words.

She hugged her again because it was easier to do that, than to say anything. How could she tell Daisy that she and Ryan were together, when Daisy didn't even know that her daddy and mommy weren't together anymore?

"Yeah it will be! We can stay at the park all day and I can play with Benjy more."

Kayla coughed lightly, and Ginny almost jumped out of her skin. Ever since her date with Ryan, she'd tried not to be in the same room as her for fear of Kayla saying something. So far she hadn't commented on it. "I've put the casserole in the oven, it should be ready in ninety minutes.

"Thank you." Ginny slowly got up from her chair, not sure how to bid farewell to Kayla.

"Let's go, Daisy. Your daddy's here."

Ginny retrieved the small package she'd hidden in a drawer, and handed it to Kayla. She took it gingerly, looking slightly affronted, then confused as she eyed it with suspicion. Ginny clasped her hands together. "It's something small. A little 'Thank you' gift from me, for all your help. I hope you'll like it."

Kayla looked at it as if it were a bomb. "What is it?"

"Open it and you'll see."

"Open it! Open it, Aunty Kayla!" Daisy cried, excitement giving her voice a high-pitched edge.

Kayla seemed stiff, and unsure, as if it were a chore to accept a gift from an enemy. Unwrapping the white and gold star spangled foil paper, her brows furrowed, then a half-smile played across her lips as she pulled out cross-stitch pattern kits. "How did you know?" She rolled her eyes. "Ryan told you. You didn't have to. This is ... not necessary. Your sisters paid me a wage for—"

"Do you like it, Aunty Kayla?"

"Yes I do. Get all your things together," she ordered her niece, stuffing the gift back into the wrapping paper and shoving it into her bag. "Thank you," she said to Ginny, "but you shouldn't have."

The difficulty Kayla was having in expressing gratitude didn't surprise Ginny. "I wanted to."

"Check you've got everything, honey," she said to Daisy. "We won't be coming back."

Ginny forced a little laugh. "It doesn't matter if she leaves something behind, I can always drop it off or—" She stopped, realizing that she was steering the conversation around to her and Ryan. "I hope you like the patterns," she said, swiftly changing the subject. "There were so many. I didn't know which one to get you."

"You didn't need to get me anything."

"It's really not a big deal, Kayla."

Kayla's face hardened. "Daisy, go and put your coat on." Cool eyes settled on Ginny's face, and she felt a prickle of agitation. "My brother has been through a lot, and he's trying to be strong for his daughter. He was supposed to make a new start, not mire himself in more drama. I don't want him to get hurt again."

Ginny's mouth went dry and the bubble of happiness she'd been in popped. Kayla was leaving and Ginny hopefully wouldn't run into her much, but poor Ryan still lived with the woman. She didn't want to make his life difficult by saying something harsh to Kayla, but the woman had caught Ginny off guard. Unprepared. Without her armor. "I would never hurt him."

"I'm sure you mean that sincerely, but you have a lot of problems to deal with. A lot of issues I'm sure you're trying to work your way through. I don't want you to take advantage of my brother's kindness or attention. He has a young daughter and he needs to be there for her. She is his priority. No one else."

The muscles along Ginny's jaw flexed. "That is something I never forget, Kayla. Thank you for all your help. I wish you well at the school."

CHAPTER 30

RYAN

"*P*ush me higher, Daddy! Higher, higher!" Daisy
screeched with laughter as he pushed her on the
swings and made her go higher each time. "I wanna do it by
myself now."

"Okay." He gave her one last push then walked back to the
picnic bench where Ginny was waiting.

"She's having so much fun," Ginny commented. "She looks
happy. Is it a good time to do this now?" They touched hands
when Daisy was on the swings, or on the slide, then moved
their hands away when she came up to them on the bench.

"I don't want to hide anything from my daughter. I want to
be able to hold your hand and not be afraid."

"Not about us, I meant telling her the truth about you and
your ex-wife."

He would have kept that a secret for longer, but Daisy had
started asking too many questions. Unlike before, Daisy didn't

talk much about her mother; these days she seemed obsessed by Ginny and Benjy, now that she no longer saw them daily after school, and she'd asked a few times if they could all live together.

At weekends she wanted to see Benjy and Ginny, and so they would meet at the park and then spend the day together. It gave him and Ginny a chance to see one another, though the two of them hadn't been out together since that first and only time. He wanted to break the news to Daisy first and they'd both agreed to bide their time.

Today seemed like a good day to tell her.

"Vanessa has gone quiet. She hasn't called Daisy in weeks, that's how maternal she is," he said to Ginny. "But Daisy suspects something. I have a feeling my little girl senses more than she lets on."

"Your little girl is wise and smart," Ginny agreed.

"I'm thirsty!" Daisy rushed up to them, breathless and bursting with excitement. He often wondered when it was that children lost that awe and wonderment with the world and every small thing in it, when they stopped finding the new and magical in the mediocrities of everyday life.

"Have some water, sweetie." Ginny held out a small bottle. She always came prepared with sandwiches and plenty of healthy fruit snacks and insisted on providing it whenever he offered to do it.

Daisy was panting.

"Why do you sound like a dog?" he asked her, tapping her on the chin playfully.

"I'm having so much fun."

She gulped down a few sips and trickles of water slid down the corners of her mouth. She wiped them away with the back of her hand and took a bag of raisins that Ginny gave her.

Outwardly, this looked like a normal day at the park, and

they were a normal family of four. It was something he longed for. Onlookers would never guess that they were two broken households coming together and finding family again.

It made his heart sing. Daisy had seemed so happy lately, and he suspected it was because of these weekend get togethers with Ginny and her son.

Benjy was fast asleep, and Ryan couldn't wait for him to start walking and running, and enjoying the park as much as Daisy did. They could play together, despite the five year age gap. Daisy was like a big sister around Benjy.

"Would you like a sandwich?" Ginny asked. "I made your favorite peanut butter and jelly."

"Not yet, I want to go on the slide next." Ginny nodded at him, a question in her eyes of whether she should start. They'd discussed how they were going to approach this, how they would gently break the news to Daisy.

Ginny cleared her throat. "Why don't you have a little rest, Daisy. Sit down next to me and get your breath back." Daisy did as asked. "Do you remember you asked me once about Benjy's daddy?"

The child looked up at her, a confused expression on her face. A why-are-we-talking-about-this-now expression.

"Well, sweetie …" Ginny paused to take a deep breath. This was obviously difficult for her and Ryan now had his doubts.

"You don't have to do this. It can wait." Not wanting to put her through this, he reached for her hand, and noticed Daisy watching.

"We agreed, Ryan. It might help."

"What might help?" Daisy asked. "Why are you holding hands?"

He slowly let go. It was time. But now that Daisy was staring at them both, he was suddenly afraid of breaking her heart and shattering her hopes. He *had* to tell her. Vanessa's silence with the phone calls made him angry, but also, he and Ginny couldn't be seen together unless he told Daisy, and he was also anxious to prevent rumors from spreading. If people saw him and Ginny together, they'd assume she was a homewrecker.

"Benjy's daddy isn't here, sweetie," Ginny told her.

Daisy blinked. "Where is he?"

Ginny winced as if it physically hurt to speak. "He ... he's in heaven. He was in a car accident."

Silence fell and Daisy's brow scrunched up as she processed the news. Then, her lower lip started to wobble. Before he could reach for her, Ginny scooted closer to her on the bench and put her arm around her, not saying a word and waiting.

"If he's in heaven, does that mean he's dead?" Daisy whispered, after a while.

"Yes, sweetie."

Daisy lowered her head. Ryan got up slowly from the bench, his breath stuck in his throat. He wished they hadn't mentioned it at all. Just as he was about to sit down next to her, Daisy jumped up and rushed to the pram. "Poor Benjy. Don't worry, Benjy. Don't be sad. Your daddy's in heaven." She looked up at the sky and a tear rolled down her cheek.

Ginny rushed to her side. "Oh, sweetie, please don't cry." Daisy stroked Benjy's face gently. "I'm going to look after him," she whispered. "I'm going to make sure he's never sad."

Ryan put his arm around her shoulder. "That's very good of you, Dee."

"I don't want him to be sad," Daisy said, again. "I want to play with him."

"You can play with him when he gets up, sweetie. Let him sleep."

He and Ginny exchanged looks. "What now?" Ginny mouthed.

He shrugged. He wanted to pick Daisy up and hug her tight, but Daisy was still stroking Benjy's face lightly, and he felt it was important to let her have this time to digest this terrible news in her own way.

"My daddy can be your daddy, Benjy," Daisy said.

He and Ginny locked eyes again. Ginny shook her head, indicating that they shouldn't say more. But he felt that there would never be a perfect time, and this moment was the best chance yet.

"Sweetie. Let's not wake Benjy yet. Let's sit back down. There's something I need to tell you." He gently took Daisy's arm and led her back to the bench.

"You can be Benjy's daddy, can't you, Daddy?" Daisy gave him a look full of pure innocence and hope, and it made him pause to reconsider if he was doing the right thing. He contemplated how to proceed. Daisy had given him a good opening, and perhaps he ought to start there. But uncertainty paralyzed him. He wasn't sure what the future held, just because his life seemed full of possibility and brimming with promise right now, who knew what might happen next?

Happiness and hope could be snatched right out of their hands at any time.

He should know.

As did Ginny.

"Daddy?" Daisy was still waiting for an answer.

With a steely determination, he decided to continue. "Dee. You remember that time you called your mom and it looked like she was on vacation?"

"When she was working at the beach?"

"Uh ... yeah." He cleared his throat. "Uh ... Mommy loves you very much, and I will always be your daddy, and we will always love you more than anything, but ... your mommy and I ... " He paused and stared at her, wanting to frame the image of her expectant expression before he broke her heart. "We're not together anymore. We're not married. Your mommy likes someone else and he's the man you saw."

"The one with no clothes on?" Daisy asked, making him wonder how out of everything he'd told her, this was the one thing she'd picked out.

"He was wearing swim shorts, Dee." He searched his daughter's face for clues. Ginny had taken hold of Daisy's hand. "Do you understand what I've told you, Dee? Mommy won't be living with us anymore, but she might ... she will ... hopefully visit us soon, and maybe you can go and visit her?"

In the past year, since Vanessa had left them, he'd offered to take Daisy to see her, but Vanessa had been too busy traveling with her boss. She didn't have time for Daisy.

"Is that man my step daddy? Helen has a step mommy."

"Who's Helen?" He was confused, more by her reaction, than anything else.

"She used to be Lara's best friend, but now I am."

"Oh." He appealed to Ginny for help.

"He can only be your stepdaddy if your mom marries him," Ginny explained.

"Is my mom going to marry him?" Daisy asked. Daisy's reaction worried him, the fact that she didn't seem upset or hadn't burst into tears as he'd expected. "I don't know, Dee."

"Mommy doesn't love you anymore?" Daisy asked, and now tears welled in her eyes.

He hugged her. "Mommy loves you *very* much, and she still loves me, but in another way." Over Daisy's head, he made a face at Ginny. "Help me," he mouthed. He'd never guessed it would be this hard.

"I still love Benjy's daddy, because he's Benjy's daddy, even though he isn't here," Ginny told her.

"Are you sad?" Daisy asked.

"I used to be very sad, but now, not so much. I have so many good things in my life, and I'm grateful for all of them."

"What good things?"

"You, for one and … your daddy. He's a good friend." Ginny's cheeks turned pink as she said it, and she avoided looking at him, instead giving Daisy her complete undivided attention.

"Do you like my Daddy?"

"Yes, I do." Ginny's cheeks turned pink.

"Is that why you keep holding hands with him?"

"Uh. Yes."

"How much do you like him?"

Ryan squirmed, sensing Ginny's unease.

"I like him … a lot," Ginny answered.

"Like you like Benjy?"

"Uh … something like that. You and your daddy make me happy."

"*We* make you happy?" Daisy asked.

Ginny smiled. "You make me *very* happy."

Daisy wrapped her arms around Ginny. "Will *you* be my step mommy?"

Ginny let out a gasp. Her eyes seeking his over Daisy's head. "Uh ... I'm … I don't think it … works like that."

He was content to let Ginny squirm for a while, seeing how the question made her whole face turn pink. If she was having a reaction, it was mild compared to his. A furnace of future possibilities inflamed inside him. A future where he was happy again, and had a home, a family and commitment.

"Then we can *all* be happy," Daisy continued. "And Daddy won't be sad anymore and he won't be lonely and –"

"I'm not lonely, I have you," he answered, quick to interrupt.

Daisy looked at him as if she didn't believe him. "… and

I'll have Benjy to play with, and Benjy won't be by himself and Ginny won't be lonely and we'll all be happy." She lifted her arms up to signify the 'all'.

"I'm not lonely, I have you," he repeated.

"And I'm not lonely because I have Benjy, and you," said Ginny.

"But why don't we live together?" Daisy asked.

"Because …" Ryan felt helpless. Ginny raised an eyebrow.

"Helen says her mommy is really sad sometimes because she's all by herself when Helen's at school, and she cries a lot. But her daddy is really happy 'cause he has a stepmom."

Ryan stifled a laugh. "*He* doesn't have a stepmom, Helen does."

"That's what I said," Daisy replied.

Just then, a noise came from the pram. A gurgle and a cry. Two tiny arms went up. "Benjy's awake!" Daisy rushed over to him.

'Phew.' Ryan mouthed to Ginny. She swept a hand over her brow in mock exaggeration.

He glanced at Daisy, making baby noises and pulling funny faces at Benjy. This had gone better than he'd expected.

CHAPTER 31

GINNY

"Can you set the table, Ginny? I've asked you twice already." Ashleigh stirred the pan vigorously. Even with her back to them, they could see that she was getting worked up.

Eloise chuckled. "Leave her alone, Ash. She's lovesick."

"I'm not, and you said it was going to take a while," Ginny protested. She finished her text message and put her phone into her pocket.

"No more than five minutes," Ashleigh growled. "Texting Ryan again?"

"Talia, actually," she replied.

"Are you two still friends?" Eloise asked. "I haven't heard you mention her name in ages."

"We're still friends." She'd blocked Talia out of her life ever since the accident, and then she'd been so blue, and in a bad place, she'd ignored her friend's calls and messages. Even when Talia had come to the door, Ginny had refused to see her. She'd been awful and she now deeply regretted her behavior. She'd taken the first step and reached out to her, and now she couldn't wait to see her. But she was nervous, because she'd been so lousy to her.

Clang. Clatter. Crash.

Ashleigh was in a mood, and the pots and pans and cooking utensils she'd been using were a testament to that.

"Tell her to come for lunch," Eloise suggested. "We have plenty of empty seats now that everyone's dropped out."

"I already did. She's on her way."

The kitchen was warm and smelled delicious with the scent of garlic and herbs and butter wafting around. It was a day off from the shop, and Ashleigh had gotten it into her head to make a huge dinner for family and close friends; there was no apparent occasion, as far as Ginny could fathom.

Ashleigh had invited Ford as well as Darcie and her family, but they were busy. Eloise maintained that her sister was copying her after the resounding success of her housewarming but, given that Ashleigh had been in a bad mood ever since Ford had called to say he could no longer make it, she now suspected that this was Ashleigh's way of reeling her former beau back in.

It didn't appear to be working.

"You said you're not lovesick?" Eloise asked, before raising an eyebrow in disbelief.

"Lovesick implies that I'm so infatuated that I'm sick, or that it's unrequited. It has negative connotations, so no, I'm not lovesick." Her life was lighter now. Lighter and brighter, ever since Kayla had left.

It was tiring being at home all day, doing chores, and making the dinner, and taking care of Benjy, but this time wouldn't last forever. She'd been reading a lot of parenting books, and books about grievance, and self-healing, and slowly, word by word, she was creating a vision for what her future might look like. Having Ryan and Daisy in her life was a big part of her recovery. "I think I'm falling in love again."

Liam whistled, while Ashleigh and Eloise gawked at her.

"What?" Ginny cried. "I am. Ryan makes me so happy."

Eloise blinked a few times. Ashleigh glanced over her shoulder and gave her a curious look.

"Good for you, Gin." Eloise clasped her hands together. She and Liam had only arrived a few moments ago. "That's all we want for you; to be happy, and in love with life again."

"She said she's in love with Ryan," Liam corrected.

"And life, judging by her recent behavior," Ashleigh added, drily.

"Aren't you happy for me?" Ginny cried, setting out the plates and cutlery.

"Of course I'm happy for you. It's the best news in a long time," said Ashleigh.

Ginny put her hands on her waist, wanting to make an announcement. "No, the best news is that Benjy slept for more than five hours last night."

"Really?" Eloise cried, carrying the food over to the table.

"Five hours and seventeen minutes."

"Yay! Gimme five." Eloise highfived her. "That's great, Gin."

It was. Hopefully Benjy would do that more often, and let her get a good night's sleep so that she'd wake up feeling energized, as she had done this morning. With all the new changes in her life, she felt blessed and she hadn't thought of Ben, or been miserable for a long time.

"That's a shame about Ford," said Liam. "It would have been good to catch up with him. I saw him at the diner the other day, with whatshername, that woman, the one who helped you with Benjy." He clicked his fingers at her.

"Kayla?" said Eloise, her voice breathless.

"That's the one, with her, but I was in too much of a rush to talk to him."

Ginny was sure she'd heard wrong.

"Are you sure it was Kayla?" Eloise asked.

"Yeah. Her. They were talking and eating. Ouch!" Eloise must have pinched him because he didn't say a word after that. They all looked at Ashleigh who was calmly pouring a glass of water for herself.

"This looks de-lish-ous!" Eloise cried, her voice abnormally high, abnormally odd.

Ginny joined in. "Those roast potatoes look tasty!"

Ashleigh let out a loud sigh. "I would appreciate it if you all ate your food and quit trying to make me feel better."

The doorbell went and Ginny jumped up, glad to have an excuse to leave the table. She opened the door to see a beaming Talia and she cried with glee. "It's *sooo* good to see you again."

"So good to see you." Talia hugged Ginny before handing her a bunch of brightly colored flowers.

"Awww. You didn't have to, but thank you!" Ginny felt even worse now. Talia had been with her through most of the crucial and life-changing moments. She'd treated her appallingly.

"And this is for Benjy. I bought him some things when he'd been born but I was able to exchange them for a bigger size."

Ginny took the shiny blue giftbag. "Thank you *so much*. You really didn't have to. I've been such a lousy friend to you and now I feel even worse. I'm sorry."

They hugged again. "I've missed you, Gin. I've been so worried about you, but your sisters kept me updated. I knew you needed your own time and space but I've always been here for you."

Ginny set down the gifts. "I'll open these later, and we'll catch up properly after lunch. Come through. Ashleigh's cooked up a feast."

"But I want to see Benjy," her friend wailed.

"He's sleeping right now. Let's go and eat and then we'll go up into my bedroom and catch up on everything. He'll be up by then." They faced one another momentarily in the hallway. "I've been the worse friend, Talia. It's nice to have you back and I'm sorry I was weird for so long."

"After the year you've had, I'd forgive you for anything. But look at you now, Gin! A complete turnaround. What happened?"

Eloise appeared in the hallway. "I'll tell you what happened but first you need to eat before the food gets cold and Ashleigh's temper gets worse," she said. "It's good to see you again, Talia."

"Thanks for inviting me."

They took her into the kitchen where Ashleigh greeted her enthusiastically and Liam nodded in acknowledgment.

"You two have met, haven't you?" Ginny wasn't sure. So much had happened in her life in such a short space of time, she couldn't remember.

"We've met," Liam and Talia said in unison.

"This looks delicious!" Talia surveyed the food. "What's the occasion?"

"There's no occasion," Ginny answered. "Ashleigh was bored and wanted to cook on her day off." A riot of laughter broke out around the table.

"I obviously have nothing else to do," Ashleigh replied rolling her eyes.

"Where's Ford?" Talia asked. A hush fell, making the awkward moment heavy.

"We broke up," Ashleigh replied. "Let's get started. Can someone pass me the potatoes?"

They ate and talked and laughed. Ginny looked around the table and felt as if the good times had returned, before she'd met Ben, when it was just her and her sisters, and their days consisted of working at the shop and having a happy homelife. Now there was Liam and Ryan, and hopefully, one day, Ford would come back to Ashleigh. Her sister looked so miserable, and Ginny felt guilty for feeling so happy for herself.

Ryan and Daisy would fit right in here. A warm and fuzzy feeling swept over her. In time, Benjy would be sitting here, too.

It would be simply wonderful.

Afterwards, they all helped to clear up and when she heard Benjy's stirring noises on the baby monitor, she made a bottle of milk for him. "Come and meet my son," she told Talia and took her upstairs.

Talia crooned and was in awe watching Benjy as he waved his arms and kicked legs frantically, but he wasn't crying. He was gurgling and making those cute baby sounds she so loved.

"You let him get this big before I could see him?" Talia cried. "Can I pick him up?"

"Why don't you sit in the rocking chair? I'll give him to you and you can feed him."

And that was what they did, not before Talia smothered Benjy with kisses. The little boy was so taken aback by a new face, a new scent, a new voice, that for a few moments he stared at her, mesmerized.

"Here." Ginny handed her the bottle of milk. "Before he realizes he's hungry and starts screaming." Talia fawned over him, and hugged him to her, chastising Ginny again for being out of her life and for all those lost months she'd been out of Benjy's life.

"We can make up for the lost time," Ginny promised. Talia smiled and babytalked to Benjy as she fed him. After a while, she lifted her head. "What's new with you?"

"New? With me?"

"Anything, or have you just been at home taking care of this gorgeous little guy?"

"I've just been at home taking care of him, but … I've met someone."

Talia let out a gasp. It seemed these were the last words she'd expected to hear.

CHAPTER 32

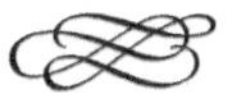

RYAN

He was looking through real estate listings online when the hairs on the back of his neck prickled.

"Planning to move?" Kayla asked. Standing behind him she set him on edge, especially now that she was looking over at his screen.

"It's time we had our own place. It's not fair to you and—"

"You want your privacy," Kayla said, interrupting. "That's what's prompted this."

No. That wasn't it. He wasn't making the move because he needed privacy or time alone with Ginny, which was what Kayla was referring to.

He needed to be away from his sister. She undermined his plans and decisions, and he didn't need that. He'd come a long way from the broken man he'd been when Vanessa had left him, but he was turning his life around and so was Ginny. What they had was precious and fragile and it needed care. After nearly four months here, he and Daisy needed to put down their own roots.

His plans to move away weren't all to do with Ginny. This new relationship was still in its early stages and they were taking things slowly.

Very, very, very slowly.

Being with her made him feel whole again, as if the fragmented pieces of himself were finally putting themselves back together again. Their news was out in the open now, and most importantly, Daisy knew. On the way back home from the picnic yesterday, Daisy hadn't stopped talking. She happily chatted away about all the different things they could do with Benjy, and the places they could visit. She'd even talked about going on a vacation, just the four of them, adding, "And Mommy and her friend can come, too."

He'd remained silent at that. He couldn't envisage a world in which he'd allow himself and Ginny to be with Vanessa and her boss.

"We need our own place, Kayla," he said to his sister. "It's for me and Daisy, not Ginny and me."

"Heaven help us."

He ignored her comment. "You need your own space, too, Kayla. I've got to move forward. It's time I started to make progress, and plans, and considered our future."

"All this because of Ginny?"

He hated that she was so bitter. Why couldn't she see how happy he was? "Can you sit down? You're making me jittery."

"Do you have something to hide?" Kayla slid into the seat beside him, but she looked pensive. Gone was that hard expression. He dared to wonder if it was because he'd mentioned moving out.

"I don't have anything to hide. You know, because Daisy has told you, that Ginny and I are trying things out."

"Trying things out. Like you would a sweater."

"Excuse me?" He pushed his laptop away and faced her. "Look, Kayla, you're my sister, and you're looking out for me, and you've been kind and more than generous in letting us stay here. I can't thank you enough for being here for me, but I won't let you talk about Ginny in that way. I like her. I *really* like her. I never thought I'd have feelings for anyone again. I didn't intend this to happen. It was the last thing on my mind and I tried to resist it for the longest time, but ... maybe it was meant to be. Daisy adores Ginny, and that means a lot to me, that at a time when her own mother can't spare any time for her, my little girl has found someone who cares deeply about her. You should see them together."

"I have seen them together." Kayla closed her eyes and pressed her hand against her forehead, as if she were in pain.

"Does the idea of me and her being together hurt you that much?"

She tilted her head and opened her eyes. "Aren't you worried about the effect all of this will have on Daisy? That girl still doesn't know that Vanessa isn't coming back to you."

"We told her."

Kayla's eyes rounded in shock. "We? Told her what?" Though judging by the tone of her voice, she knew.

"Ginny and I explained it to her." He went on to recount the conversation.

"She didn't cry? She wasn't upset?"

"That's the thing. Her reaction wasn't what I expected. You have to remember she hasn't seen Vanessa for months."

"That woman is an abomination," Kayla muttered under her breath. "You're better off without her. She's been so careless about Daisy."

"We told Daisy about Benjy's father, and that he'd died and then I told her that Vanessa was in love with someone else."

"Was that wise?"

"She hasn't stopped asking questions ever since she had that video call with her mom and she saw that guy in the background."

"I worry about Daisy and the damage that woman has done to her."

"I would worry too, but Ginny has been wonderful. Daisy confided in her. She heard us arguing that time, and she burst out crying to her, she thought she was to blame for Vanessa leaving. She took something she heard and made it mean something else. It kills me to think that she blamed herself. Thank goodness she opened up to Ginny, otherwise I would never have known."

Kayla's jaw fell open and she put a hand to her mouth. "That's what I worry about. That child deserves all the love we can give her."

"And Ginny has been great with her."

Kayla shrugged. "As long as you know what you're doing."

"We got a lot for selling the house, and even after splitting our assets, I have enough to buy something nice here."

"Don't move away too far from here."

This surprised him. "I wasn't planning to. If I'm not mistaken, you sound sad." He was looking for something close by, in between Kayla's place and Ginny's, so that Daisy's school wouldn't be too far.

"I'll miss you both. It's been nice having you and Daisy here after years of living alone. It will be hard to adjust to being alone again."

"You don't have to be alone," he said, softly, sensing a vulnerability around Kayla that he'd never seen before. He was surprised at how solemn she'd become, as if the fight had gone out of her. "You should let your guard down and let someone in. You're too young to live alone."

"Young? I'm going to be forty next year," Kayla snapped.

"That's young! You're only halfway through your life. You shouldn't let what happened between me and Vanessa scare you."

"I'll help out with the school runs as soon as I've got my courage back behind the wheel."

Ryan blew out a groan. For now, Lara's parents had kindly offered to help with the school runs. "Sorry. We should go out on a drive. I've been so busy with work and … things." The last few weekends he'd spent with Ginny. He waited for the quip, but it didn't come.

"It's okay."

"I'll take you. I will."

"There's no rush," she insisted.

But he still felt bad because he'd promised Kayla he'd take her out in her car to build up her confidence, and he'd have to do it soon because she was planning to return to work. "You're going back to work soon, aren't you? Do you have a date fixed?"

"That's on my list of things to do."

CHAPTER 33

GINNY

"We have two hours," said Ginny, as she curled up on the sofa with Ryan.

"Not quite. I'd rather leave half an hour before your sister said she'd be back."

"My sisters like you. They think you're good for me.

Ryan wrapped his arm around her shoulder. "And what do you think?"

"I *know* you're good for me."

He nuzzled her ear. "I like snuggling up with you in front of the TV. That's all I need and want." She squealed as he kissed her earlobe and a prickly heat sensation fanning out from her belly.

This was nice. Being able to do this with Benjy asleep upstairs, and just the two of them here, and to not have her sisters watching their each and every move. Daisy was at a sleepover at her friend's house and Ginny had invited Ryan over. They'd had dinner together, with Ashleigh, but then she'd suddenly announced that she was going over to Eloise's place and would be back 'around nine.' Ashleigh had given her a pointed look when she'd said that. As if she wanted to give Ginny and Ryan some alone time.

Ginny appreciated the thought, because otherwise they would have just been going to the park with the kids.

She sensed that Ryan was slightly worried about Daisy being on the sleepover, even though he wouldn't admit it. They'd both been startled that Daisy had taken the news so well. *Too* well, Ginny thought. But Ryan had the view that Ginny had been instrumental in helping Daisy deal with the absence of her mother, and maybe that was the reason why Daisy seemed to be dealing with her parents' breakup.

While Ginny didn't at all consider herself to be a replacement for Daisy's mother, she felt good that she had helped the little girl in some way. "She must have been deliriously excited about the sleepover?" Ginny asked.

"She was. She feels that she's finally been accepted by her new friends. A sleepover is a big deal."

"True."

"She's been a little sad, lately. Maybe what I told her about her mom is finally sinking in. She's been a little less *Daisy*, and a lot subdued."

"Has her mom called?"

He shook his head. "No, and it's a real shame, but I'm not surprised. That woman is a waste of space." He huffed out a sigh. "I shouldn't say things like that but it makes me mad. She's been out of the picture for so long, and she's stopped calling lately. I've texted her and told her to call and she texts back and says she will but then she doesn't. She also says there's a lot going on for her."

Ginny's ears pricked up at this. "A lot going on? Like what? Another vacation, a quickie wedding in Vegas?"

"I wouldn't put anything past her."

"Don't think about her." Ginny reached back and touched his face. It was enough to sit in this man's arms and do nothing but talk or watch TV. Ryan wanted to get to know her, wanted to know about her life and everything up until they'd met.

This was different. This told her that he was a man who wanted to know more than surface level things. He wanted to know about her past and all the things that made her who she was. He wanted to understand everything completely, and she had never felt more seen or more heard.

"Daisy has some crazy notion about going on a vacation."

"That would be nice."

"All four of us," said Ryan. She sat up and turned around to face him, kneeling. "*All* of us?" An idea, like a tiny firework, popped off in her mind. Ryan looked at her, and she wondered if he was thinking the same thing.

"What are you thinking?" he asked, his gaze bouncing across her face.

"What are *you* thinking?" she pushed back.

"I think … I think that would be a wonderful thing."

"It might be difficult with Benjy, and … maybe a little too soon." It was too soon for them to go on vacation, even for a weekend. She and Ryan were only getting to know one another. What they needed was more quality time like this. Or a day trip somewhere.

"Maybe we can decide on something once I find a place and we get to spend more time together," he said, making an apologetic face.

"I haven't taken Benjy away anywhere for a night and it might be better to go away for a few days when the weather is warmer." The more she thought about it, the more she liked her idea. "But that doesn't mean we can't go on a long drive somewhere and do something fun."

He pointed at her as if she'd hit the jackpot. "That's what we should do! A day trip. We could test the water with Benjy, and it would be a wonderful surprise for Daisy."

Ginny agreed. "A surprise. Yes! Let's spring this on her." Daisy needed something good to happen in her life. "We could go to Starling Bay. It's a couple of hours' drive away, or visit a national park or something."

"Starling Bay is meant to be nice."

"It's not too far, and when we're there we could go to the cinema, or just amble around. We could alternatively go to a national park or somewhere like that."

Ryan winced. "A national park might be too much for Benjy. We've only taken him to the park so far."

We.

For a moment it felt as if they were making decisions for their little family, and Ginny loved the feeling of belonging. "We just need to get away and have a change of scenery," she said, poking him in the chest lightly before giving him a kiss.

"I'm happy to go anywhere, as long as it's with you."

She sighed, overcome with joy, and fell back against his chest. He circled his arms around her, clasping them against her stomach. "Maybe in the summer, we can plan a longer trip away," he suggested.

"I like the way you think." She placed her hands on his. "Hopefully I'll have returned to work by then, and it would be nice to have a short vacation to look forward to."

"You've made up your mind?"

She'd told him about her plans to get back to the bridal shop. "I love being a mom, but that's not all I am. And because I'm lucky enough to work in the family business, I'm sure Ash and Eloise will be okay about me doing limited hours, and about taking Benjy in."

"Have you told them yet?" Ryan asked.

"Not yet."

"I'll have found a place by then, hopefully sooner."

"Have you seen anything yet?"

"I've shortlisted a few places for possible viewings next week and I'd love for you to come with me. I'd like your opinion."

"I'd love to."

"Obviously, it's just for me and Daisy, for now," he said, carefully.

"I know."

"But I'd want to find somewhere that has potential, for later, maybe."

She understood. "Yes."

Lying with Ryan on the sofa, in his arms, feeling secure, and happy, and making plans for their futures was something she could never have envisaged a few months ago, and it showed her how far she'd come, with Ryan's help, and that of her sisters.

CHAPTER 34

RYAN

"Want me to do that for you?" Kayla asked.

Ryan stopped sewing the button on his jeans. "I've got this. I do know how to sew on things. Kayla. I've had to do all that ever since ..." He didn't need to finish the sentence. They both knew. There was a divide in his life; life as he knew it before the split, and life after. Not that Vanessa would sew on buttons for him; she'd take his clothes to various tailors and alteration shops and get what needed to be done there.

Two timelines of his existence. He was determined to make the 'after' timeline be happier and more colorful and vibrant than before. It was his duty as a father to create a world for Daisy where she wouldn't feel that she was from a broken home, or motherless, or unwanted. More than anything, he didn't want her to be scarred. His main goal in life was to provide meaning and a better life for Daisy.

"We'll be setting off early," he reminded Kayla once Daisy had gone to bed. He and Ginny had planned this trip for over a week and they were finally leaving early tomorrow. He couldn't wait to see Daisy's face once she discovered the surprise.

"Is it wise to go on a long trip with a baby in tow?"

"We're not hiking up a mountain, Kayla. We'll have the pram, and Ginny will carry Benjy in the baby carrier most of the time, or I will. We need a day away."

"I suppose it will do you all some good to get away, and it will be a nice surprise for Daisy."

"That's why we're doing it. It was Ginny's idea. We're both worried about Daisy. She seems subdued. I'm not sure it was wise to tell her so much when we did."

"I noticed she was quieter, too."

"Maybe I shouldn't have said anything about Vanessa and me breaking up."

"That's what we agreed," said Kayla, stiffly. "Why did you?"

"It seemed like the right time."

"For you?" Kayla hit back. She was right. He didn't want to keep lying to Daisy about Vanessa, but he'd also done it because he didn't want to hide from her that he and Ginny were starting to see one another.

"It's nice what you and Ginny are doing for her."

He was surprised to hear such high praise from his sister instead of more I-told-you-sos. "Let's hope it cheers her up. We'll be back late at night," he told her. "Do you have any plans?" Not that he would have invited her along, but the hard edges around Kayla seemed to be softening. Maybe she was feeling sad about him and Daisy moving out.

"I'm having some driving lessons," she announced. "I had one a few days ago. It was my first time behind the wheel."

"What? When?" This was news. "Why didn't you tell me?"

He was supposed to have made time to take her and he felt bad that she'd gone by herself.

"You didn't ask."

He put down his jeans, feeling guilty for letting his sister down, especially considering how much she'd done for him. "I'm sorry. It's been a busy week at work—"

"You're busy. I understand."

"We could have gone at the weekend, Kayla."

"When?" she asked softly. "You're going on your trip tomorrow, and you're often busy with Daisy, Ginny and Benjy."

"I'm really sorry. I've let you down."

She let out a nervous laugh. "It's okay Ryan. It's not a big deal."

"Were you scared, going out by yourself?"

"Stop apologizing, and I didn't go by myself—" A knock at the door, this late, on a Friday evening when they weren't expecting visitors, interrupted her. She frowned. "Are you expecting anyone?"

He stood up. "No. You?"

"No."

"I'll get it." He walked towards the door, his heart starting to race. Late night unexpected knocks on the door meant bad news. He opened the door, thinking that it might be Ginny passing by and wanting to discuss some last minute things about the trip; even though he knew she wouldn't turn up, unannounced like this.

"Hi Ryan." His ex-wife flashed him a smile that might as well have been a five-alarm fire for the severe shock it caused him. He was left speechless.

"What are you doing here?" Kayla asked.

"Hey, Kayla." Vanessa chirped, cheerily, as if she and Kayla were the best of friends, something that was so far from the truth it would be hilarious. Vanessa swanned inside with her bright pink wheeled trolley.

His heart sank. "What's that?" He glared at her in disbelief. This didn't appear to be a quick, casual visit. Questions bounced around in his head. What was she doing here?

"Where's Daisy?" she asked.

"She's asleep." He grabbed her by the arm and walked her into the living room. Kayla followed.

"Why are you hear? We haven't seen you for months," he asked, sensing that something was very wrong. That she was hiding something behind that plastered on fake niceness.

"I wanted to see Daisy." She paused, then, "And you, too, Ryan. I've been wanting to see you both for a while."

"It's been a long time," he said stiffly. They all stood, in a triangle, all on edge, as if preparing for combat. "And it's late."

"I wanted to surprise you."

"You did." Though shock would have been a better word. The cogs in his brain whirred furiously as he tried to make meaning out of this madness. That his ex-wife had the nerve to show up here, this late, after such a long time, unannounced, made his blood boil. A slow burning anger simmered inside him; seeing her here, in his space, disrupting his and Daisy's lives when they were finally starting to move on.

This woman didn't have the right.

"Mind if I sit down?" She slipped off her shoes and made herself comfortable on the couch, curling her svelte legs under her. She was tanned, her face slightly fuller, her figure thinner than he remembered. Her eyes raked over him slowly as she gave him the once-over. "You look well, Ryan. Small-town life obviously suits you."

He shoved his hands into his pockets. "It does."

"And how are you, Kayla?" Vanessa asked, throwing her a cursory glance.

Kayla's expression tightened. "All the better for seeing you." If Kayla's tone was icy when she spoke to Ginny, it was glacial now. "Don't get too comfortable. I presume you intend to stay the night?"

"I was hoping to stay a *few* nights."

"What for?" Ryan growled.

"A few nights?" Kayla repeated.

"Maybe a week?" Vanessa gave a shrug.

"Why?" he snapped, hating that this woman had so casually breezed back into his life so easily and casually. His plans for tomorrow with Daisy and Ginny disintegrated before his eyes.

Vanessa threw her hands into the air. "What do you mean 'why?' To see my daughter and to spend time with her, of course."

"Why now when you haven't bothered before?" The blood in his veins coursed with quiet rage.

"There are B&Bs in town," Kayla offered. "They'll put you up for a month if need be, if you really want to spend quality time with the daughter you haven't seen for so long."

Vanessa grinned good-naturedly. "I thought you *were* running a B&B. How long has Ryan been here?"

"Only for family, and you're not family," Kayla answered. "I certainly won't put you up."

Ryan could have hugged Kayla.

"What do you really want?" he asked the woman who had torn down his life. Something was going on. Vanessa hadn't just turned up because she'd found her heart. There was more to it. "You can't waltz in like this, unannounced. We're getting on with our lives now."

"Mommy!" Daisy flew into the room. "I thought I was dreaming!" She rushed into Vanessa's outstretched arms. "I missed you so much, Mommy."

"Oh, baby. I missed you, too. I missed you so much." Vanessa hugged Daisy tightly.

"*This* was my surprise!" Daisy squealed. "Daddy, it's the best surprise."

"What does she mean?" Vanessa asked. He turned away, furious.

"Are you staying, Mommy?" he heard his daughter ask, joy bursting from her like streaming sunshine.

"Of course, baby. Of course. Oh my. Your hair has grown so long! Baby, you've grown taller, too. I've missed you so much, my baby girl."

RYAN

He couldn't sleep. He would never be able to sleep, not while that woman was under the same roof.

He had so many questions, but he had to suffer being silent, and to simply observe. He didn't dare risk leaving Daisy alone with Vanessa.

She wanted to stay for a week?

It was his idea of hell.

The next day he was up at the crack of dawn, and when he went downstairs to the kitchen, Kayla was sitting at the table, doing the cross stitch that Ginny had given her. She looked up. "You couldn't sleep either?"

"Haven't slept a wink all night." He rubbed his jaw, felt the prickle of his five o'clock shadow.

"You're dressed. Surely you're not still going on the trip?"

"How can I?" He let out a long sigh. "I have to tell Ginny, and I didn't want to do it over the phone."

"Take your time. I'm not going anywhere while that woman is under my roof. I dare not leave her alone."

"You, too." He snorted. "I'm sorry about this. I'm going to sort this out."

"Sort what out?"

"What she wants and why she's here."

But that wasn't the most important thing. Seeing Ginny was.

CHAPTER 35

GINNY

"Have a great time." Ashleigh hugged her.

"We won't wait up." Eloise winked and kissed her on the cheek.

"We're going with the kids. It's not the romantic escape you seem to think it is," Ginny retorted, indignantly.

"No?" Mischief flashed in Eloise's eyes.

"No." Ginny continued to pack the food hamper with cupcakes and sandwiches she'd made for the road trip. She couldn't wait to see Daisy's reaction when they told her where they were really going.

"But you might get stuck in a storm somewhere, and have no choice but to check into a motel." Eloise winked at Ashleigh.

"Leave her alone." Ashleigh dismissed the nonsense with a wave of her hand. Ginny ignored them both. This trip with Ryan and Daisy was nothing like what her sisters were insinuating. She and Ryan were taking things slowly. They'd only ever kissed, and nothing more than that. Neither of them was in a rush to take things further, and it suited her.

Just spending the day with Ryan and Daisy was more than enough for her and she couldn't wait to get on the road and get away. She hadn't left Whisper Falls in a long time and this, for her, signaled the start of a new chapter in her life. She felt a tingle all over when she thought of Ryan. She was seeing life in bright colors, instead of the dull, grey misery she'd been wrapped up in.

"Of all the things I'm looking forward to on this trip, being away from the likes of nosy good-for-nothings like you two is a major one." She looked at her watch. Benjy would be up soon. She was showered and ready for Ryan who'd told her he would be over at eight, so when the doorbell rang soon after her sisters had left, she rushed to answer it.

She instantly knew something was wrong, not because of the somber expression on Ryan's face, but because he was alone, without Daisy. Ginny's enthusiasm vanished.

Ryan marched in and paced around with his hands on his hips.

"What's wrong?" she asked, getting worried.

"I'm ... I'm really sorry to do this." His face drained of color and alarm bells went off in her head. She braced herself for the worst. "Is Daisy okay?"

"Yes. Yes. She's fine. She's more than fine."

"Then what?"

He scratched his jaw, and that's when she noticed he hadn't shaved. On closer inspection his eyes looked haggard and he looked so dishevelled. She'd never seen him like that before.

"Vanessa's here."

Her heart stopped and missed a few beats. Somewhere in

the depths of her mind, that vaguely familiar name had bad connotations. And then she remembered.

His ex-wife. Was here. The thought sank and settled like a heavy stone in her stomach. "What for? When?"

"Last night. She turned up on the doorstep, out of the blue."

"Why?"

He shrugged. "I wish I knew. I have no idea." He went on to tell her how Vanessa had appeared unannounced, then made herself comfortable in Kayla's house. How Daisy had woken up and come rushing to find her. How she was so excited. How she thought *this,* Vanessa's visit, was the surprise they'd been saving for her. "I didn't have the heart to tell her. It was sheer luck that we didn't tell her about today."

"Why?" Ginny asked, her voice shaky. Did he want to hide what they had? Did he want to keep their romance a secret from Vanessa?

"Because it would only have added more complication."

Complication? How? Ginny felt resigned. She looked at the cupcakes in the plastic Tupperware box and the sandwiches she'd lovingly made and put into Ziploc bags, and for what?

Ryan observed her silently. She hated that. She wanted him to explain, and him being silent made her uneasy. "Isn't it odd, her turning up on your doorstep like that? She gave you no indication that she was coming?" Ginny asked, irritation making her grouchy.

"None. I had no idea. It is odd. This doesn't make sense and now she's waltzed in and ruined our day. We'd planned a trip and today was supposed to be our day, and now we can't go. I'm sorry. Daisy won't want to leave and—"

"I understand you wanting to cancel." She wouldn't have enjoyed herself anyway. Not now.

"She says she wants to spend time with Daisy. She came with a suitcase." He blew out his breath. "Why? Why does this keep happening to me? Why when things start to work out for me does everything go wrong??

"Why indeed?" Ginny felt miserable. Her bright and wonderful day had dulled to monochrome grey. "You didn't probe further?"

"I didn't. It was late, then Daisy woke up and came rushing downstairs, and then she got overexcited at seeing her mom. I couldn't keep asking Vanessa what she wanted. But clearly, something's up. I just need to find out what."

Something was up, and this was what Ginny feared. Her opinion of Vanessa, from the little she knew from Ryan, was of a selfish woman who thought mostly of herself. She let out a disappointed exhale. At least Benjy was too little to know anything, and Daisy hadn't known about the surprise trip. The only upset person was her. She'd been looking forward to it.

She needed it.

They needed it.

It would have been lovely, just the four of them spending the whole day together exploring a new town.

Ryan dangled his car keys from his fingers. "I don't know what she wants but I'm going to find out. Kayla doesn't want her in the house. She let her stay last night because it was so late but she's told her to find a room at a B&B."

Ginny folded her arms and listened, fighting the urge to give her thoughts on the matter.

"She's up to something," Ryan continued. "Vanessa doesn't do anything because it's the right thing. She does what's right for her."

"I made these cupcakes and sandwiches. Take some."

His eyes settled on her. "You're angry."

"I'm disappointed."

"I'm sorry, Ginny, this is as much as shock to me as it is to you." He moved towards her to hug her but instinctively her body hardened.

A knowing look passed through his eyes. "I didn't want to cancel our day. She's here, and there's nothing I can do about it. Daisy's over the moon. She even slept with her mom. Kayla and I are annoyed. I haven't slept properly. I didn't want to tell you over the phone. I wanted to see you and tell you face to face. I'm sorry this has happened. I feel terrible but I'm helpless to do anything, at least until I find out why she's here." He sounded genuinely upset.

The tiny sliver of doubt that had wormed its way into her head ebbed away and she softened. "You're right. It's not your fault. You need to find out what she wants."

"I *am* going to find out." Ryan sounded determined as he scratched his cheek again. "We'll do the trip another time. We will, Ginny. And there will be another time. I hate that she's swept in like a storm and is wreaking havoc in my life again, but Daisy ..." He lowered his head and sighed. "Daisy is so happy." He looked up at her, and she could see he was sad. "She's the happiest I've seen her."

"She would be. It is her mother, after all. Daisy's been pining over her for months."

"The woman doesn't deserve it. I should get back before Daisy wakes up. I don't like leaving Vanessa alone with her. She often has ulterior motives." He moved to hug her, but stopped. Maybe it was her posture, the way she'd folded her arms across her chest, effectively putting her guard up, that stopped him.

RYAN

He returned home to the sound of laughter and singing.

When he walked in, the Disney film 'Frozen' was on and Daisy and her mom were singing along. It looked like a typical, normal, average family weekend at the family home.

Kayla was nowhere in sight.

He stood in the doorway watching Daisy who was so caught up dancing around the room and singing, that she didn't notice him. She looked deliriously happy. Her eyes shone and she beamed with joy.

All this because her mother was back.

"Daddy!" Daisy stopped dancing around, and ran up to him, suddenly feeling very self-conscious. She buried her face in his legs. "I didn't know you were watching, Daddy."

He laughed. "You were good, sweetie. Don't stop. Your voice is amazing."

Vanessa was sitting on the couch in her purple short satin nightshirt. It didn't look as if she belonged here among Kayla's paisley printed cushions and wallpaper with the pale colors.

"You're back," Vanessa commented, leaving the sentence dangling in the air. Her smooth, unlined forehead belied the myriad of questions she undoubtedly had.

"Where did you go, Daddy?" Daisy extricated herself from him.

He had no intention of answering that in detail. "Out. Where's Aunt Kayla?"

"She's having a shower," said Daisy as she sat herself down beside her mother. Vanessa always managed to sniff something suspicious and she was looking at him like a Doberman with ears on alert. "You haven't answered Daisy's question. Where did you go so early this morning?"

Incensed by her question and her nerve, he gave her a withering look that would have made a lesser woman squirm.

"When are we going to the park with Ginny?" Daisy asked. This was what he and Ginny had told her. They'd pretended that they were going to the park at the weekend and then planned to spring the surprise while on the drive.

"Ginny?" Vanessa echoed, never missing a thing.

"Can we see them at the park today, Daddy?"

"Not today, sweetie."

"Tomorrow?"

"No."

"Why not?" Daisy demanded to know.

"We can't," he answered, lamely. He hated this. Vanessa being here. Ruining his plans. Disrupting the quietness of his new life. An anger started to build in the pit of his belly. He should have been on the road with the people he really wanted to be with instead of pandering to his ex-wife.

"But I want to see Ginny and Benjy, you said we would."

"No, sweetie. We can't go to the park today."

"Who is this Ginny person?" Vanessa asked.

Daisy turned to her mother. "She's my friend. She's really nice and she's got a baby. His name is Benjy and he's really cute."

Vanessa stared at him with her eyebrow raised. That myriad of questions had surely quadrupled. "A baby? How cute. I would love to meet this Ginny person."

"And Benjy," Daisy added.

"Him, too." Vanessa stared at Ryan expectantly, waiting for answers he wasn't prepared to give. "A baby. Isn't that interesting?"

He glared at her in disgust, guessing what she was thinking. Her mind was in the gutter and he could imagine her trying to figure out if baby was his.

"I want to show you what Ginny got me, Mommy." Daisy ran off upstairs.

"Who is this Ginny?" Vanessa demanded for the third time. "You haven't answered my question."

"Daisy's told you." He tried to calm himself down; tried not to let his temper soar.

"She must be very close to you if she's buying things for Daisy," Vanessa remarked.

"She's none of your business." Rage simmered just below the surface and Ryan fought to stay calm. "You need to find a place to stay. Kayla doesn't want you here another night."

"Come." She patted at the space next to her. "We need to talk, Ryan."

"We do. I need answers."

"Not here. Not with Daisy around. Let's go out somewhere. Just you and me."

The idea repelled him. "I'm not going anywhere with you," he growled, growing increasingly resentful of her presence, and hating himself for it. She was the mother of his only child and he shouldn't be feeling this level of anger despite what she'd done. He wasn't ordinarily a vengeful man, but he hated that she'd ruined a wonderful day out for him, Ginny and the children, and it hadn't gone unnoticed by him how quiet Ginny was when he left her.

"But I need to speak to you in private, and I don't have anywhere to go."

Before he could tell her to find a room at a motel, he heard Kayla talking to Daisy. He needed to speak with his sister. Daisy rushed back in with the coloring books and pencils that Ginny had bought for her. "Look, Mommy. Look what Ginny got me."

"My, my." Vanessa's voice was cold and calculating. "She bought you all these things?"

Ryan stepped out of the room and almost bumped into Kayla. "Can I have a word?"

"Is she still here?" Kayla walked into the kitchen and poured herself a cup of coffee.

"She's still here, and she wants to talk. I need answers, so, please can you keep Daisy occupied for a while? *Please*," he begged.

"I was going to help Ford."

On a normal day this sentence would have stopped him in his tracks, but this wasn't a normal day. "Please, Kayla. Please. Something big has obviously happened and I need to find out what it is. Then I'll get her to leave. I only need half an hour."

"If that's what it will take." She headed back towards the living room and he followed her. "Bring your coloring books and pens into the kitchen, Daisy. We'll do some coloring."

"You, Aunty Kayla?" Daisy sounded as surprised as him. "You don't do coloring."

"I do now."

"What do you want, Vanessa?" he asked, closing the door when they left. "What's the real reason you're here?" He sat on the other sofa away from Vanessa, but she moved over to his side so that she was next to him. "I wanted to see my daughter."

"It's been a long time."

"I know. I'm sorry. It hasn't been easy for me."

He choked at her words. "It hasn't been easy *for you*? You walked out on us. You abandoned your daughter."

"I don't want to talk about the past, Ryan. I want to look to the future."

He opened his mouth to protest but words evaded him. This woman was as selfish now as she was the moment she'd walked out on them. Before then she'd been normal. Lovely. Understanding. A woman he'd considered his soulmate. Or so he'd believed. But something had changed when she started working at the new company.

And this now, with her telling him it hadn't been easy for her, and not wanting to talk about the past but the future, this was surreal. He didn't recognize this monster.

"I've been waiting to find the right moment to talk to you but you've been avoiding me, Ryan, and your sister hates me being here. She doesn't even try to hide it anymore, not that she's changed much." Vanessa rolled her eyes.

"We don't have much time. Kayla is going out soon because she has plans—"

"Plans?" she snorted. "Where? At the monthly knitting circle for spinsters?"

"Speak fast."

"I've left Avery."

He sucked in a breath. He'd suspected something along those lines. It was the only reason a woman like her would come back, because she had nowhere else to go. "And?" he asked, shrugging. What the heck did she expect him to do about that?

"He's a cheat."

"A cheat? Then you both deserve one another." It gave him the utmost satisfaction to say that, and when a muscle flexed along her jawline, he knew he'd hit a nerve.

She stared down at her hands. "I found a gift box filled with expensive lingerie in a drawer in his Paris apartment, but he never gave that gift to me. We were there for a few meetings, or rather, he was, and some nights, he went out alone. I had access to his laptop so I went through his emails, and that's when I found out. He's seeing someone else. He didn't have a meeting that night. I remembered some other places we'd been where he'd left me alone for the evening, so I went back in his diary and checked. It wasn't the first time he cheated on me. He's got women everywhere."

Her words gave him a strange sense of satisfaction. Vanessa had discovered what it was like to be on the receiving end of pain so searing it branded into the skin and marked you forever.

Until something or someone came along to heal you. And his someone was Ginny. "Did you think you were the only one? A man like that, the globetrotting CEO of a company who had no qualms about *you* cheating, did you really believe that you were the only one for him? That you were somehow special?" he growled.

It was cruel, yet he couldn't stop himself. Vanessa's lower lip trembled and he felt as if he'd penetrated her hard, glacial veneer, but she managed to recompose herself quickly, sitting taller, her spine rod straight, holding herself together. "I was, in the beginning. He made me feel like I was the only woman in the world, but now … now he's broken my heart."

"You broke mine."

She leaned across and placed her hand over his but he wrenched his away. "When?" he asked.

"When what?"

"When did you leave him?"

"A few weeks ago."

She moved fast. "You've come back from Paris and made your way here, and *this* is what it takes to remind you that you have a daughter?" Her insensitivity knew no bounds. Every muscle across his body tightened when he remembered the times Daisy missed her mother, when she was making her Valentine's Day card, and when she asked him why Mommy didn't call.

It was only now, when she was alone, that she conveniently remembered the family she'd left behind. His anger exploded. "I don't care that you forgot me, or that you didn't care about me—"

"I care about you. I care about you more than you know and Ryan I'm sorry—"

He didn't want to hear it. "I don't care that you don't give two hoots about me, but you have a young daughter, and you broke her heart."

"It doesn't look very broken to me."

He gasped at that. "She's so happy to see you, but it doesn't take away from the unhappiness you caused her."

"I'm going to make it up to her."

He pushed back, unrelenting. "You hurt her."

"But she's so happy now! I'm going to make it up to her, I promise I will, just give me a chance." Vanessa sat forward, wringing her hands, staring at him with big, sad eyes. "I made a mistake, Ryan. It's taken me a while to realize how monumental a mistake it was, but I want to make amends. I want us to be a family again, and I'm asking for your forgiveness."

He felt winded, her words were a hefty boxer's punch that

left him too stunned to answer. She could never make amends, not if she lived to be a hundred. The damage she'd caused to their lives, to their family, was something she'd never be able to fix. It saddened him to see Daisy so happy again just because this woman had come back. "I can't trust you. I can't trust you to not hurt Daisy again with your false promises."

"I want to fix things. I don't want to hurt her," Vanessa said. "Also, who is this Ginny? Is she someone important?"

"I won't discuss her with you."

"Are you seeing her?" she asked.

He bit down on his teeth and looked away, refusing to answer.

Vanessa chuckled. "You are. You didn't waste any time."

He snapped his head towards her and glared. "It's nothing like what you think it is. You have no idea. I'm not like you, Vanessa. I begged you to come back and I would have taken you back for our family's sake, but that time has passed."

"It's not too late."

"It is for me." He meant it. That time had passed the moment he'd upped and left the city to come here.

"Surely you can't mean that, Ryan?"

He got up and walked away, his hands shoved in his trouser pockets as he fought for composure. "You've caught up with Daisy, and now it's time for you to leave. When you get settled, I'll bring Daisy to see you. But, please, if there's nothing else you can do, try to maintain regular weekly phone calls with her. It's the very least you can do."

"You're not listening, Ryan." Vanessa raised her voice.

"I've heard enough," he spat back.

She patted a place beside her on the couch. "Come sit, Ryan. Don't sulk. You wanted me back and now we have a second chance."

"Did you hear me?" he cried, trying to rein in the contempt

he felt for her. "I'm not interested in talking to you. You turned our lives upside down and you didn't care while you were gallivanting around the world with your boss. I don't know why you've come back now thinking I'd roll over like a puppy at your feet."

Her eyes grew bigger, before brimming with tears. "I made a mistake, Ryan, and now I want to come back. Daisy wants me to come back. We can be a family again—"

"No. We. Can't," he hissed, putting up his hand. "We can never be a family again. You killed that dream a long time ago but you will always be Daisy's mother, and I will always be her father."

"It's a dream that can come true. We can make it happen. Daisy wants us to be together. She asked me if I had come home forever."

"This isn't home."

"But we can build a home. We can set down roots here."

He stumbled back a few steps, overwhelmed, confused and dazed. "You'd stay in a small town?" he asked in disbelief.

"I would do anything. I regret what I did. I regret that I broke your heart. I regret what I did to our little girl. Please, I'm begging you, Ryan. Please give me a second chance. I have a beautiful family. It was losing you both that made me realize how much you meant to me. I was stupid to throw it all away."

He rattled his head as if something had come loose and was now shaking about inside, messing with his thoughts and his logic. Vanessa sidled up to him. "Please, Ryan. Don't do this. You want revenge. You want to punish me." She placed her hands on his chest. "You might think that I don't deserve a second chance, but I've learned my lesson. Daisy looks so happy. She keeps hugging and kissing me."

"As if you care about Daisy," he snarled. "You didn't get in touch with her. You didn't come and see her. It's been ten months. TEN. MONTHS.”

“I had a lapse of common sense. I don't know what came over me, Ryan. I don't know what happened to me.”

“She's your daughter for goodness sake! You gave birth to her. She's your own flesh and blood. She's five years old and she was younger when you left.” His eyes turned glassy.

“I’ve been despicable. I am a despicable person. What I did was unforgivable. It’s like I took a drug, a love drug, and it made my brain turn to mush, but now I just want my family back.”

He couldn’t believe what he was hearing. This was so much worse than he’d anticipated. He’d thought she might want a place to stay, that something had happened with her lover. But not this; her wanting to get back together and to set up home here. He wasn’t convinced. “No.”

“Please, at least think about it. Daisy is so happy. She's so happy, Ryan. Are you willing to give that up?”

“You did.”

CHAPTER 37

GINNY

She returned home, feeling better.

After Ryan left, having broken the news about his ex-wife, Ginny had taken the food she'd packed for the trip and gone to see Talia. The last thing she wanted to do was to sit at home and be miserable.

They ate the sandwiches, followed by the cupcakes, and she told her friend everything. What surprised her was that she hadn't fallen apart. This was just another doomed romance. For her, it was not to be. She was better off being single and she didn't need romance in her life, or a man. She had Benjy and he was enough.

Ryan's life was complicated, and with his ex-wife back, she sensed a shift in his loyalties. She'd learned that love was not always smooth sailing. Her romantic encounters had never been easy, and meeting Ryan had just been a stroke of luck. He was a ray of light in the tunnel of darkness. Through him, and maybe because of him, she'd found the courage to change, to lift herself out of her misery.

But now things were out of her control. It wasn't Ryan's fault that his ex had turned up unexpectedly, but it was something he needed to deal with. She wasn't going to sit around waiting for him.

Later, when she and Talia went to the mall, her friend encouraged her to buy some clothes to cheer herself up, but Ginny didn't yet feel ready. She didn't like the baby weight she still carried and she refused to buy clothes a size bigger. She had plans to work out, get fit, lose the excess weight, and return to work, in some capacity. She was going to make it work. Life for her and Benjy was going to be an adventure.

While she bought nothing for herself, she bought a whole heap of cute little outfits for Benjy. She got back home and bathed and fed him, and he fell asleep in no time. She was sitting at the kitchen table, flipping through the pages of a magazine, when her sisters returned.

They looked shocked to see her. "What are you doing here?" Eloise cried, putting grocery bags on the countertop and rushing to her side.

"Why are you back so early?" Ashleigh sat down beside her and held her hand, obviously expecting tragedy. Eloise left the groceries and pulled up a chair alongside her. Ginny felt hemmed in, almost claustrophobic, as they gaped at her with worried faces.

"I didn't go," she told them.

"What?" Ashleigh cried.

"Why?" Eloise asked, as she and Ashleigh exchanged looks.

"Ryan's ex-wife arrived last night, and this morning he came here to tell me."

"His ex-wife is here?" Eloise shot up from her chair, then

started unloading the groceries, slamming them into cupboards and the refrigerator with such force and noise that Ginny was afraid she might break something.

"It was unexpected," she said, watching her sister warily. "She just turned up on his sister's doorstep and stayed there last night and obviously, we couldn't go on the trip with things being the way they were."

"What is she doing here?" Eloise slammed the cans into the cupboard.

"Go easy on the eggs." Ashleigh got up and started unpacking the bags, noiselessly. "Darcie said that cheating woman is to blame," she snarled, a packet of pasta in her hand.

"Why is she even here?" Eloise asked, charging over to the fridge with a carton of milk.

"I don't know why you two are so worked up." Ginny watched her sisters in amusement. It was touching, and funny, seeing them so worked up. Once upon a time she would have reacted like this, getting out of control with no rein on her actions. She'd have felt sad and sorry for herself.

Today, she'd chosen to respond, and it meant she was in control of her emotions. She'd considered the situation and she didn't blame Ryan. It wasn't his fault. He had no idea why that woman was here, and the only thing Ginny felt bad about was Daisy. That child had missed her mother and was obviously ecstatic to have her back. Yet Ryan was suspicious, and Ginny too, wondering about the real reason for Vanessa's return.

"Don't you care?" Ashleigh asked.

"Aren't you upset?" Eloise sat down beside her again and Ashleigh followed suit.

"It happened, out of the blue, and that's all there is to it," Ginny replied calmly.

"What did you do all day?" Eloise wanted to know.

"Is Benjy okay?" Ashleigh asked, her eyes filling with worry.

"Why wouldn't he be?" Ginny asked slowly.

"What did you do?" Eloise asked again. "You're remarkably calm." She and Ashleigh looked at one another again.

"I went to Talia's place and then we took Benjy to the mall."

Ashleigh got up, surveying Ginny as if she were a serial killer. "I should maybe go check on him."

Ginny laughed in shock. "What do you both take me for? What do you think I've done to him?"

Ashleigh remained standing as if she couldn't make up her mind whether to go upstairs and check, or stay here.

"Oh my goodness." Ginny placed her hands on her face, suddenly understanding. Her sisters thought she was crazy. They mistook her calmness for insanity. "I'm not falling apart. I'm not. I'm fine. Come and sit down Ash, before you wake Benjy up." Her voice was a sharp rebuke.

To her surprise, Ashleigh sat back down again. "I hate that your plans were ruined because Ryan's ex-wife showed up," she said.

"Like I told you both, it wasn't his fault. He felt bad about it, but he has bigger things to sort out. I had a good day. You don't need to worry about me." Ginny yawned, a wave of exhaustion sweeping over her. She'd been up early making the food and packing things for Benjy for the road trip, and Ryan's news had knocked her for six. That, along with the visit to Talia and the mall, had made for a very busy day, for all the wrong reasons. "I might go to bed now. It's been a long day." She was starting to feel sleepy, and the thought of watching TV in her room with her headphones while Benjy slept, appealed.

Her sisters did it again. From the periphery of her vision Ginny saw her sisters look at each other. Ashleigh reached for her hand again. "Are you sure you're okay, Gin?"

Ginny counted to three silently, then slowly withdrew her hand. "I'm fine, but if you're both going to treat me like I'm some deranged, escaped lunatic from an asylum, it's not going to help."

"Okay. Okay. We have to give her some space." Ginny didn't appreciate Eloise talking about her instead of to her.

"And Ryan? How is he?" Ashleigh asked, not one to let things lie unless she had all the answers.

"I haven't heard from him since."

"He hasn't kept you updated?" Ashleigh asked.

"With what?"

"Gin." Eloise started. "You told us a few weeks ago that you were falling in love with him. Now his ex-wife is back ... I mean ... how do you feel? That's all me and Ash want to know. We worry about you."

Ginny stood up. "Then don't. Please don't. I'm not a delicate flower you have to nurture and protect. Thank you for being here for me, but I really am fine. I'm sad, but I am *not* heartbroken. I don't know how I feel because I don't know what's going on. Ryan doesn't know. I can't jump to conclusions. I like him. I like him a lot, but things don't always go according to plan. I have Benjy to focus on now. So, don't worry about me breaking down and neglecting him because that's never going to happen. I'm trying to look at this all through Daisy's eyes. That little girl has been pining for her mom, and now she's finally here. I can only imagine that she's deliriously happy. I know I would be if mom and dad miraculously came back."

No one said a word, and she was sure they were all now thinking of the mother and father they'd lost.

"Well that's ... that's wonderful, then. You seem to be handling things okay, so I'm going to go back to my place," said

Eloise, standing up. She kissed Ginny on her head. "You're going to be fine, honey."

Ginny was sure of it. "I am. I'm not a baby anymore."

"No, you're not," Ashleigh said.

"I'm going upstairs to watch TV," she announced.

"We can watch something together," Ashleigh suggested, looking hopeful.

"I'd like to be by myself." As she edged towards the door, she heard Eloise whisper, "She's got this. I think she's going to be fine."

Ginny smiled. They were finally getting it. Just before she left, she turned around. "And another thing I've made my mind up about." She hadn't planned to tell them yet, but it seemed like the perfect time. They stared at her with mouths slightly open, waiting expectantly, on edge. "I'm planning to come back to work. Not yet, but soon."

Ashleigh looked confused. "When?"

"I was thinking maybe I could do a few hours starting in the summer."

Eloise raised an eyebrow. "You want to come back to work with *a baby*? What about Benjy?"

Luckily Ginny had answers. "I can bring him with me. We have a family business. We don't have a boss, collectively we *are* the boss, so we can bend our rules for me. I won't be on the shop floor. I'll be in the background, in the office, only for a few hours, but I need to do something."

CHAPTER 38

RYAN

Thankfully, Vanessa had moved into a B&B. She said she was staying here for a week, and he was counting the days until Friday.

He was only halfway through, but work kept him occupied, even if his mind drifted to the new and strange turn of events in his life. Daisy was at school. He'd seen the marked difference in his daughter. She was the happiest he'd seen her in a long time. She'd even begged him to let Vanessa do the school runs, and when Vanessa had hired a car, he had no excuse not to.

Today Vanessa planned to take Daisy to a movie after school. Yesterday she'd taken her out for pizza. These things made Daisy so happy. Who was he to get in the way?

He'd made his feelings clear to Vanessa—about her wanting to get back together again, and wanting them all to be a family living under the same roof—it wasn't going to happen. She hadn't broached the subject with him again. The problem was he knew his ex-wife well, and he didn't expect this to be the end of the matter. Vanessa was likely finding a way to hook her claws into him.

"It's getting late." He glanced at his watch again. He and Kayla had finished their dinner. "It's a school night. I should have said 'no' to the movie."

"She needs this time with her mom."

"I told Vanessa to have Daisy back home by seven thirty."

Kayla shrugged. "She's only a little late."

"So far." Movies were long, and Daisy had probably been hungry so might also have had something to eat. He should have told Vanessa to take her at the weekend, but hopefully by the weekend she would be gone.

"You shouldn't worry about school, not while Vanessa is here. Let them spend time together. At least Vanessa is staying at a hotel, instead of here. And Daisy loves her mom. She's so happy, Ryan. Let it go. It's only temporary."

He wasn't sure about that. "Vanessa doesn't do things out of the kindness of her heart. She's up to something."

"She's already told you what that is. She wants to get back with you.

"Not going to happen."

"She wants you all to live together."

He groaned. "Definitely not going to happen. She can get her own place and live close by, but all of us living under the same roof? No." He didn't trust her. Couldn't find a place in his heart for her. She'd been so deceitful that he could never trust her again or forgive her. As for Vanessa following through on her claim that she could live here? He couldn't really see that either. She'd always loved the big city vibe, the fast life, the tall skyscrapers, men in suits, the scent of money.

But maybe she was changing? He had to give her the benefit of the doubt. Perhaps having her heart broken and being cheated on had made her consider other life choices—like being a good mother and building a relationship with her daughter again? He hoped she wouldn't break Daisy's heart again. He started to clear the dishes away.

"At least she's helping with the school runs and is being of some use," said Kayla, getting up from her seat.

"Yes, at least that's something."

"I'll be able to do that soon."

He set the dishes down and placed his hand on the back of his neck, feeling bad. "I'm sorry. Vanessa arriving was a shock and it's thrown me off course. We'll go for a drive this weekend once she's gone. "

"You're being optimistic."

"I mean it. I'll put a few hours aside," he insisted.

"I meant about Vanessa leaving."

He groaned loudly. He was worried about the same thing.

"She might decide to stay if she's serious about starting over. If she really has split up with her boss and is at a crossroads, she might be hurting and reconnecting with you and with Daisy might be best for her right now."

He felt uneasy. "I don't know what to think. Vanessa can be selfish when it suits her. She put her own happiness before Daisy's, and she didn't care about breaking up the family, but now she expects me to jump for joy because she thinks it's something she wants again." Something in his gut told him not to trust her.

And there was also Ginny to consider. He cared about that woman; was falling in love with her, and he had no intention of letting her go.

"Whatever you decide to do, Ryan, I'll support you no matter what."

"Thanks." He appreciated Kayla so much. She'd been a rock for him, even though they'd had differences in opinion. "I will always be bound to Vanessa, in some way, because we were married once and she's the mother of my child, but I'll never trust her again. What makes me angry is that she thinks she can walk back into my life and expect everything to be fine. I begged her not to leave, but did she listen? Did she care? No. She didn't care about Daisy. And now I'm at a point where I don't feel so bad about her walking out on me, but my heart breaks for Daisy. How could this woman walk away from her own daughter? Vanessa didn't listen to my pleas because everything was fine in her world and now she's suddenly decided that she wants us back. I know why." He waggled a finger at Kayla. "Because she doesn't have anywhere to live. She lived with her boss. We sold our house and she moved in with him. Now things have changed. She has money and she'll have to start over, but this is an easier option for her. She thinks she can worm her way back into our lives until the next time."

"Until the next time?"

"I don't doubt that she'll cheat on me again. I don't care about me, but she'll hurt Daisy when she takes off again and I can't let that happen. She won't last in a small town. She'll get bored in no time. I've discovered that there isn't a maternal bone inside Vanessa. How can there be when she neglected her daughter for as long as she did? Unfortunately, Daisy doesn't know any better. She's like a little puppy dog besotted by her owner. But as long as Vanessa is being good to Daisy, and genuine, I'm willing to have her spend time with her. It's what Daisy needs."

Kayla didn't look so hopeful. "That's the question, isn't it? Is she being genuine, or just using you both?"

"Like I said, she's here because it suits her."

"Obviously."

The doorbell rang and he felt relieved. It wasn't too late on a school night. Kayla disappeared to get the door, and returned with Daisy and Vanessa in tow. Daisy rushed to him. "We had so much fun, Daddy! We had burgers and then we watched a movie! It was fun."

"I'm glad you had fun," he said, hugging her to him and smoothing his hand over her hair.

"Can we go again tomorrow. Mommy says she'll take me if you let her. Please Daddy, please can we go tomorrow?" Daisy stared up at him, her arms still encircled around his waist.

"To watch another movie?"

"Yeah, there were lots of them. We saw all the posters and I want to see—"

"Tomorrow is another school night, sweetie." He looked down at his daughter. She was radiating pure joy. "Too many late nights will pile up and you'll be exhausted by Friday." Daisy made a sad face. "But ..." he shrugged and relented. It was so obvious that Daisy was enjoying this rare and precious time with her mother.

"Maybe we can go on Friday, then?" Vanessa suggested. "And it doesn't matter how late you sleep in the next day because there's no school, and Daddy can come with us?"

His head jerked up. "Friday? You're leaving on Friday, aren't you? You said you were only staying a week."

Vanessa shook her head. "Are you counting down the days, Ryan? I'm having a great time with Daisy. We're *both* having a great time, aren't we, pumpkin?"

Daisy nodded. "Please Daddy, please can we all go to the cinema on Friday?"

"Come with us, Ryan. It can be a family night out," Vanessa smiled at him and Daisy jumped up and down.

So, it was just as he'd thought. Vanessa wasn't leaving so soon. "It's time for bed, Daisy." His voice was sharper than he intended. Daisy stopped jumping. He'd dampened her sparkle. "Come on, sweetie. We'll see, okay?" He didn't want to give her false hope, but he was hoping for Vanessa's miraculous departure between now and Friday.

~

"Snuggle down. It's getting late." He put away the book he'd been reading to Daisy, then tucked her in and sat on the bed.

"I love having Mommy here. I like it when she picks me up after school. Now no one can say my mommy doesn't love me."

It struck like an arrow, straight through his heart, hearing his little girl say that. "Who said that?"

"The other girls."

"Which girls?" A knot fisted in his belly. "Lara? Helen?" The muscles in his body tightened at the thought that his daughter had suffered at school. His wish had been for her to settle in well and be happy.

"No, the others."

"What others?"

Daisy's face turned sad. "The other girls. Not Lara and Helen. They're my friends. And Shelby. They tell the others to stop being horrible to me."

"Oh, sweetie. It sounds like you have some good friends. Friends who stand up for you are special." He tucked away a lock of hair behind her ear. "For now, try to ignore the nasty girls. Pay no attention and stick to your real friends." But he made a mental note to speak to her teacher about it.

She nodded. "But now that Mommy's back, they don't say anything to me."

He bent down and dropped a kiss on her cheek. "Your mommy loves you. And remember even when she's not here, you still have a mommy. Hopefully you'll see her a lot more now."

"Yes, Daddy! Please can I?"

"That's not up to me to decide, but let's see." He wasn't yet ready to tell Daisy about Vanessa's plans to live here.

"Yay! We have so much fun together!"

"That's nice," he replied.

"Please can we go watch a movie on Friday? *Please*, Daddy? I want you to come with us. It will be so nice."

"Yes, it will."

"Mommy really wishes you came today."

"I was working." He took her hand in his, struggling to reconcile the edginess he felt about Vanessa with the wonderful effect it was having on their daughter. Daisy loved her mother unconditionally, as all children did.

"I love it. Daddy. I really, really, really love having Mommy here. I miss her so much when she's not. She said she's going to live here for ever and ever and never leave me."

A muscle twitched along his jaw. "She said that, huh?"

Daisy's face turned sad again. "I thought it was my fault that mommy left me."

"No, sweetie. It was never your fault. It's never, ever, *ever* your fault."

"Mommy said she doesn't love the other man."

He couldn't believe his ears. Had Vanessa discussed this with Daisy? "She talked to you about that?" He hated her dragging a five-year-old child into their mess. It was a conversation strictly for adults.

"I asked her. 'member that time you said Mommy loves someone else? That man on the beach? So I asked Mommy and she said Daddy shouldn't have said that."

"I shouldn't have," he muttered under his breath.

"Mommy said she wants to meet Ginny." Daisy twittered on incessantly, unaware of the deeper connotation of what she'd said and blissfully ignorant of her mother's calculating mind.

The hell he'd let Vanessa anywhere near Ginny.

"I haven't seen Ginny and Benjy for a long, long time. Can we go see them?" Daisy asked.

"We'll see sweetie, we'll see."

"Can we see them on the weekend? At the park?"

"I'm not sure, yet, Dee." There was a lot to process here, but there was no way in hell he'd ever let Vanessa meet Ginny.

"Mommy said that when we live together, we can have a little brother or sister."

He blinked. Time stopped for a few seconds. "She said what?"

"Mommy said I love Benjy so much because I'm always talking about him and she asked me if I wanted a little brother or sister."

He tried to calm down his breathing. "What did you say?"

"I said I want a little sister."

He managed to hide his shock. "Okay, sweetie. You need to go to bed now so that you wake up on time for school."

"'Nite, Daddy."

CHAPTER 39

RYAN

The sound of Daisy's voice should have made him happy, but his mood darkened on hearing Vanessa's voice.

In the next moment, Daisy came flying through the door. "Daddy, you should have come! It was brilliant!"

Vanessa walked in after her, and his mood soured even more. "Why didn't you come with us, Ryan?"

"I had things to do," he mumbled.

"But it's the start of the weekend for goodness sake! You need to learn to relax more and stop being so uptight."

"Not possible at the moment," he replied, through gritted teeth.

"Oh, why's that?" she asked, coquettishly.

"Sweetie, can you go and help your Aunt Kayla?" He'd already primed Kayla to take Daisy so that he could have this one final conversation with Vanessa.

"Help with what, Daddy?"

Ryan scratched his forehead, but thankfully Kayla walked in. "Hey, honey."

"Are we doing some coloring in?" Daisy asked.

"We can do whatever you want."

When they left, Ryan closed the door. "You came here a week ago and I just want to know when you're leaving." Vanessa made a face as if his question had wounded her. "That's all you can think of? I came to you with a proposal, Ryan. You haven't spent any time with me."

The thing he had been dreading, the way her stay might drag on, was actually happening. "I don't want to spend time with you."

Vanessa made a face as if she didn't understand. "Have you thought about what I said?"

"About what?"

"About getting back together and being a family."

"I don't love you, Vanessa. I don't want to be with you and I don't approve of you putting ideas in Daisy's head that we're going to be a family or live together. Why on earth are you talking to Daisy about having more babies?"

Kayla opened the door. "Keep the noise down. Daisy can hear." She closed the door again.

Vanessa moved closer, her long, thick, heavily mascara'd eyelashes reminding him of a cartoon character. "Ryan, I understand your anger, and I'll wait for as long as it takes. I'm trying. Give me a break."

"Why don't you give me a break?" he snapped. "You've come here and disrupted our lives."

"Disrupted? Daisy loves that I'm here. I'm the mother of our child and I'm trying to mend things."

"You're only here because you have nowhere to go. When I begged you to stay when you first told me of the affair, you didn't care. I was even willing to sleep in a separate room and do whatever it took to keep our family together, to try to make things work. I prayed that you would come around."

She clasped her hands together. "I *have* come around."

"It's too late."

"It's never too late!"

"We are nothing more than a convenient pit stop for you. This ..." He flicked his hand between them. "This is temporary, because your boss has dumped you, or you've dumped him, it's irrelevant who came to their senses first, but you've led a very glamorous life up until now and all of a sudden you're alone, and you have no job and nowhere to stay. You think you can come back here and weasel your way back into our lives, but you're wrong. Daisy loves you, and maybe she needs you, but I don't love you. I won't ever trust you again."

Her eyes turned shiny, and her lips trembled as if she was going to cry, as if she were deeply hurt. For a second he caught a rare glimpse of the woman he'd fallen in love with; she'd been a different person back when they'd met. But ever since she'd started at the new job where she'd met her boss, that was when it all started to fall apart.

'People become more of who they really are.' Kayla had once said that to him when they'd been discussing his marriage and how it had come to this. Maybe there was some truth in that. He'd always earned well, had always been driven, but not ruthlessly. Vanessa's new boss had opened the door to a lifestyle she'd mostly dreamed about until then. She was a gorgeous woman, and naturally she'd caught the man's attention.

"Can't you see how happy Daisy is?" Vanessa hissed, her façade dropping like a bomb. "You're prepared to ruin that?"

He'd lain awake at night thinking about his options, of what would be the right thing to do for Daisy, for her life and her happiness. While he could put up with Vanessa, if she really meant what she said about coming back, he couldn't ever be with her again. "I'm prepared to tolerate you."

"Tolerate me?" she shrieked. *"TOLERATE?"* she scoffed, clearly taken aback. "You really do hate me that much, Ryan. I never thought you'd be capable of so much hate."

"I didn't realize until now how much audacity you had to waltz back into our lives and assume you could slot back in again."

"I love my daughter and I want to make a fresh start, Ryan. We don't have to break up our family. We can live here in this small town, if that's what you really want and we can get a house here, for us all to live in."

He squeezed his eyes shut, and pressed his fingers in the space between his eyebrows, releasing the ball of tension there.

Could he do this?

Live a lie?

For Daisy?

He could live *half* a lie. "I'll do anything for Daisy. Anything. But there's nothing between us. We can live under the pretense of sharing a house, but we'll have separate bedrooms. There will never be anything between you and me."

Vanessa's lips pinched together making her jaw jut out above her graceful neck. She was livid. "It's that woman, Ginny, isn't it? Daisy told me all about her. How convenient for you."

His temper flared. "Leave her out of it. She has nothing to do with this, and my opinion of you has nothing to do with her. I can't trust you. I will never trust you. You're not a good person."

"You're heartless," she snarled.

He wasn't going to win this, nor did he need to. He'd said

his piece and made his feelings clear. "How long do you intend to stay at the B&B?"

"I don't know."

"Another week?"

"You've always been so literal, Ryan. It was one of the things about you that grated on me the most."

He was about to tell her that there were many things about her that grated on him, but he didn't want to lower himself to her level. She always managed to get under his skin and rile him. He wasn't going to fall for it anymore.

"I love my daughter and I'm getting to know her all over again. I told you, Ryan, you need time and I'm more than happy to give you all the time you need."

"Then what?" he asked, unsure how this was going to work. "You plan to stay in a B&B for weeks or months?"

"I'll rent a place if I have to, but Daisy said you were looking to buy a place. We could do the right thing by her and buy a bigger place. I could give you my share of the divorce settlement and then we'd also be able to send Daisy to college later. Think about it, Ryan. We're better parents to our child if we stay together."

He tightened his jaw, trying hard not to answer back. To not let her manipulate him and cause his temper to soar. But he failed. "I don't love you, Vanessa. Don't ever make the mistake of thinking that we'll ever get back together, because it's not going to happen."

CHAPTER 40

GINNY

Ryan sounded agitated. Nothing like the calm and cool guy she'd come to know.

When he asked to meet, telling her he was desperate to see her and he missed her and wasn't thinking straight, she agreed and told him to come over.

They hadn't seen one another since he'd come to tell her about his ex-wife's sudden appearance. In the meantime, they'd called and texted and spoken to one another and she sensed he was deeply torn and didn't know what he should do. She'd tried not to think too much about him, but hearing his voice every night made that impossible. Reading his texts made it even harder.

But in the last day or so, she had sensed a shift in him. Ryan was such a good father, he'd do anything for his daughter, and if Vanessa begged him to forgive her and try again, Ginny believed he'd do it.

"Who's having a party? Is it Lara or Helen?" She was making him a cup of coffee and he'd been telling her how he'd dropped Daisy off to a birthday party at one of her friend's houses.

"Shelby."

Ginny didn't recall that name. "A new friend?"

"Yes. A nice girl."

"Nice girl? Are some of them not so nice?" Then she listened as he told her what the mean girls were saying to Daisy about her not having a mother. Ginny's heart sank. Poor Daisy. Schoolkids could be cruel. She hoped Benjy never had to experience that. Funny how lately, any time she heard something bad, or watched the news, her mind went to her precious son and how she would feel if anything bad happened to him. Until she'd become a mother, she'd never thought like that, and now she was a vulnerable mess, worrying about all the things that might happen to Benjy.

"But ever since Vanessa's been picking her up from school, that nastiness has stopped."

"That's a relief. Vanessa's been picking her up from school?" Ginny asked, dropping her voice as she led him into the living room. Things were starting to sound very cosy with Ryan and his family.

"She hired a car, and then suggested it. Daisy leapt at the idea, and it's always better to have your mom pick you up rather than someone else's parents."

Ginny nodded. She could see that he was in a difficult position, and might be considering his options. "That must be so nice for Daisy."

Ryan took a sip from his cup. "She's so happy. I've not seen her like that for a long time."

It was as Ginny feared. She sat down. "She has her mom back. What have you decided?" He'd been keeping her updated daily on things, and of the last conversation between him and Vanessa, of what she had proposed, of wanting to try again.

"It's a mess, Ginny. I can't give her what she's asking. To be a family again and to forgive her. It's such a mess, and in all this mess, Daisy is happy and I don't want to make her sad again."

He was a father and he was thinking of his daughter first. It's what parents did; the ones who cared. She'd gone through this thought process herself when she was pregnant with Benjy. Two parents were better than one, surely? "What do *you* want?"

"I don't want Vanessa."

"Are you sure about that? Can't you find it in your heart to forgive her?"

He stopped and stared at her in disbelief. "I'm one hundred per cent sure. Why would you ask me that?"

"Because I know what it's like to be in that situation. To want to do the right thing for your child. To be completely selfless. I got back with Ben. My instinct told me it maybe wasn't the right thing for me but I did it for Benjy's sake. He needed a father. I couldn't be a single mother and I convinced myself that he might have changed."

"Had he?"

"No. He hadn't. But I gave him a chance, and my conscience is clear. I did what I believed was the right thing for my son." Looking back now, she should have known, but she wanted things to be a certain way. She'd wanted a happy ending in her future and as a child who'd grown up with no parents, she wanted her son to have both.

Ryan set down his cup and clasped his hands together. He rested his forehead on his hands, looking every bit as wretched as he must have felt.

"Ryan?" She was worried about him.

He lowered his hands. "Are you saying I need to give Vanessa a chance?"

She didn't want him to. For her own selfish reasons she didn't want him anywhere near that woman, but she wasn't thinking of herself. "She's been begging you. She wants to try again."

"She cheated on me. Ginny. She had an affair."

"Maybe she has regrets and she really does want to make it up to you both. Maybe she's finally realized how priceless it was, the family she threw away."

"The only reason she's come back is because she's found out that the man she's left me for has been cheating on her. Not with one woman either. He has numerous women. He's a filthy rich CEO."

"What if you don't make it be about that? What if you reframe it?"

"What?" His eyes bore into her. "Are you pushing me away, Ginny? Do you not want what we could have?"

He took her hands in his. They felt warm and familiar. Him looking at her like he was now gave her comfort and security; it hinted at a chance to love again. A new and deeper love. She didn't want to give Ryan up. She didn't want to push him away but she'd never forgive herself for getting in the way of something that might save Daisy's family. For something that would be the best thing for Daisy. "You have to do what's right for your family."

"But Vanessa isn't right for me."

"She's Daisy's mom and Daisy's happy, that's all I've heard from you this week." She tried to wrench her hands away but Ryan wouldn't let go.

"She's deliriously happy, but I can't see how things will work out. I've seen a side to Vanessa, and I don't trust this sudden change of heart. I'm sorry that you're caught up in all this. I miss you, Ginny. I miss being with you."

He wasn't making this easy. "I miss you, too." But she

wasn't holding her breath. She was stronger now, and she didn't need a man in her life to make her life perfect. She had Benjy and he was enough. "We do what we have to for the people we love, Ryan."

"I'm in love with you."

She jolted back in shock, wondering if she'd heard right. She raised her eyes to his and held them there, seeing so clearly before her the face that consumed her as she went about her day, and as she lay down at night. He was in her thoughts all the time.

She swallowed, wanting to say the same words back to him but keeping them at bay—words she never dreamt she'd ever say again. "Think of your daughter," she said, her voice fading as if she were in pain.

"I am trying to. I told Vanessa if she really does mean it, she can live here, in this town and she should rent a place and be a part of Daisy's life."

"What does Daisy say?"

"Daisy." He blew out a breath. "I haven't had a proper discussion with her. Every time I talk to her she gushes about her mom and how much she loves her and wants us all to live together."

Benjy's cries pierced the conversation. Ginny let out a gentle sigh. "I am being summoned."

"Can I see him?" Ryan asked. "I've missed him. I've missed you both. This week has been a nightmare for me."

"But think how wonderful it's been for Daisy," she said, her voice shaky. They stood up together and this time when she prised her hands away, she succeeded. Or he gave in.

"Are you going to push me away and tell me that Vanessa is the answer?"

"Look at us, Ryan. We both have responsibilities and commitments. We're not single people. We have children and we must do what's best for them." She steeled herself, because it would be wrong of her to come between Daisy's chance to have her family back again. Just because hers was broken, didn't mean that Ryan shouldn't try his hardest to reclaim his.

She went upstairs, and Ryan followed. By the time she picked Benjy up from his cot, the ear-splitting cry-shrieks he usually let out when he awoke had softened. She hugged him to her chest, then turned him towards Ryan. "Look who's come to visit you, Benjy."

"Hey, little man." Ryan made a funny face and Benjy giggled, so he did it again, and Benjy giggled some more. "Can I hold him?" Ryan held his arms out.

Ginny watched as Ryan hugged and talked and made Benjy laugh. He scooted around the room with him, carrying him high in his arms, sailing him through the air.

He was so good with her son. Benjy had no male role models in his life, and she was aware of that.

Ryan would have been perfect.

Would have.

Ryan's future was not going to be a part of hers.

"He's such a happy baby." Ryan held him up and nuzzled noses with the child. "You're such a good boy, aren't you, Benjy?" Then he let out a gasp. "Daisy! I have to pick her up." He quickly handed the baby to Ginny and rushed down the stairs, without so much as a backward glance or a goodbye.

"And that is how it should be," Ginny whispered, cradling Benjy in her arms. "Family always comes first."

CHAPTER 41

RYAN

He wasn't too late. Five minutes. Six, maybe, and parents were still picking up their girls.

"Good party?" Ryan stared apologetically at the harassed looking woman who answered the door. He remembered meeting her on the night of the school play. "I've come to get Daisy."

The woman looked at him oddly. "Daisy? And you are?"

"Daisy's father, Ryan. We met at the school play." He'd also met the birthday girl's father earlier when he'd dropped Daisy off. The woman opened her mouth and stared at him blankly, and he understood that a house full of unruly five-year-olds might have fogged her brain over. But then she said something that stabbed like a knife. "She already left. She went home with Lara's mom about fifteen minutes ago."

"Lara's mom?" Ryan echoed. "I don't understand." Why would Daisy leave, and with Lara's mother?

The woman looked even more confused. "Daisy told me that you were okay with it."

"She said that?" Beads of sweat sprung up on Ryan's forehead and his underarms turned damp. This couldn't be right. "She knew I was coming to get her. What else did she say?"

"That she was going to *Jeanie's* place?" The woman shook her head as she pronounced the name wrong. "I'm sorry I don't know who that is. Lara's mom said she knew where it was, and that it was on her way home."

"And you let her go? A five-year-old?" He raised his voice and a hush fell in the air. Shelby's mom slapped a hand to her cheek and looked sheepish. "I'm sorry. It's been so busy here and I was handing out the party bags. I'm sure she'll be okay."

Ryan blinked. Maybe it had been someone else. "Are you sure it was Lara's mother?" Maybe Vanessa had decided to come.

The woman looked annoyed. "I'm good friends with Lara's mom. I know what she looks like. She was in a rush and had to leave early, and Daisy wanted to go home with them. I'm sorry, maybe I should have checked. The girls are such good friends, I thought it would be okay."

Ryan forced a smile because after all, it wasn't this poor woman's fault. "I'm sure it's fine." But still, a thought gnawed away at his gut, and he wondered if Daisy had heard him and Vanessa arguing last night. "How was Daisy?"

"She seemed happy enough."

"And they went to Ginny's place?" he asked, completely flummoxed and not understanding why his daughter would do such a thing.

"Yes." The woman frowned, not liking the interrogation.

He backed off. "Thank you for the ... the party. For inviting Daisy."

"My pleasure."

He rushed back into his car and raced back to Ginny's place, his heart in his mouth. When he got there, he sprinted to the door, and banged on it until Ginny opened it with Benjy in her arms. His head was resting on Ginny's shoulder and when Ryan looked closer, he was asleep.

"Is Daisy here?" He sped inside, desperate to see his daughter.

"Daisy?" Ginny followed him in. "Ryan, what are you talking about? Daisy hasn't been here."

He turned around, the blood freezing in his veins. "Lara's mom didn't come here?"

Ginny's expression said it all. "Who? You said you were going to get her."

"I went but I was told Lara's mom had already picked her up and was bringing her here." He started to shake. His daughter, his precious five-year-old, the one person he'd give his life for, wasn't here. Worse, she was acting out of character.

Ginny laid a tender hand on his cheek. "Are you sure she said she'd drop her off here?"

"Here." He hadn't misheard. And, clearly, something was wrong. His baby girl was missing and he didn't have a clue where she'd gone or why she would do this. It was his fault. He was convinced that she'd overheard them arguing yesterday.

That's what had done it.

Daisy didn't feel loved and now she'd run away because she was so miserable. "Vanessa." He grabbed his phone. It was possible that Daisy was with Vanessa. "Is Daisy with you?" he asked, the thudding of his heart growing as loud as thunder.

"What? No. She's at a party, isn't she?"

"She's not with you?"

"I'm in a department store. Ryan, what's wrong?" He

pressed his fingers against his forehead, and walked around, trying to guess where his daughter might be.

Think. Think. THINK.

There was a chance Daisy might have gone to the hotel. "Can you go back to your B&B and check. Daisy might be there."

He heard the sharp intake of breath at the other end. "She's not with you?" Vanessa shrieked.

"No. I went to get her from the party but she wasn't there."

"What?" The word was a wail. "What do you mean she wasn't there? Where is she?"

"She left with one of the moms. Lara's mom, apparently, and I was told that she took Daisy to Ginny's place, but I'm there now and she's not—"

"Ginny's place?" Vanessa snarled. "What the heck, Ryan? You don't know where my daughter is, but *you're* at Ginny's place?"

Trust Vanessa to miss the point. "Go back to your B&B," he said as calmly as he could. "You've taken her there before, haven't you? There's a chance Daisy might have gone looking for you."

"How would she get there? She's only five!" Vanessa was hysterical.

"I don't know, Vanessa. Just do it. Just go and check."

He hung up when Vanessa started hurling insults at him.

"Have you got Lara's mom's number?" Ginny asked. The fear in her eyes reflected the fear he felt. He couldn't think and he fumbled blindly on his phone before realizing that he didn't have contact details for any of the school parents. He'd only met a few of them at the school play and he'd never swapped numbers. He barely knew them, and now he was paying the price. "I … I d-don't…"

Ginny placed a hand on his chest. "Deep breath, Ryan. Calm down. We're going to find Daisy. I'm sure she's safe."

"How can I calm down when my baby girl has run away? Where's Benjy?"

"I've put him in his cot. We don't know that Daisy's run away. Eloise must know Lara's mom because she was at the housewarming." She reached for her phone and made a call.

He left Ginny to it and started to look around the house, under the table, behind the sofas. Standing at the foot of the stairs, he glanced upwards and considered searching there, but Ginny appeared. "Eloise and Liam are on it. They're calling Lara to find out what she knows and then they're coming over."

"They don't need to come over."

"Ryan, Daisy's five years old. We all need to start brainstorming and looking for her."

"But you told me not to worry, you said she'd be okay." He wanted to believe her, even though deep inside he had never been so worried in his life.

"She is going to be okay, but we need to retrace our steps and figure out where she might have gone, so, tell me again what you know."

He marveled at Ginny's poise. "All I know is that Lara's mom dropped her off here." He opened the front door and went outside to look around, but in the open and empty space, there was nowhere for Daisy to hide. "She's not here, Ginny." His voice sounded strangled. "Why would the mom just leave her? Daisy can't even reach the doorbell. Did you hear her knock? Maybe you opened the door and ..."

"Ryan." Ginny walked up to him and grabbed his hand. "No one knocked on the door. I've been in the kitchen the entire time."

"But if my baby girl isn't here, *where is she*?" He was this close from having a full break down. Ginny stroked his face again. "You're worried. I'm worried. It feels like I've lost Benjy. I'd be a wreck, but know this; we *are* going to find her." She walked around then looked around the corner. "I've already checked, she's not here."

It was hopeless. He clutched at his chest, felt his insides hollow out, felt his legs start to buckle. His five-year-old had vanished into thin air. The world could be a terrible place for a child so young. "Why would she do this?" he cried, helpless and paralyzed.

"Did anything happen to upset her?" Ginny asked, the calmness in her voice confusing him. "How was she when you left her at the party?"

"She was happy. She perked up when she saw her friends."

"Perked up? Was she not happy before?"

He tried to think. She had been quieter this morning when he'd woken her up. "She might have heard me and Vanessa having a disagreement last night."

Ginny chewed her lower lip. "You think she heard?"

He had a sneaky feeling she might have. Kayla had interrupted them to tell them to be quiet. As far as he could remember, they were being quiet, but Vanessa had a way of getting him worked up. "I tried to be quiet. I thought we were."

"Maybe she heard?" Ginny suggested.

That's what he feared, and now he blamed himself even more. "Wherever she is, she's not here." His life didn't feel worth living anymore.

As they stood outside the house, talking, Eloise and Liam pulled up in Liam' truck. "Did you find her?" Eloise asked, rushing towards them. Ginny shook her head. Liam strode over and gave Ryan a reassuring pat on the back, before mumbling something about finding Daisy. Then they all went inside.

"I called Lara's mom." Eloise sounded breathless. "She says

she left Daisy here, outside, then she drove off once Daisy was at the door."

"Then why isn't she here?" Ryan growled. He couldn't believe that the woman had left Daisy. He wiped his hand across his brow, an uneasiness spreading across him like a thousand crawling ants. It wasn't right they were all standing around talking. Doing nothing to find his daughter. "I need to speak to her," he begged. "Can you call Lara's mom again? I need to talk to her."

Eloise seemed reluctant. "Lara's mom is at the hospital. Her mom had a fall and a passerby called 911 and took her to the hospital. That's why she rushed off. I'll call her, but keep it quick. She sounded pretty frantic when I spoke to her." Eloise dialed the number and handed him the phone.

The others talked while he waited for Lara's mom to answer. Liam suggested they look around the house, and Ginny told him they'd already done that. Eloise asked if they'd looked upstairs, and Ginny said Daisy hadn't even been in the house, but they all disappeared upstairs anyway.

Lara's mom picked up. "Have you found her?"

"It's Ryan, Daisy's dad. Look, I appreciate you dropped Daisy off but she knew I was coming to get her."

"Oh, hi." The woman's voice turned quiet. "You haven't found her?"

"I wouldn't be calling you if I had." He didn't mean to snarl.

"I'm so sorry." In the background he heard sirens.

"I can't believe you left her at the door, that you didn't even wait to see her go inside?" he growled, wondering what kind of woman would do that.

Someone like Vanessa would.

"I thought I saw her knock. I thought I did." The woman sounded as if she was going to burst into tears. "I'm so sorry. I wish I'd seen her to the door and waited. I wish I had."

"She knew I was coming," he snapped, growing angrier with himself than anyone else.

"Daisy said she wanted to go to Ginny's house. She said it had all been arranged."

Ryan scratched his head because he didn't understand why his daughter would lie. "I … I don't know why she would say that. We didn't arrange anything like that."

"I wish I could help. I had to leave quickly because my mom had a fall and I was rushing to get to the hospital. I shouldn't have just left your daughter. I'm so sorry. Please forgive me, but I wasn't thinking straight. I'll try and come over to help look for her as soon as I'm done here."

He felt bad for her, and realized that he'd made her feel even worse than she might have already felt, on top of that, her mother had had a fall. "No. I'm sorry. I hope your mom gets better soon."

"I hope you find Daisy."

"Me too." He hung up. "I was only five minutes late," he muttered to himself as the others returned.

"She's not upstairs," Ginny announced. The doorbell rang again and they all rushed to the door. Eloise opened it.

"Is this *Ginny's* house? I'm Vanessa, Daisy's mother."

"Come right ins—" Eloise started to say when Vanessa charged towards him like a raging bull.

"She's not at the B&B. Where is she, Ryan? Where is my baby girl? How could you let something like this happen?" She poked her skinny fingers into his chest.

He stumbled back. "Keep your voice down. There's a baby asleep upstairs."

"The baby? Is that all you care about? What about your own daughter?"

"Let's go into the kitchen," said Liam calmly as he ushered them in that direction.

"How could you do this?" Vanessa shrieked. It was the most distressed that Ryan had ever seen her, and now his thoughts turned inward, to a dark and dangerous place. Daisy was nowhere to be found, and he feared the worst.

"My baby girl is gone." Vanessa started to cry. "How could you do this?" she wailed.

"How could I do what?" he hollered back. "I was five minutes late, but parents were still picking their children up."

"Five minutes late?" Vanessa cried, in between wiping her eyes. "Why were you late?"

"It's not because I was late that she's missing. This isn't helping, you finding any excuse to blame me."

Vanessa's nostrils flared. "Blame you? And rightfully so!"

"Calm down both of you," Ginny hissed. "My son is sleeping."

"And my daughter is missing!" Vanessa shrieked.

"I said, *quiet* or I will have to tell you to leave." Ginny was calm in the face of such hostility. "Ryan was here, talking to me."

"I'm sure he was. He seems stupidly besotted by you." Vanessa glared at him. "You were talking to her? You dropped your daughter off and you snuck back to here for a secret rendezvous?"

He saw red. "Don't you dare go there!" he yelled, sick with worry, and fed up with Vanessa's sniping. "If you want to talk about being sneaky I can tell you a thing or—"

"Enough," Ginny hissed, her voice deathly quiet.

CHAPTER 42

GINNY

"*E*nough."

Ginny couldn't take the bickering anymore. Their daughter was missing, and Ryan and Vanessa were at each other's throats. Ryan's ex-wife was not a nice woman and Ginny could see why Ryan had such reservations about her.

"Stop." With gritted teeth, she eyed Vanessa squarely. "Stop attacking Ryan and looking for someone to blame. This shouldn't be a blame game. You need to calm down and stop sniping at one another. Daisy is five years old. She's much too young to be out on the streets alone. We need to focus on her and you two being at each other's throats isn't helping."

Ryan looked defeated and Ginny wanted to reach out and hold him, to reassure him that everything would turn out fine.

But she wouldn't.

She couldn't.

She wasn't willing to give Vanessa even more ammunition

against her ex-husband. These two hated each other, and it didn't make any sense to Ginny why Vanessa claimed to want to get back again with Ryan.

She felt helpless as she watched him, wanting to comfort him, but having to stand back. Ryan pinched the bridge of his nose. "I was five minutes late and parents were still there, picking their girls up. Daisy would have waited. I know she would have. That's why I'm convinced she must have been upset about something."

"She loves me, and she doesn't understand why you don't want us to work on getting back together again," Vanessa snarled.

"You've discussed this with her?" Ryan asked in disbelief.

"Yes I discussed it with her."

And off they went, bickering again. This wasn't working. At this rate, they were nothing but a hindrance. Ginny stepped between them, her back to Ryan's ex. "Ryan, no. Stop. Let's not go there. We need to focus on Daisy."

Ryan looked over her shoulder, unable to contain himself. "Why are you talking to our daughter about our problems?" he growled.

"There you go. Blame me about it, why don't you," Vanessa shot back.

"Okay guys. Guys. *STOP*." Liam raised his voice and put his hands out in a prayer motion.

The doorbell rang again, and Eloise sighed then left to see who it was.

"We need to call the police. We need to get an amber alert set up." Ginny wrung her hands together. She was scared, and worried, and her insides were trembling. Daisy was so vulnerable. Anything could have happened to her. What if someone had taken her? Bile crawled up her windpipe. She clasped a hand to her throat, recoiling in fear.

Ashleigh marched in, like a woman with a mission. "Anything? Any ideas? What's the plan?" She looked around at everyone.

"You didn't have to come, Ashleigh, but I appreciate you being here," Ryan told her. "I don't want your business to suffer and we've got things covered here."

Ashleigh stepped towards him. "I left the assistants in charge. The shop isn't important at a moment like this. Tell me, what do we do now?"

"After we've called the police, we need to start looking for her, around this area. We'll go off in different directions because she can't have gotten far," said Ginny, trying to get inside Daisy's mind.

The doorbell rang again. "Oh my word!" Ashleigh cried. "I thought everyone was already here. I'll get that." She disappeared.

Ginny's mind worked furiously. From what she'd gathered, Daisy's parents had been arguing again. It was possible that Daisy felt unloved, like the last time.

Where would she go?

What would she do?

Before she could think of an answer, Ashleigh walked back in. She'd turned pale, as if she'd seen a ghost. Kayla rushed out from behind her, her arms outstretched as she rushed to her brother's side. "I heard. Oh, Ryan, what are we going to do? We need to find her."

Ford walked in, his huge frame making the kitchen feel even more cramped. "I'm sorry to hear the news. We jumped in the car and came as fast as we could."

Ginny looked at Ford, then Kayla, then at Ryan, and finally at Ash.

We?

Had she heard him right?

In the time she began to process why Kayla and Ford had walked in together, Benjy started to cry. It was a loud, piercing shriek. Like he'd been disturbed from a deep slumber and was furious about it.

Ginny sighed. Benjy was important, but in this instant they needed to search for Daisy. "I'll go." Ashleigh vanished, lightning fast.

Ryan filled his sister in, while Ginny racked her brains.

"What can I do to help?" Ford asked her. "Want me to get out there and start driving around?"

"No. Just give me a few moments. Let me think." She couldn't concentrate with all this noise and commotion. She glanced at Ryan, but he seemed to have frozen. He looked miles away, staring out of the window. Vanessa was blowing her nose into a bunch of tissues, and Eloise and Liam were trying to soothe her.

Then Ashleigh walked in with a crying and screaming Benjy.

It was pure madness. Ginny reached for Benjy and held him tight, trying to imagine what it would be like if Benjy ever went missing.

Never.

She would never let this precious little boy out of her sight. This happy baby who loved nothing more than to lie under his musical play gym and kick his legs high in the air. This child was her blessing and she was lucky to have him.

In that moment, a lightbulb went off in her head. She had an idea, and it was worth exploring. She handed the baby back to Ashleigh, but he immediately started to shriek and flail his arms, clearly wanting his mom. "Sorry, baby." She grabbed Ryan's hand. "Come with me."

"Where?" Ryan asked.

She prayed she was right. Leaving through the kitchen door, she started to walk fast, before breaking into a run.

"Ginny?" Ryan ran along to keep up with her. "Where are you going?"

"To Eloise's house," she cried, getting quickly breathless.

"You think she's there?"

She prayed Daisy was somewhere around there.

"Shouldn't we get the keys?" he asked, but she ran past Eloise's house and headed for the beach.

"Ginny?"

She sped up as soon as she saw her, an anguished cry coming from deep in her chest at the sight of the small solitary figure walking along the seashore. There, in the distance was Daisy. She had her back to them and looked as if she was collecting shells.

Ginny let out another shriek, a heartfelt cry of huge relief because the girl was safe, and found, and here, within reach. She turned and waved to Ryan, pointing to Daisy who now looked their way. "It's her!" Ginny cried out and raced towards the child.

Ryan screamed. Hours of pent-up worry and frustration released in one loud scream. "Deeee!" he yelled. They reached her within seconds and Ryan scooped his daughter up in his arms and twirled her in the air before hugging her to his chest and raining kisses all over her face. "Dee! We were so worried. Why did you go, sweetie? Why did you leave with Lara's mom?"

Ginny clasped her hands to her chest, relief, joy and the many emotions in between washing all over her.

"Daddy." Daisy flung her arms around Ryan's neck and buried her face. "I'm sorry." She burst into tears. He hugged her again, his face losing all the tension that had been imprinted on it. "We were so worried about you, baby girl. Why did you leave? Why didn't you wait for me?"

In answer, Daisy snifled, but said nothing and kept her face buried in his neck. "How did you know?" he asked Ginny.

"I remembered how happy she was that day, at Eloise's party when we all went for a walk. Where else could she have gone around here?"

Ryan placed Daisy on the ground gently, before crouching down and smoothing back her hair. "We've found you now. Thank God, we found you and you're okay." The little girl's face was downcast.

"You had us so worried, Daisy," said Ginny, crouching down alongside Ryan.

"Why did you come here, sweetie? Why didn't you wait for me at the party like I told you?" Ryan asked.

Daisy chewed her lower lip, her eyes still downcast. Ginny put her hand on his shoulder. "Ryan, calm down. Not so fast," she whispered in his ear. The poor child looked cold, and miserable and she probably thought she was in a lot of trouble. "There's time for that later."

Then Daisy burst out crying again. "Aw, Daisy." Ginny placed a comforting hand on her shoulder. Ryan held her hands, telling her not to cry. Ginny leaned towards her. "We're so glad you're okay, Daisy. Please don't cry. We're so happy that we found you."

"That's all that matters, Dee. I promise I'm not angry now. I'm over the moon happy that you're okay."

"Am I ... am I in trouble?" Daisy asked, in between sobs.

"No, sweetie, you're not in any trouble." Ryan wiped away her tears. Kneeling on the sand, he threw his arms around her again.

"You scared us, that's all," Ginny told her, "but now it's all fine. Everything is fine."

"I was so worried, Dee. Your mommy was so worried. We didn't know where you were, but Ginny thought to come here. She knew where you'd be." Ryan couldn't stop hugging his daughter. Ginny understood. She'd never want to let go of her either.

"I like this place," said Daisy. "It makes me happy."

"Aren't you happy?" Ginny asked, her voice turning soft, as Ryan backed away. Daisy stared at the sand, unable to meet their eyes. Ginny stroked the girl's face, and wiped the tears away. "Everyone loves you so, so, so much, Daisy. Your Mommy and Daddy do, I do, Benjy does. You'll see so many people here are worried about you and wanted to look for you. You are so loved."

"But Mommy and Daddy are always fighting. And Mommy told me that she was leaving soon. She said she'd come back another time but I don't believe her."

Ryan's face turned hard as stone, his looked so furious he could barely get his words out. Ginny tugged his hand, motioning for him to calm down.

"You're sad because your mommy said she was leaving you again?" Ginny asked softly. Daisy nodded, her eyes still fixed on the sand. "I heard them fighting last night. They were being mean."

Ginny let out a sigh. "It's not nice when mommies and daddies fight." She looked at Ryan, unsure of what to say. She thought better of it and changed the topic. "Why did you leave with Lara's mom?"

"I was angry with Daddy. I didn't want to go with him."

"Dee, sweetie." Ryan's voice choked up. "I'm sorry I made you feel that way. It's all my fault."

Ginny raised her hand to tell him to wait. They needed to let Daisy talk; they needed to get to the bottom of this. "So you went with Lara's mom because you were mad at your Daddy?"

"And because I wanted to see you." This time Daisy looked up at her and in that moment Ginny's heart flipped inside her chest, like it had jumped for joy. "Because you always make me happy."

"Awww." Ginny tried to hold herself together and not burst into tears. Daisy lunged towards her, throwing her arms around Ginny and causing her to fall back. Her bottom hit the sand as the girl fell into her arms. "I wanted to come and see you but then I remembered I haven't seen you for a long, long time and I thought you didn't love me anymore so I ran away. I ran and I ran and I went back to that other house. I remembered it was close and I ran all the way there and then I saw the beach where me and Lara collected shells."

Tears rolled down Ginny's face. She didn't quite understand why. She blanketed Daisy with her arms and stayed like that for a while until Daisy stared up at her and asked her why she was crying.

"Because I'm so happy that we found you." Ginny snifled, wiping her eyes quickly.

"You found her!" Eloise cried as she and Liam reached them. They were out of breath.

"Aw, man!" Liam highfived Ryan. "That's awesome."

"They found her!" Eloise yelled, cupping her hands to her mouth. Kayla came running and stopped, then immediately burst into tears of happiness. "Daisy!" She held out her arms. Daisy slowly got up and walked towards her aunt who embraced her tightly. "You had us so worried," said Kayla, fussing over her.

A feeling of triumph blossomed in the air.

Ryan got up slowly and held out his hand, helping Ginny to her feet. They fell into an embrace. "Thank you," he whispered in her ear.

"Don't thank me, Ryan. I'm just so relieved that we found

her and that she's okay. Where's Ashleigh?" she asked, pulling away, and realizing that they'd left her son alone in the house.

"Oh, shoot!" cried Eloise. "I should tell her. They were trying to calm Benjy down. Ash," she yelled into her phone. "We found her!"

"Daisy, my baby!" Vanessa came hobbling along, her high heels sticking in the sand, the wind blowing her bouffant hair all over the place. She grabbed Daisy away from Kayla and hugged her.

Ginny didn't miss the way Kayla rolled her eyes. She started to run back towards her house, desperate to get back to her baby.

CHAPTER 43

ASHLEIGH

"Shhhhhh" Ashleigh tried to calm the crying baby but Benjy wasn't quietening.

"What does he need?" Ford frantically clapped his hands and clicked his fingers, then quickly fetched a baby rattle from the other room. He waved it in front of the baby's face but Benjy's howls grew louder to glass-shattering levels.

"You're not helping." She turned her back to Ford and walked around the room, rocking Benjy in her arms and hoping this might soothe him. She was at a complete loss on what to do. She'd never dealt with babies much, apart from Darcie's son when he'd been born, and the upside to that was she'd been able to give him back as soon as possible.

She and Eloise had taken care of Benjy when he was newly born, and he slept a lot, then Kayla had come along. This screeching, screaming baby with his ear-piercing shrieks scared her.

"We're not too good at this, are we?" Ford attempted a chuckle, but Ashleigh was furious. She couldn't bear to look at him.

Ford and Kayla?

How had that come about?

She held Benjy a few inches from her face. "Are you hungry, Benjy? Is that it?"

"Shall I get his milk ready?" Ford hovered around, as useless as a duck. She didn't want to answer and was glad that the baby's screeching blocked Ford's voice.

"Ash? I asked you if I should get Benjy's milk ready?"

Ash.

He had no right to call her by that name. She was *Ashleigh* to him from this point on. "Do you know how to get his milk ready?" she asked, forcing herself to face him.

"No, but you could tell me, if you calmed down enough."

"Calmed down?" she hissed, pressing the baby to her shoulder and bobbing around with him. "I'm calm. I'm very calm."

"You're not."

She snorted with derision. "I *am* calm. Benjy's hollering doesn't make it easy."

"Is that so? I thought it was the sight of me and Kayla walking in together that made you get all riled—"

"I. Don't. Care." But she sounded exactly as if she did. Proving his point. She took a big breath, trying to quell her jealous rage. "You've made it perfectly clear to me that you're not interested in resolving our problems, or fixing our relationship."

He looked at her, his lips pressed together. He had no reply for her. But she now had the answer she'd been trying to find. Ford's silence spoke volumes.

"Is she a rebound?" Ashleigh asked, unsure whether stupidity or blind courage prompted the question.

"Rebound?" Ford's eyes narrowed, and he cocked his head as if he didn't understand. "From who? You?"

She managed to suppress the gasp, even though her body froze from the shock. He'd never had any intention of getting back with her. Ever. "From Susan."

"Susan?" His eyes turned wide and his surprised tone made her doubt her earlier suspicion. She hadn't had an accurate read on this man for a while now. She'd misjudged and misunderstood him completely. She'd been so focused on him having feelings for Susan, that the whole Kayla situation had blindsided her. "What's Susan got to do with anything?" he thundered. She squirmed under the weight of his glare. That hardened look was filled with anger and resentment; everything bad he felt for her.

She couldn't stare at his face any longer. Luckily, magically, Benjy had quietened down. She glanced at him; his cries had turned to soft whimpers and his eyelids were starting to close. He was tired, the poor little baby.

"How is he?" Ginny cried, rushing inside, and causing Benjy to start crying again. Ginny's eyes were filled with worry, and she rushed at Ashleigh like a Mama bear trying to get her cub. "Oh, Benjy. Benjy, baby. Come here my precious baby boy." Ginny scooped him away and cooed and fussed over him.

"What about Daisy? Did you find her?" Ashleigh asked.

"We found her. She was near the beach, collecting shells."

Ashleigh let out a long sigh, a huge weight of worry lifted off her chest. She'd been praying for this. It was the best news.

"That's good. That's great! The best news." Ford wiped a hand over his face, looking relieved. "It's the outcome we all wanted."

In his mother's familiar arms, Benjy had fallen in a deep sleep.

"He must have exhausted himself," whispered Ashleigh.

"I wasn't sure if he needed milk," Ford added.

"He's not hungry." Ginny stared down at her son, a look of pure love on her face. "He's had so many interruptions today. His routine is out of whack. I'm going to put him in the crib."

"I'll come with you." Ashleigh moved so fast, she was in front of her sister. The last thing she wanted was to be stuck in the kitchen with Ford when Kayla returned.

CHAPTER 44

RYAN

He carried his little girl into the house then set her down gently on the sofa. "You okay, Dee?"

Daisy yawned and nodded. Vanessa sat beside her, then patted down her hair. "You scared us, baby."

"I'm sorry, Mommy."

"How about I get you something to eat?" Kayla offered. "You must be hungry. The party was hours ago."

Ryan crouched on the floor in front of his daughter, grateful that she was safe and sound and at home again. "How about a peanut butter and jelly sandwich, sweetie?"

"That sounds good. Can I have four please, Aunt Kayla?"

"You can have as many as you want, honey." Ryan mouthed a silent thanks as his sister left the room. Vanessa put her arm around Daisy and hugged her. "I am *so* glad you're back home."

"But you're leaving me again, Mommy." Daisy's voice was barely audible. Ryan wanted to have words with Vanessa about this, but now wasn't the best time. Daisy had run away because of the disagreements between her parents, and she believed she wasn't loved. He had to be careful about his words and not fall for Vanessa's baiting.

"Oh, baby." Vanessa waved her hand dismissively. "I'll be back. I won't be gone for too long."

"You said you were going to live here, and you said you were never going to leave me again," Daisy countered. Ryan listened quietly, curious to see how Vanessa would answer. "I will come back, pumpkin. I promise."

"That's what you said before," Daisy protested. Ryan lowered his head and tried to keep calm. Tried to hold it together while he listened to the excuses his ex-wife made. "Why are you going?" He couldn't hold back any longer, but kept his voice level.

"I have an interview."

"A what?" Of all the answers he'd been waiting for, this hadn't been one of them. Kayla walked in with the sandwiches on a plate and a glass of milk. She surveyed the situation. "I'll put this on the kitchen table, and you come and get it when you're ready," she said, before leaving abruptly.

"You have an interview?" he said, trying very hard not to snap.

"Avery's friend owns a luxury chain of hotels and he has an opening for someone like me."

I'll bet he does.

He swiped his hand over his face. "Avery's friend?" Someone else she'd met, no doubt rich and powerful. "Did he head hunt you or did you ...?" He was about to say, 'go begging to him?' but he bit his lip and forced his mouth shut.

"The job has great benefits and perks and I'm more than qualified for the position. The money's great, too. It's ideal."

Ryan wondered how it was ideal, or for whom? "Then,

good luck," he said, tightly. "It would be great if mommy got the job, huh, Dee?" For Daisy's sake he had to look like he supported Vanessa's decision. Daisy needed to see that her parents were a team, that they were united, even though this woman continued to disappoint him so much. Surely she could have delayed her departure for a few days, given that Daisy had been found and that she was obviously upset? Surely a mother would feel for her child and be willing to do whatever it took to assuage that child's fears?

Any mother would stay.

Not Vanessa.

Ginny would, but Ginny was the antithesis of Vanessa, and that's why he was in love with her.

"Will you promise to come back and live here, Mommy?" Daisy's face filled with hopeful innocence.

"We'll see, baby." Vanessa smoothed back her daughter's hair again.

"Where's the job?" he asked, curious.

"Seattle."

He stared at the floor, a heavy feeling weighing him down. Vanessa wouldn't be back for a long time, irrespective of whether she got the job, or the guy, she wasn't planning on coming back here. His heart broke for Daisy.

"Would you like to stay with your mommy tonight?" he asked Daisy, in the spirit of solidarity and needing to do something to cheer his daughter up. Apart from that first night when Vanessa had first arrived, Daisy and her mom hadn't spent a night under the same roof. He was loathe to let Daisy out of his sight, but he had no idea when she might get another chance like this with her mom.

"I've got an early flight tomorrow." Vanessa pouted, trying her best to put on a sad face. "Sorry, pumpkin. Next time."

His fists clenched, and he couldn't believe his ears. Even

now, after everything, the woman had casually dismissed an offer that would have meant so much to Daisy.

"Can I stay at Ginny's?" Daisy asked, not missing a breath. Ryan was speechless. Vanessa did a double take. "Who?"

"Ginny. My friend. Benjy's mommy." Daisy looked at him, her eyes suddenly filled with hope. "Please Daddy, can I?"

Something light and fluttery, hope with wings, soared inside him. He recalled the reason Daisy had gone to the beach instead of to Ginny's place, and how Ginny had hugged his little girl and held her. He could see how much she loved his daughter. "Sure you can. Maybe tomorrow might be better? It's late now, and Ginny and Benjy will be tired."

"Thanks, Daddy!"

He felt better now, seeing the smile back on Daisy's face. That she had so easily asked about Ginny when Vanessa rejected her gave him hope that Daisy would be fine. Maybe on some level, his little girl knew who could be depended on and who could not.

Looking back on the day, Ryan was in awe of how Ginny had handled things; of how she'd been so calm and in command while he'd lost his mind from worry. In the end, when it really mattered, she'd known where to look for Daisy, and she'd found her.

CHAPTER 45

GINNY

Ginny couldn't be happier. Daisy was coming over for a sleepover.

Ryan had called her last night to ask. He updated her on events, and sounded skeptical about the so-called job interview Vanessa claimed she had in Seattle. Ginny was shocked to learn that Vanessa left early this morning.

Then he told her that Daisy had been the one to suggest the sleepover after Vanessa had turned her down. This made Ginny so mad. How could that woman be so callous and self-serving? She herself was overjoyed about Daisy coming to stay.

Sleepovers were for friends of the same age and Ginny wondered if all the little girl wanted was a mother figure. She felt honored and privileged that Daisy had picked her and her heart broke for the child. She was even more determined to make tonight even extra special.

She had a whole slew of girlie things ready; face masks and

nail polish, as well as the things Daisy liked, such as coloring books and crayons.

Hearing her plans for tonight, Ashleigh offered to stay at Darcie's place. Her sister had been moody and quiet since yesterday when she'd seen Kayla and Ford together. Which reminded Ginny that she needed to ask Ryan what was going on there.

Ryan arrived late in the afternoon with an ecstatic Daisy who didn't stop talking from the moment she walked in, telling her that she'd brought her pink Barbie pajamas, and glitter and glue and a new coloring book that Daddy had bought her.

When she saw Benjy in the bouncer she ran to him squealing, and he did the oddest thing. He waved his arms, then made gurgling noises as if he was excited to see her. Daisy dropped to the floor and played with him.

Ginny and Ryan looked at the two children. Daisy was behaving much like a big sister would behave, to Benjy. The thought warmed her heart.

"Thank you for this," said Ryan, his voice turning low as he stepped towards her. The familiar clean and soapy scent of his cologne took her back to the time when they'd kissed.

"Don't thank me. I'm so excited about the sleepover myself. I really am. Doesn't that sound insane? I have the girlie toiletries ready, cookie and cake mixes galore, a range of suitable girlie movies to watch, and some delectable but healthy snacks. I made pizza as well."

"You *made* pizza?"

Ginny nodded. "Don't you?"

"I order in."

"You can't beat homemade pizza."

"That's true. My daughter is in for a treat tonight."

"My son is in for a treat. Look at him, Ryan." Ginny loved watching the two of them play.

"She really does want a sibling," he murmured.

"Yeah?" Ginny turned to him.

"Vanessa put that idea in her head. Daisy told me. I'm guessing it was Vanessa's way of presenting an idyllic life, hoping to get Daisy on board with this new vision of hers to live here. But look at what's happened. The first opportunity Vanessa had, she's gone."

Ginny touched his arm, wanting to show support, wanting to show she cared. Ryan took her hand, making her pulse quicken, and slowly rubbed his thumb over it. Gently, he led her into the hallway, away from the children. "You were pushing me to consider Vanessa's proposal. To go back to her, for Daisy's sake, and I told you I couldn't do it. I didn't want to."

"That was then … when I believed Vanessa had come back for the good of the family," she whispered, her insides doing cartwheels as his thumb slowly caressed her skin.

His eyes raked slowly over her face before settling on her lips. She almost tilted her face upwards in readiness for the kiss she hoped was coming.

"Vanessa never changes. I knew she was only here temporarily, getting Daisy's hopes up for no reason. I didn't fall for her empty words. I don't love her, Ginny. I have no feelings for her. I was prepared to make it work, maybe have her live close by, but not as a couple. I can't lie or pretend, and I would have had to do that with Vanessa. But I'm not that guy, and I wouldn't have lied or pretended for Daisy." He gently cupped her face with his hands, causing her insides to freefall. "Don't you see? It's you I'm in love with. It's *you* I want. That's it. You and Benjy. Me and Daisy. We need each other."

His lips pressed against hers and his hand cradled her face. Her heart missed a beat as the scent of his cologne washed over her, making her skin tingle. A low current thrummed between them as their kiss deepened. He reeled her closer to him until their bodies were touching. She could feel his heat, and hear the blood pounding through her ears as she savored the sweet taste of him. All her senses were in his control, and she gave in like an obedient servant.

"Oh my goodness! Now *there's* a sight I thought I'd never see."

She and Ryan pulled apart to see that the front door was open and Eloise was standing in the doorway with a huge ear-splitting smile on her face. "Sorry to interrupt. I hate to break something so beautiful up," she said, her gaze bouncing between her and Ryan.

"It's about time you handed back the key to the house," Ginny told her.

"Sorry." Eloise sailed past them and headed into the kitchen. "I wanted to borrow some milk. Oh, hey kids!" She crouched down to talk to them.

"We always get interrupted." Ryan swiped his thumb over her lower lip, and looked like a man who didn't want to move away. For the record, she was content to continue with the kissing once her sister left. Hopefully in the next few seconds.

"It's awful," Ginny agreed. She blinked at Ryan, as a crazy idea formed in her mind. "That trip we were going to go on, the surprise for Daisy," she whispered, glancing at the kids in the kitchen. "Why don't we do that tomorrow?"

Ryan's face lit up and his eyes sparkled. "Tomorrow? It would be perfect."

After Daisy going missing, and all the commotion in that young child's life, this trip would be a good break from everything. It was exactly what they all needed. "Tomorrow, then, you can come by and say you're picking her up after the sleepover and we could pretend to go to the park."

"And then go on our drive like we were supposed to." Ryan

pressed his forehead against hers, and she didn't care who saw or what anyone said.

"Thanks for the milk. I'll buy you some back." Eloise walked past them and headed for the door.

"Why have you come in this way?" Ginny asked, because her sister usually came in through the entrance at the back, through the kitchen.

"We were driving past. Liam's parked outside."

"Say hi." Ginny was relieved to hear this. Maybe Ryan could stay for dinner, and they could plan tomorrow's trip and ... it was all unraveling so wonderfully.

"Uh … what's this about a sleepover?" Eloise asked. Ginny wished she would leave now that she had the milk.

"I'm not having a sleepover," Ryan answered, quickly.

Eloise raised an eyebrow. "No?"

"No. It's Daisy. She wanted to come here and have a sleepover with Ginny."

"Right." Eloise didn't look as if she believed him. Ginny ground down on her teeth, trying to keep calm, trying to go along with the teasing, but it was so unfair. Eloise had moved out into her own home where she had plenty of her own privacy. Could she not let Ginny have the same?

"Where's Ash?" Eloise asked.

"At Darcie's," Ginny said, with a sigh.

"Drowning her sorrows, no doubt. "I didn't know that Kayla and Ford were an item." Eloise set down the carton of milk on the hallway table and folded her arms as if she were getting ready for a discussion. Ginny inwardly groaned and was tempted to sarcastically ask her if she wanted something to drink and eat now that she was here. The fear that Eloise might say 'yes, please,' stopped her.

"They're not," Ryan countered. "It's not what people think. At least I don't think it is."

"What do you think it is?" Ginny asked, curious. From the way Ryan was talking, he didn't seem so sure himself.

"Kayla's helping Ford take care of his mother and he's offered to give her a few driving lessons in return."

Eloise grinned. "That's how these things start."

"It's not like that," Ryan insisted.

"But did you see the way your sister looked at Ford?" Eloise pushed back. This revelation surprised Ginny. She'd been too caught up in worry yesterday to study Kayla and Ford in depth.

"Kayla wouldn't do anything to upset Ashleigh. Though I'm not sure if she's aware that she and Ford were together. Kayla hasn't been interested in anyone for as long as I can remember."

"I don't know what the truth is," said Eloise.

"You should go, before that milk goes bad." Ginny picked up the carton and handed it to her sister.

"It's like that is it?" Eloise winked at her. "Enjoy the sleepover." This was aimed at Ryan.

"I'm not sleeping over," he protested.

Ginny closed the door after waving to Liam who was sitting in the car. "I thought she'd never leave." She turned around and fell into another kiss with Ryan. "Stay for dinner," she said later.

"Are you asking me?"

"I'm ordering you to."

"I'll stay."

He pressed another kiss on her lips.

"We can plan our trip for tomorrow." She placed her hands around his neck, while he slipped his around her waist, pulling her towards him until their bodies were flush again. She relaxed against him, finding the warmth and understanding that she'd craved, finding love again, a deeper love, something she'd stopped believing in.

Despite their brokenness, she and Ryan had found one another, and life had given them a second chance.

"I could get used to this," Ryan husked.

She could, too. This was magical. Her possible-future-family. She leaned in for another kiss and was justly rewarded.

"Ew!" Daisy cried.

They pulled apart, but their arms were still wrapped around one another. Ginny sensed the muscles in Ryan's body tense. This wasn't easy for him, having his daughter see him with someone who was not her mother, standing with their arms around one another.

"You can kiss her again!" she shrieked, running off again to Benjy.

"That was … surreal," said Ryan, starting to relax again.

"You heard her, didn't you?" Ginny licked her lower lip. "She said you can kiss me again."

"That's right." He nodded, and his gaze fell to her lips but before he moved in, he stared into her eyes. Thin lines crinkled from the corners. Benjy and Daisy's laughter filled the air, along with animal noises coming from Benjy's favorite keyboard.

Ginny inhaled a deep breath.

It was going to be okay.

They were all going to be okay.

Thank you for reading THE WINTER BEACH. I hope you enjoyed reading Ginny and Ryan's story!

There will be a fourth and final book in The Rose Sisters series and this will release in 2024.

This book is available as a preorder at all major retailers

SIGN UP FOR MY NEWSLETTER to find out when new
books release:
http:/www.siennacarr.com/newsletter

I appreciate your help in spreading the word, including telling a
friend, and I would be grateful if you could leave a review on
your favorite book site!

Thank you!
Sienna

BOOKLIST

The Rose Sisters:
The Bridal Shop
The Summer House
The Winter Beach

Starling Bay books:
Whirlwind Kisses
Winter's Kiss
Maid for Him
Love Letters
Escape to Starling Bay (Books 1-3)
From Faking to Forever
Winter's Vow
Guarded Hearts
Table for Two
A Bouquet of Charm
A Christmas Wish

ACKNOWLEDGMENTS

I would like to thank my amazing group of proofreaders who check my manuscript for errors, typos and inconsistencies. I am eternally grateful for their help and support:

Marcia Chamberlain
Dena Pugh (a special 'Thanks' for coming up with the title)
Carole Tunstall
Charlotte Rebelein

I would also like to thank Tatiana Vila of Vila Design for creating this awesome cover.

ABOUT THE AUTHOR

Sienna Carr has been writing romance since 2013. She lives in the UK with her husband, three children, and a parrot.

Connect with Me

I love hearing from you – so please don't be shy!
You can email me at: sienna@siennacarr.com

Newsletter | Goodreads | Bookbub | Website

BB bookbub.com/authors/sienna-carr